Acclaim for Dan

FAMILY H

"Shapiro's small observations of motherhood are keen and astute; they demand empathy. . . . Realistic and heartbreaking."
—*The San Diego Union-Tribune*

"A brutal firecracker of a novel that chronicles the dissolution of a cinematically perfect New England family." —*Newsday*

"Shapiro has both a bestselling writer's instinct for plot and pacing and a fine literary sensibility. . . . A powerful, penetrating illumination of the hidden agendas and consequences of family relationships."
—*Elle*

"A gripping, contemporary story of guilt, love and redemption."
—*Rocky Mountain News*

"Keeps us flipping pages late into the night. Through seamless writing and a good plot, Shapiro manages to impart to us Rachel's frenetic desire to understand the past." —*The Oregonian*

"Riveting." —*Harper's Bazaar*

"Shapiro displays a sharp eye for the tiny epiphanies of everyday life, the quiet contentments we all have taken for granted."
—*The Charlotte Observer*

"Dani Shapiro has the gift. That a book as harrowing as *Family History* can be such a page-turner is testimony to the primal power of storytelling and the saving grace of art." —David Gates

"Absorbing . . . elegantly written, wry and unsettling."
—*Fresh Air*, NPR

"A gripping account of a contemporary Massachusetts family of four unraveling as problems with the eldest daughter start to rip the delicate fabric of love and partnership."

—*Seattle Post-Intelligencer*

"From the first page to the last, *Family History* is virtually impossible to put down: a beautifully structured, tightly woven exploration of the mysteries of adolescent pain, and the brutal efficiency with which a crisis can engulf a family and transform it into something unrecognizable."

—Jennifer Egan

"Start reading Dani Shapiro's *Family History* and you'll be wishing you didn't have to put it down for anything. Let the kids wait for their ride home from school; let the phone ring; cancel the doctor's appointment you waited six weeks for. This writer has a story to tell."

—*Calgary Herald*

"Dani Shapiro's new novel strikes at the heart of every mother who has ever worried that she has failed her child . . . readers will fly through this book. A contemporary domestic drama . . . a quick powerful read."

—*Chattanooga Times Free Press*

"Graceful."

—*Glamour*

"Shapiro's suspenseful novel movingly explores the fragility of family life. . . . The overall effect is to create a web that lures readers in, curious to find out who is guilty of what and whether the ending will be happy."

—*People*

"Spare, compelling, and heartbreakingly authentic. . . . Shapiro has fashioned a deeply moving, beautifully crafted story. Once begun it is impossible to put down."

—*Denton Record-Chronicle* (Denton, Texas)

DANI SHAPIRO

FAMILY HISTORY

Dani Shapiro is the author of three acclaimed novels, *Playing with Fire*, *Fugitive Blue*, and *Picturing the Wreck*, and the bestselling memoir *Slow Motion*. She teaches in the graduate writing program at The New School, and has written for *The New Yorker*, *Granta*, *Elle*, and *Ploughshares*, among other magazines. She lives with her husband and son in Litchfield County, Connecticut. Her Web site is www.danishapiro.com.

BOOKS BY DANI SHAPIRO

Playing with Fire

Fugitive Blue

Picturing the Wreck

Slow Motion

Family History

FAMILY HISTORY

To Veronica,

FAMILY HISTORY

A NOVEL

With warm wishes,

DANI SHAPIRO

ANCHOR BOOKS
A DIVISION OF RANDOM HOUSE, INC.
NEW YORK

FIRST ANCHOR BOOKS EDITION, AUGUST 2004

 Published in the United States by Anchor Books, a division of Random House, Inc., New York, and simultaneously in Canada by Random House of Canada Limited, Toronto. Originally published in hardcover in the United States by Alfred A. Knopf, a division of Random House, Inc., New York, in 2003.

Grateful acknowledgment is made to Alfred A. Knopf for permission to reprint excerpts from the poem "The Man in the Tree" from *Reasons for Moving* by Mark Strand. Copyright © 1973 by Mark Strand. Reprinted by permission of Alfred A. Knopf, a division of Random House, Inc.

The Library of Congress has cataloged the Knopf edition as follows:
Shapiro, Dani.
Family history / by Dani Shapiro.—1st ed.
p. cm.
1. Brothers and sisters—Fiction. 2. Teenage girls—Fiction.
3. Infants—Fiction. I. Title.
PS3569.H3387 F3 2003
813'.54—dc21 2002030183

Anchor ISBN: 1-4000-3211-3

Book design by Virginia Tan

www.vintagebooks.com

Printed in the United States of America
10 9 8 7

For Michael

I shall never know why
our lives took a turn for the worse, nor will you.
Clouds sank into my arms and my arms rose.
They are rising now.

—Mark Strand, "The Man in the Tree"

FAMILY HISTORY

1

I LIE IN BED THESE DAYS AND WATCH HOME MOVIES—A useless exercise, to be sure, but I can't stop myself. Ned's an amateur filmmaker, and ever since we got our first video camera when Kate was born, he has documented our family's life, not just birthday parties and anniversaries but smaller, more telling moments. When I appear in these tapes, I'm usually laughing and covering my face, saying *No, no, I look terrible.* Ned is almost always behind the camera. *Kate, Kate, Katie,* his deep voice cajoles, *come here, baby doll.* And then, after Kate as a baby, a toddler, a blurry little blond girl, she begins to become sharper and clearer, her features morphing themselves into a face of such extraordinary beauty that sometimes I felt shocked to realize she was my daughter.

My bedroom is dark, the shades drawn against the sun. Even though no one is home, the door is closed. Outside, the occasional car. Voices rise and fall. The dull thud of heels on the street. The walls of this old house are thick, but the windows are made of ancient wavy glass. We had always planned to replace the glass, but we never got around to it. I used to like the way I could hear everything going on outside. It made me feel like part of the world. Now, all I want is to be sealed off. People come and go. They drive their cars to and from work. They take their children to one another's houses. They go out to dinner and drive slowly, carefully home, protecting what is theirs.

The people on the screen are strangers to me: that pretty young woman, her hair pulled back in a messy ponytail; that man next to her, with faint laugh lines under his eyes. Everything was so easy then. That's what I see in Ned's home movies. I had no idea my life was easy. We didn't have enough money, or space, or hours in the day. The boiler had a leak; the dog needed a bath. Little things got the better of me. Now, all that seems absurd. If I could reach a hand back to that last summer, I would slap myself. Hard. *Snap out of it!* I would scream.

KATE WAS THIRTEEN. SHE HAD BEEN A SKINNY LITTLE KID with long stringy hair, always coming home with scrapes and bruises. She'd broken more bones than I could count, playing field hockey, soccer, basketball, softball. Kate was single-minded about winning. She threw her whole body into the final assist, the winning goal, even if it meant a torn ligament, a sprain, a fracture. And to listen to her tell it afterward, after the casts or Ace bandages, the hot and cold compresses, it was a saga: "Jenny McCauley fouled me, but the referee—that would be her father, *Mr.* McCauley—didn't call it. And then I got mad and told myself I wouldn't miss a single other shot," she said. Her cheeks were bright pink circles, and her blue eyes were framed by long dark lashes. Kate had a sense of competition—we called it "healthy competition" but secretly I wasn't so sure—that amazed Ned and me. She got straight As and was captain of everything in school. Ned and I hadn't been like that as kids, and we certainly weren't overachievers as grown-ups. Of course, we each had our ambitions, but they had changed over time. We wanted our family to be safe and happy. We wanted to make enough money to keep our roof over our heads and have a nice dinner out every once in a while.

Over that last summer Kate had gone away to camp, and I

could tell, even through the tone of her letters, that something had changed. *Dear Mother,* she would begin. Mother? She didn't say she missed us or dot her *i*'s with hearts the way she used to. She didn't write about archery or color war. She sounded hot and querulous when we called her on the phone. I wondered what was going on, but truthfully I put it out of my mind as much as I could and tried to enjoy the quiet, our new freedom to leave the house whenever we felt like it or to climb back into bed on a Sunday morning. For the first time in thirteen years we had nowhere to be: no car pool, no soccer practice, no Sunday school. I was almost scared, when Kate first left. I wondered how it would be, alone with my husband. So much of our time together had been spent discussing Kate and the logistics of Kate. "All Kate, all the time," we joked. And while we were immersed in the details of parenthood, the years were rolling by and we were getting older. I worried that having Kate early in our marriage had made us prematurely middle-aged. But it turned out I had nothing to worry about: within days of Kate's leaving, we were like newlyweds, enjoying each other, falling into long late-night talks, sleeping wrapped together for the first time in years. We blinked, and time fell away.

Our first Saturday night alone in the house, Ned cooked dinner. I had been out all afternoon, doing the usual errands—dry cleaner, butcher, grocery store, buying a baby shower gift—and when I returned, Ned had set the picnic table in the backyard with our best crystal, china plates, linen napkins rolled into napkin rings. His grandmother's hurricane lanterns rested in the center of the table, beeswax candles already flickering in the pale-orange early evening light.

"What's this?" I set my bags down on the kitchen floor. The house smelled sweet, a mix of Indian spices. Ned didn't cook often, but when he did, whatever he made was ambitious and elaborate. I saw several open cookbooks; three pots simmered on the stove.

"Never you mind. Just go outside," said Ned. He pushed my hair away from my face and kissed my ear.

"But I need to—"

"You need to do nothing," he said. He uncorked a chilled bottle of wine—one of our few really good chardonnays—and poured me a glass. "I'll be out in a bit."

I was confused. Was this a special day I had somehow missed, an obscure anniversary? Through all the years we had been together, we still celebrated the day we met and the day we got engaged, along with our wedding anniversary.

"Relax, Rach," Ned said, reading my mind. "I just wanted to make you a nice dinner."

The screen door slapped shut behind me as I walked out back. I particularly loved our backyard in the summer. We mowed the lawn just around the perimeter of the house, and the rest was meadow. Tall grass rustled in the breeze, blowing bits of dandelion fluff through the air. The sun was setting over the tin roof of the barn.

I kicked my shoes off, climbed into the hammock, and balanced the glass of wine on my stomach. It was an odd sensation, having this empty, quiet time. I didn't exactly mind it, but I wasn't sure how to do nothing.

"Here you are." Ned crouched down next to the hammock. He popped something into my mouth.

"What is it?" I asked, chewing. It was delicious.

"A date stuffed with ground almonds and wrapped in bacon."

"Yum. A nice low-cholesterol snack."

"Yeah, and after this we're having that lobster curry thing."

"You've been a busy boy."

He squinted up at me and grinned. His dirty-blond hair flopped over his forehead, and he shook it away, a gesture I had seen a thousand times in our daughter.

I grabbed Ned's hand and turned it, palm up, then held it to my cheek. I felt a familiar stinging against the backs of my eyes, tears I was embarrassed to let him see. Some people were able to take this for granted—this beauty, this *bounty.* But no matter how many years we had been together, I still felt it as something amazing, thoroughly undeserved. How had I gotten so lucky?

Ned kissed me on the forehead. Then he stood up, with a slight middle-aged groan, and went back inside the house.

WEEKS DRIFTED BY BEFORE WE ADMITTED TO EACH OTHER how much we missed Kate. Sure, there were advantages to not having her around: sex with the bedroom door open, a clean kitchen sink, listening to Coltrane instead of 'N Sync. But by the time she was due home, we longed for her. At the end of the summer, we picked her up in the parking lot of the A&P. She got off the bus wearing a flowery little tank top I had never seen before, her hair was bleached orangey-yellow, and she had a tattoo of a leaf on her ankle.

Here she is, standing in a group of new camp friends, exchanging hugs and phone numbers. "Katie!" Ned's voice cracks in the video as he calls her, waving with one hand and holding the camera with the other. I am standing next to our old Volvo wagon with the hatchback open and ready for her mountains of dirty laundry. Ned turns the camera on me for a second, and I grin self-consciously. I'm wearing big dark glasses and no makeup, and again I am struck by how young I look. I was thirty-eight that summer but I could have passed for thirty, especially with the dark glasses.

The camera jerks as I grab it and focus on Ned. He looks like an overgrown college boy himself, wearing a Red Sox baseball cap and a faded sweatshirt. I'd been looking forward to seeing Ned and Kate together. It was a secret pleasure of mine, quietly watching them as they played basketball or watched television or went over Kate's math homework at the kitchen table. I start to move toward Kate, but she shakes her head, her eyes narrow in warning, and I stop. She turns her back, squaring her little shoulders resolutely away from me. The movie ends there. I turned off the camera and stood alone in a crowd of parents, my arms dangling uselessly by my sides.

DOWNSTAIRS, THE DOORBELL RINGS. I CLIMB OUT OF BED, the bottoms of my socks collecting dust on the floor. The windows are covered with heavy blue curtains. I peek out, squinting in the glaring light. A Federal Express truck, with its cheery purple-and-orange logo, is parked by the curb. It can be nothing good: a legal document, a collection notice. I go back upstairs. The digital clock reads 1:57. I have to pick up Joshua at preschool at three. I should get out of my pajamas. Slap some cold water on my face, under my arms. Run a comb through my hair. Have I even eaten today?

This was once such a happy house. The sunny kitchen with its refrigerator covered with magnets and drawings; the dining room dwarfed by an enormous old pine table, a bowl of fresh fruit in a ceramic bowl at its center; flowers arranged in empty wine bottles along the windowsills and side tables. I took pride in our house, in the accumulation of objects that had character and meaning for us. Other people could buy expensive photographs, but they wouldn't have the framed black-and-white photo Ned took of a fence curving along the dunes on Nantucket one summer, when we were visiting our old friends Tommy and Liza Mendel. Our summers with the Mendels are another thing I miss. Every August, our families spent a few weeks together at their house on the beach; their daughter Sophie was a year younger than Kate. Tommy and Liza had done phenomenally well over the years. Tommy had started a series of restaurant and hotel guides, then sold his company to a big German corporation. And Liza was a senior partner at a small prestigious Boston law firm. Our daily lives may have been worlds apart, but the Mendels were like family to us.

That photograph, along with a lovely one of Kate and Sophie, still hangs on the landing. And then this room, the bedroom: the bed is soft and creaky, and the wing chair needs reupholstering. The Art Deco vanity we found in a flea market on the Cape before we were married is gathering dust. My perfume bottles, seven of them, are arranged on a china tray, next to a jumble of jewelry: African silver earrings, a pair of gold hoops, some dangling semi-precious stones. The good pillows and sheets I bought from a catalog a few years ago have served me well. Who knew how much time I would spend here, by myself?

If I let my mind wander, I can recall nearly every moment we spent in this house, in this room. I don't need Ned's video to see Kate at two, climbing onto the bench at the foot of our bed and flopping down on the old patchwork quilt we used to have there, giggling. Or Ned, up on one elbow, his gray-green eyes looking down at me as my belly swelled with Joshua, whispering that he was so lucky to be a new father all over again. On the mantel above the fireplace is a photograph in a hammered silver frame: Ned, Kate, and I are standing together near the base of Stratton Mountain. (There are no photographs of the four of us—not a single picture of Kate and her baby brother together.) It is early fall, and we are dressed lightly in sweatshirts, shorts, and hiking boots. I remember Kate's confusion when I said I wasn't hiking. I was always first one up the mountain. "Do you feel okay?" she asked, in a rare moment of concern. I wasn't ready to tell her the reason why. Too soon. The waistband of my shorts was a bit snug around my waist, and my breasts were sore and heavy, but no one would have known. "I'm fine, honey," I said. I sat at a picnic table and watched over my newspaper as my husband and daughter began climbing until they disappeared from sight.

THE PHONE RINGS ALL MORNING, BUT I DON'T PICK IT UP. The caller ID flashes UNAVAILABLE. I want to know who's calling me before I answer. A thin stream of light from between the curtains plays against the wood beams, shadows of leaves from the elm tree out front flickering against the chipped white paint. Ned and I made love countless times in this bed. Sleepy too-tired-to-do-it sex. Wild, scratching, grasping sex. Makeup sex, both of us bruised and tender. All of it here, under this quilt, in this place where I now lie with so little sensation in my body it's hard to imagine ever having given or received pleasure. I try to bring Ned into bed with me in my mind. I've lost his smell. It was the first thing I loved about him, breathing him in and knowing, inexplicably, that I was home. I remember his long fingers and the way he brushed my skin lightly with the back of his hand until I shivered. I can describe it, but I can no longer feel it. I still see him, though: his strong, powerful chest with just the right amount of curly blond hair; the way that hair got thicker below his belly button and thicker still until it ended in a soft tangle. The phone rings again, and I reach over and unplug it.

Lately, I've come to think about what it takes to unravel a life, not just one life, but the fabric of a family, carefully woven together with love and faith over the years. It doesn't happen in a moment but in series of moments—insults, improbabilities, just plain bad luck—that finally begin to pile up until all hope is gone. Recently, I saw a story on the news about a man who lived somewhere out west. He went into his attic after dinner, loaded a shotgun, and killed his whole family: wife, two kids, and then himself. When they interviewed the neighbors on the news, they shook their heads and described him the way these people are always described: quiet, no trouble, never saw it coming. But it turned out that the man had been fired from his job and had no prospects and no health insurance; his wife was having an affair; the younger child had a chronic illness. It must have seemed to him, that cold and starless night, that there was nothing left to do but destroy what remained.

There are things I still do, even if I walk through them like a robot. I wake up when Joshua cries and take him a bottle. I rock him to sleep with the same lullaby I sang to Kate: *Hush, little baby, don't say a word, Mommy's gonna buy you a mockingbird.* What a crock that lullaby is. I used to think it was good for them, to believe that no matter what went wrong I'd be able to fix it. I feed Josh his breakfast and take him to preschool. I pick him up on time. I can't afford to be late or to miss a single day. Everyone is watching me. They think I don't know it—that with their good manners they're fooling me—but I know what it feels like to be judged. I must have brought my own misfortune down around myself, is what they believe. They have to believe it. If it was all just a random series of events, if it could happen to anybody, where would that leave every one of them?

I glance at the clock. Time to get up. The bathroom is dirty, with strands of hair—mine—in the sink and tub and fingerprints all over the mirror. Even though the afternoon sun floods through the grimy window, the black-and-white tile floor is cold against my feet. My eyes throb as I squint into the medicine cabinet mirror. I try to look at my face only in pieces: my mouth, when I brush my teeth; my hair, when I try to arrange it into something other than bed-head. It's too awful to take in all at once. I was never particularly vain, but now that my looks are gone, I miss them. Ned has only improved since all this began. He's lost his middle-aged bloat, and he looks edgy and angry. He bought himself a black leather jacket and wears it around town with his oldest pair of jeans. It's as if he's dressing the part of the bad guy, giving the finger to all the people who have doubted him, who assumed his guilt. And I guess at the top of that list would be me.

The sweater, jeans, and boots I wore to drop Josh off this morning are where I left them, on the wing chair. My bra, panties, and socks are crumbled into a ball on the floor. I throw it all on again, smear a little lipstick on the apples of my cheeks, rubbing it in. Maybe if I look healthy, people will leave me alone. The stairs creak as I walk downstairs. Sure enough, a Federal Express envelope is lying on the faded old rug outside the front door. I pick it up without glancing at it. I head into the kitchen and pour myself a cold cup of this morning's coffee, heating it in the microwave. The *Globe* is unopened on the kitchen table, where I left it this morning. I sit down and try to focus. All I have to do is drive ten blocks, pick up Joshua, and come home. Usually he goes down for a two-hour nap, exhausted from a whole day of playing. Then I can take off all my clothes again and climb back into bed.

The answering machine is blinking with five messages. I hesitate for a moment, then push the PLAY button.

"Hi, Mrs. Jensen, this is Bill Sommers, from New England Gas and Electric. I'm calling about an outstanding bill—"

DELETE.

"Rachel, this is your mother. Enough is enough. I haven't heard from you now in at least—"

DELETE. Whatever she's saying, I can't bear to hear it.

"Mrs. Jensen, this is Charlotte Meyers, from Stone Mountain. There's a small problem with Kate. Please call us as soon as you get this."

My heart starts to race. Small problem?

Beep.

"Mrs. Jensen? Charlotte Meyers again. I'm going to call the next person on our list of contacts. I guess that would be . . . let's see . . . Mr. Jensen."

Beep.

"Rachel? What the hell is going on?" Ned's voice fills the kitchen. The air is as thick as molasses, and I'm having a hard time taking a breath. Ned sounds concerned and angry. "You can reach me on my cell phone. Where are you?"

I dial the number for Stone Mountain, which is posted on an index card and taped to the wall above the phone. I frantically look for the school's brochure, which is wedged between grocery receipts and take-out menus in a drawer. I need to see where Kate is, to hold it in my hands: the bucolic campus with its Tudor buildings, old trees, tennis courts. The thick glossy pages of the brochure are designed to make parents feel better about having to send their child to such a place. Inside, there are pictures of normal-looking girls doing normal-looking things: sitting in a circle on the lawn, walking in pairs along wooded paths. The high fences, the infirmary with its antidepressants and sedatives, the outer buildings where girls are kept in isolation—those are not part of the picture.

Finally someone answers.

"Hello, this is Rachel Jensen. I'm calling about my daughter, Kate?"

I'm put on hold. I look wildly around, trying to find anything of comfort to focus on, but instead my gaze falls on the knives in the knife block; the glass cupboards full of crystal; the wall of family photos—the three of us in the snow or on the beach—looking so perfect we could be modeling for *Parenting* magazine. I grab a pen and start to doodle. Blocks within blocks within blocks. I check my watch. If I don't leave home in the next five minutes I'll be late to pick up Josh.

"Mrs. Jensen? Frank Hollis here."

Hollis is the head of the school.

"What's wrong?" I ask, too loudly.

"Well, I don't want to alarm you, but we'd like you and your husband to come up here," he says.

"Did something happen?"

"Not one specific thing, but—"

"Is Kate okay? Is she hurt?"

"There's been an incident, a fight with another girl, and—"

"Fight? That's impossible."

"I'm sorry, Mrs. Jensen." He pauses here, waiting for a reaction from me. But I have no words. I try to imagine Kate, her skinny arms punching someone, her nails scratching. I feel like we're talking about somebody else, someone I know so slightly that I would have to call her a stranger.

"Also, a pill—the hallucinogen ecstasy—was found in her pocket during a random check."

"Well—isn't it possible that one of the other girls put it there?" Even as I ask the question, I know how lame it sounds.

"No," Hollis says slowly. "She admitted it was hers."

"How did she get it? Aren't you supposed to make sure that kind of thing doesn't happen?"

"We do our best, but it does happen sometimes. It's under investigation—"

"I thought the whole point of your school is to protect her," I blurt out. I've been gripping the table so hard my fingers hurt.

"Look, let's discuss this when we meet. I've spoken with Dr. Esposito, and he agrees that we should all sit down and come up with a game plan."

A game plan. I try to picture Hollis, sitting in his slightly shabby office. He's a pale stooped-over man with bags under his eyes. The night—nearly a year ago—when we first left Kate at Stone Mountain, I kept staring at the framed degrees on the walls of his study (A.B. Harvard, Ph.D. Cornell), trying to make myself feel better about leaving my daughter in the care of someone who looked like he hadn't taken a deep breath in a couple of years.

"In the meantime, she's back to Level One," he says.

Level One is where all the girls start when they come in, no matter why they're there. It's pretty much isolation, along with daily therapy. Going to classes, contact with other girls, even eating in the cafeteria are all privileges they have to earn. Kate hasn't moved past Level Two since she's been at the school.

My teeth are chattering. I wrap my arms around myself, trying to stop the shaking. I agreed to put her in that school because I thought it was the only place we could keep her safe. They promised to watch her twenty-four hours a day and make sure nothing happened to her. In the meantime, she would grow, grow up and out of the terrible twisted confines of her own mind.

Stone Mountain is two hours away. If I leave now, pick up Josh, and find someone to watch him, I can be there before dark.

"I'm on my way."

"We were thinking about tomorrow, Mrs. Jensen."

"I need to see her now."

"We would prefer that you wait. This is something that has to be carefully orchestrated. I'm sure you can appreciate that."

He's talking to me in a slow, careful monotone. This is how they talk at the school. They're used to crazy people, parents and children both. I try to take a deep breath, but my chest hurts. Fights? Drugs? The words don't even belong in the same sentence as Kate. Her skin is so pale you can see the network of veins in her arms, close to the surface—just like the rest of her.

"How would noon tomorrow be?" Hollis asks.

"Fine," I say. "I'll call my husband and let him know."

I look down at the paper on which I've been doodling. There must be a hundred boxes there, each smaller than the next, until finally you can't tell that they're boxes at all.

MY MIND IS RACING, THOUGHTS COMING TOO FAST TO SORT out. I try to take a couple of deep breaths. Baby-sitter for Josh; that's the first thing I need. I have a list of names on a scrap of paper tucked under the kitchen phone—Hannah, Lily, Kristen, Grace—local girls Kate's age. She would have been a high school sophomore if things had been normal. I see them around town sometimes, Kate's old friends. They have long hair and wear tight jeans and little tie-dyed tank tops, their new breasts bouncing as they walk down Main Street. They wear aviator sunglasses and go-go boots, little sixties redux girls standing in line at the ice cream parlor. They always ask after Kate when they see me. *How's Kate, Mrs. Jensen? When's she coming home?* They all grew up together in Hawthorne, went to the same nursery schools, kindergartens, grade schools. They went to each other's confirmations and bat mitzvahs and stayed friends even when Kate went to the academy as a day student because we had free tuition there. They were jealous of her then. Lucky Kate. But now Kate is in New Hampshire in a place that calls itself a school but has a locked fence around it and guards twenty-four hours a day. And Hannah, Lily, Kristen, and Grace are taking their PSATs and getting their learner's permits.

Those girls are all in school during the day. Besides, I don't think I want any of them knowing my business. I suppose I could take Josh with me tomorrow if I absolutely have to, but I don't want him to see his sister in that place, with its bars on the windows. His sister. He would look at her with the affectless, curious eyes of a toddler and wonder who she is.

So I do something I swore I would never do: I dial Ned's mother's office. It has been months since I've called her. I can picture the phone ringing on the other end, in the old brick house at the top of the village green, with its cobblestone walk and the ivy growing up the sides and along the tops of the windows.

"Jensen Realty, how may I help you?"

"Gladys, this is Rachel Jensen."

A brief, almost imperceptible pause.

"Hello, dear, how are you?" my in-laws' longtime secretary says. Her voice is polite, but still I hear the girding up, just beneath the surface. My whole life has become a foreign-language film and I'm sitting in the dark, reading the captions. What she's really saying is, *You! What the hell do you want?* I am no longer a member of the clan.

"Is Jane in?"

"I'll check."

The offices of Jensen Realty are state-of-the-art, spread across two floors of one of the nicest pieces of commercial real estate in Hawthorne. From where Gladys sits, at her antique desk in the foyer, she can see Jane's office, and she knows full well whether Jane is there or not. Even if the office door is closed, Gladys can just look out the window and see whether Jane's hard-to-miss black Range Rover is parked on the street.

"It's an emergency, Gladys," I blurt out.

"Goodness, I hope nothing too serious, dear."

She puts me on hold without waiting for an answer, and Muzak drifts through the phone. I wish I hadn't used the word emergency. Everybody in this town seems to know my business, sometimes even before I do. I can just hear Gladys Oberman talking to Joe the butcher while he cuts her some pork chops. *That poor family.* She would shake her head. *Seems like one thing after another.*

"Rachel? What's the matter?"

My mother-in-law has a thick Boston accent and the Yankee sensibility to go along with it. She calls women "broads" and "gals." *What's the maddah?* So Ned hasn't called her yet. I had wondered, thought he might have, especially when he couldn't reach me.

"I have to drive up to New Hampshire tomorrow morning, Jane. I was wondering if you could pick up Josh at The Little Acorn after preschool and keep him for the afternoon and maybe the evening."

"Did something happen to Kate?"

I stare out the window at the bird feeder hanging on the lowest branch of the elm in back. It used to be Ned's job to fill it with seed. Now it swings back and forth, empty for so long the birds don't even check.

"A small problem," I say.

Jane and Arthur are paying for Kate to be up there. Ned and I couldn't possibly afford the school's tuition. It's a rarefied place; you have to be extremely fucked-up and extremely rich to go there. Ned and I barely had enough money to pay our household bills, and though his parents don't know it, we broke into our IRA to deal with the costs of therapy and lawyers. There's nothing left.

"Now what?" Jane asks. I can practically see her long polished red fingernails tapping her polished wood desk. I can't tell her the truth. That's probably why Ned didn't call her; he realized Jane would go berserk at the idea of fighting or drugs, with all the precautions they take. Jane likes getting what she's paid for.

"I'm not sure," I say. "That's why I'm driving up there."

"Hmmph."

She doesn't believe me, but I don't care. All I want is for her to take care of Josh. Not that he's going to be too happy about it; he bursts into tears when he's left with his grandma. I know she keeps him safe and takes good care of him, but she doesn't get down on the floor and play hide-and-seek. And she makes him sit in his high chair until he's finished all his green beans. Grandma No-No, he calls her. I think she takes it as a compliment.

"I'll have to cancel some appointments."

I roll my eyes.

"Of course that's the least of it," she says, almost as if she can see me. "Anyway, I'll call you back in a bit and we'll make arrangements."

"Okay." I hang up. She's calling Ned right now; that, I'm sure of. And he's going to be furious because I didn't call him like he asked me to, but right now all I can do is put one foot in front of the other, go to the foyer, and gather my keys, wallet, and raincoat from the console table where I left them this morning. Josh's letter blocks are scattered on the floor of the back hall, next to a green plastic worm that says all the letters of the alphabet. Josh hasn't yet learned to put words and thoughts together. He doesn't ask questions. I try to talk about Kate with him, so he won't forget her, but she has disappeared deep into the land of toddler memory. Sometimes I see a little wrinkle in Josh's brow, a shadow cross his eyes, and I wonder if he's seeing an image of his big sister, her blond hair falling over his soft cheeks as she bent over to kiss him good night.

MY CAR IS PARKED ON THE STREET IN FRONT OF THE house. It's five past three, and Josh's teacher is probably getting annoyed. Rachel Jensen can't even get it together to pick up her kid on time. I pull out of my parking space and into the midday traffic. Somewhere, I register the gorgeousness of the day, even though the forecast is for rain. Springtime in Massachusetts lasts only a few weeks. The dirty gray blanket of February lifts, and suddenly the sky is bright blue, and the small yellow heads of crocuses peek up from the ground. This has always been my favorite time of year. Now, like most other things, it feels like a slap in the face, something to be enjoyed by other people, people who are going about their lives, who have not been swallowed up whole by the earth.

I used to wish people only the best. What was the point, I wondered, in wallowing in envy? Other people had more than we did: more children, more money, more houses, more success. I never cared, because I was happy with what we had. But now I am driven sick with envy for the women I see in town with their families, their sturdy husbands and healthy kids. *Why you and not me?* I want to scream at them. And I find myself horribly, secretly wishing harm to befall them. A husband collapses of a heart attack while shoveling snow. A child wakes up one morning with a headache and is deathly ill by afternoon. *It happens!* I want to tell them. *It happens to all of us!*

On the car radio, the weather report predicts that the approaching storm will be a spring blizzard. I slow to a stop in front of the red light by the stone-columned entrance to Hawthorne Academy, on the edge of town. A bell is clanging in the church tower. Fair-haired kids, their down parkas unzipped and swinging open, cross the wide brick driveway in their mud-splattered L. L. Bean boots on their way to class. Once, I would have looked out for Kate. She was hard to miss, even from a distance: tall and lanky, with a long easy stride. And I still expect to see Ned, walking along the common, carrying a briefcase bulging with papers to grade, surrounded by a bunch of kids. They lined up to see him in his office and signed up for whatever sport he was coaching. If you had asked any of them who the most popular teacher at Hawthorne was, they would have said Ned Jensen. He had gone to Hawthorne himself as a kid, and he knew the language of adolescent privilege and its discontents. They came to him with problems they couldn't tell their parents, and he kept their confidences as if he were a priest. Now say his name and watch them scatter.

The Little Acorn is just down the street from the academy, past Merrill's flower shop. It's one of four or five preschools that have started in recent years; this town has exploded as the Boston baby boom has moved north—much thanks to Jane and Arthur, who built subdivisions on farmland in North Hawthorne, catering to the Jacuzzi and granite kitchen set. The parking lot of the preschool is filled with minivans and SUVs. Several moms are standing there, car doors open, bouncing their toddlers up and down in their arms as I pull into the lot. They glance over at me, then away.

I leave my car in the lot with the keys in the ignition and run inside. Through the glass door of the Twos' classroom I see Joshua, sitting in a tiny chair, turning the pages of a Dr. Seuss book. His head is down, dark curls spilling over the round curve of his cheek, his mouth pursed in concentration. I'm not the last mother here, thank goodness. There are a few other toddlers playing with a yellow metal bus, their overalls smeared with paint. Josh is the only one who is all by himself. Even while I was pregnant with him, he was so quiet inside of me that sometimes I'd eat ice cream just to get him moving.

He looks up and sees me through the door. His little mouth opens and he shouts "Mommy!" as he pushes his chair back and runs to the door. He reaches for the knob and tries to twist it.

"Sorry I'm late," I say to the assistant teacher, a college girl. I grab his jacket and hat from his cubby and swoop him up in my arms.

"Hands red, Mommy," says Joshua, and I look down just in time to see his fingers, covered in red chalk, leaving powdery streaks all over my pink sweater. I kiss the top of his head and smell the sweet scent of Play-Doh.

"Did you do some painting, Joshie?" I ask. "Did you make a picture?"

He looks at me blankly, and my heart does the little skitter dance it does a hundred times a day. He isn't like the other two-year-olds. He doesn't answer questions, but I keep asking them. *Is that a flower? A house? Who's inside the house?* I look hard into his eyes, as if I might be able to see all the way inside his head.

Two other moms from Josh's class walk down the hall behind me as I carry him out of the building.

"Have you signed up for the music-for-tots class?" I overhear one ask the other. "It's a lot of fun—a bunch of us are going." They pass by me without saying hello.

Once, I would have cared. Certainly when Kate was a little girl I tried harder to fit in. I hung around the parking lot and joined the other moms for midmorning coffee. We talked about our kids, mostly—exchanging tips about feeding, or good music classes, or toddler discipline. Most of the other mothers had given up their careers, and being around them made me wonder if I was doing the wrong thing—if maybe I should give up my art restoration work and get back to it once Kate was in grade school. *You never get these years back,* they said. *Time goes by so fast.* Their days were spent shuffling their kids between preschool and play dates. They seemed so sure of themselves, wearing their spitup-stained T-shirts like badges of honor. I was always rushing off to appointments in my black city clothes, holdovers from my old life in New York.

I avoid those women now, the ones who still live here. I don't want them to see what's happened to my family—if they would even notice or care. I can read their minds as clearly as if there were cartoon bubbles above their heads: Rachel Jensen really thought she was better than us, didn't she? Well, she sure got hers.

2

WHEN I WAS IN MY EARLY TWENTIES AND A STRUGGLING graduate student, I used to imagine my life as a grown woman. Often, I'd think about the year 2000, far, far off in the future. Another century, another millennium. I'd be thirty-eight, positively ancient. Certainly I'd be living in New York City. New York was where I had to be, if I wanted to have a career in art restoration. That's where the paintings were; that's where the artists lived. I was more than halfway through the graduate program at New York University—a program that only admitted five students a year. I knew what I wanted when I graduated: one of the rare plum jobs as a conservator at the Metropolitan Museum. I spent much of the time that I wasn't in class at Veselka, a Ukrainian diner on Second Avenue. It was a crowded, noisy place that served big cheap bowls of chicken soup, doughy pierogis, and strong coffee. I brought my books and spread my papers out over a back table, preferring the din to the oppressive quiet of the NYU library.

I was far less ambitious when it came to my personal life. My parents' marriage hadn't exactly made the whole endeavor appealing to me. I thought that if I married and had kids at all, it would probably be later—much later, like the year 2000—once I was firmly established and when motherhood wouldn't rob me of my identity. I hadn't counted on the tall, blond, rangy artist who sat by the window of Veselka most mornings, drinking cup after cup of black coffee and alternately sketching on a pad and staring out the window at the traffic on Second Avenue. Ned claims he had noticed me for weeks, buried under my pile of books. But I think I saw him first—he was impossible to miss. It wasn't so much the way he looked (though there was that) but a sense of contained melancholy that drew me to him. He had a face that begged you to ask him what was on his mind.

When we finally spoke, it was something as banal as *Have you tried the babka?* But it didn't matter. There was something between us. *There you are.* The thought came to me, bizarre and unbidden. I simply knew I had just met the man I was going to spend my life with. I sat for hours at Ned's table and we talked about everything we cared about, our conversation zigzagging from art to our families to life in the city, the friends we quickly discovered we had in common. By the time the sun went down, we were holding hands and the current running between us was somehow both electrifying and safe.

Ned was thirty-one. He had been working as an artist since being invited to the Whitney Program ten years earlier and had watched as the careers of some of his friends had skyrocketed. It wasn't that Ned had had no success—he had good galleries in other cities: Boston, Los Angeles, Paris—but he hadn't been able to crack New York. He made ends meet by doing legal proofreading at night and on weekends. I was impressed by his lack of bitterness; he seemed to have a sense of historical context. He'd shrug. *Who knows where all of our work will be a hundred years from now?*

It was a while before he worked up the courage to take me to his studio. A month after we had begun to date—spending almost every night together from the start—we walked down from his apartment on the Lower East Side to his studio in Chinatown, beneath the Manhattan Bridge. We stopped for some pasta and a glass of wine first, in a tiny storefront restaurant on Mulberry Street. Ned kept stalling; I could see he was nervous. After dinner, he finally led me up a narrow dark staircase to his studio. He walked around the space, turning on six or seven spotlights clamped to ceiling beams. I looked through a dozen canvases piled against one wall. As I studied them, I slowly began to understand the problem. The paintings weren't quite there yet. They weren't completely *his.* Ned hadn't achieved a unified vision—though to my highly educated if still naive eye, there was no question when it came to talent. He was gifted. He just needed more time.

I didn't think it would be helpful to critique Ned's work—and I certainly didn't think it was my place. I knew enough to know that he was in the midst of finding his way, and I had no doubt he would get there. I never shared with Ned my certainty that it was all going to work out—not a hundred years from now but in this lifetime. We'd get married, eventually, I'd land the Met job, and Ned's talent would win out; he'd break through, be represented by one of the best galleries, like Leo Castelli. We'd be like those famous low-key couples you see on the pages of *Architectural Digest,* lounging in their fabulous sun-filled Tribeca loft with their two beautiful children.

I GOT PREGNANT WITH KATE AFTER NED AND I HAD BEEN together for a year. I had two semesters left to go in the doctoral program, and Ned was hard at work on a new series, leaving our tiny apartment at the crack of dawn and spending long days in the studio. A good SoHo gallery had expressed interest, and he was gearing up for a studio visit from the owner. Pregnancy wasn't the plan—it wasn't even on the periphery of the plan. I was only twenty-four. The people we knew didn't have babies. They didn't even have pets.

"What am I going to do?" I wept in Ned's arms. I already was feeling sick to my stomach and exhausted. My whole body felt bloated.

"We," said Ned. "What are *we* going to do."

"I don't know."

"I think you do."

"I'm sorry!" I cried. "I just can't imagine doing anything—"

"We'll have the baby."

"But my school—your work—"

"We'll figure it out. Maybe we can fix this place up."

I looked around our apartment, which consisted of two tiny rooms, with a hotplate and minifridge in lieu of a proper kitchen.

"I don't think so," I said.

"Well, maybe we'll move to a loft."

"With what money?"

"Pat Hearn is coming next month—she seemed really interested on the phone. One show, Rach. If I sell even one painting to a collector, we'll be fine. That's all we need."

I SPENT THE NEXT FEW WEEKS PUSHING MYSELF TO GO TO class, keeping my little secret. But I didn't know how long I could hide it—or even how long I could keep going. I was working with all sorts of chemicals. Could I be exposing the baby to toxic material? Finally, as I was getting closer to the end of my first trimester, I met my friend Liza for breakfast. She was still Liza Masters in those days—she had just started dating Tommy, who was in the business school—and she was a student at NYU Law. She and I had shared a sublet together until I moved in with Ned.

Liza flew into The Bagel on Bleecker Street a few minutes late. She was glamorous even then, before all the money and success, with an innate sense of style and self-possession that made people look at her and wonder who she was. Her hair was pale blond, her skin almost translucent, and she was wearing skinny black jeans, high-heeled boots, and a white tank top.

She hugged me hello, then pulled back and looked at me.

"You look awful. What's wrong?"

I was taken aback. I had planned to ease into telling her.

"Nothing," I said, then burst into tears.

"Oh, Rachel." She slid to my side of the table. "Is it Ned? What?"

"I'm pregnant," I said.

"Shit."

"We're having it," I said.

Her eyes widened. "You can't!"

"Well, we are."

"Is this Ned's idea?"

"No—it wasn't anybody's idea. It just happened."

"But I can give you the name of a good doctor who can—"

"That's not what I want," I interrupted.

"But Rachel. Listen to me. How are you going to have a baby here—now?"

I found myself wishing I hadn't said anything to her. What was I hoping for? She couldn't understand.

"Ned just sold a painting." I lied so smoothly that I almost convinced myself it was true.

"Wow, that's great!" said Liza. She was trying to be a good friend to me. And I was a liar, a traitor. Ned wouldn't understand at all if he could have heard. I didn't understand it myself.

"And a good SoHo dealer is taking him on," I continued. Because, why not? One little lie led to another. The fact was, the dealer was visiting sometime soon, and I had no idea what was going to happen. But I was trying to paint a picture of the life I wished we had.

Liza shook her head. "Still, wouldn't it be better to wait? We're so young now—it's such a huge thing. You can't ever take it back."

"This is what I want," I said.

2 7

WHEN I CAME HOME THAT NIGHT, NED WAS SITTING ON the edge of a crate, smoking a cigarette and drinking a big glass of whiskey.

"Hey," I called out. I crouched over and put a quart of milk into our minifridge.

He looked up at me with bloodshot eyes, and I stopped in my tracks.

"It was today?" I asked.

Ned hadn't told me when the studio visit was going to be; he felt superstitious and didn't want to jinx it.

"Uh-huh." He looked back down at the floor.

"What happened?"

"No go," he said.

"But wait, what do you—"

"She wasn't into it. She was there for five minutes, tops."

I lowered myself down next to him. My mind was going in a thousand directions: embarrassment about the ridiculous lie I told Liza, sympathy for Ned, and for the first time the faint thrumming of real financial worry. We were down to about twenty dollars. How could we have a baby, living this way? We didn't even have health insurance.

"I've been thinking," said Ned.

I swallowed hard, bracing myself. I was terrified that he was going to say we should abort the baby.

"Maybe we should move away for a while," said Ned. "It wouldn't be the end of the world. You can take a leave—"

"But what about you?"

"I can paint anywhere." He paused. "It's not like it's going so well for me here."

"Where would we go?"

Ned got up and walked over to the window, which overlooked the fire escapes across the inner courtyard.

"I called my parents, Rach. I told them—and asked for a loan. But they don't see art as something they want to support indefinitely. They told me about this house in Hawthorne. It's in foreclosure, and they'd lend us the down payment." He paused and then added, almost as an afterthought, "There's a barn in the back that my mother says would be a perfect studio."

A long silence. Ned had never expressed any affection for his hometown.

"Ned! You can't go back there. You need to be here—to do your work here. You'll go crazy living so close to your parents."

"Not if I have you. And anyway, it makes sense. We're going to need some money, right? Babies cost money."

"You'll hate me."

"I love you," he said softly. He put a hand on my still-flat stomach. "This—this will be an adventure."

He got up and walked over to the bookshelf and pulled down a tiny black-velvet box. I caught my breath as he handed it to me. Inside was an intricate antique diamond engagement ring, with white-gold scrollwork and tiny diamonds along the sides.

"It was my grandmother's," Ned said.

I slipped it on my ring finger, speechless.

"Do you like it?"

In truth, it wasn't a ring I would have chosen for myself. It was large and ornate—my style would have been simpler—but I didn't care. I didn't come from a long line of ancestors passing heirlooms down through the generations. Most of my family's possessions had been lost when they fled Europe before the war. I loved the idea that I was joining a family who had roots and things to pass down from generation to generation. Great-grandmother Ruth's Limoges and her silver tea set. Great-great-grandfather Edmund's leather and crystal hip flask that, it was rumored, he carried with him while battling the Indians.

But more than any of that, it was the idea of Ned—the idea of forming a family with this man I believed in—that made me love the ring. It was physical, tangible evidence that he felt the same way about me. I turned my hand this way and that as the tiny diamond chips caught the dim light inside our apartment.

"It's beautiful," I said.

I AVOIDED TELLING MY MOTHER THAT NED AND I WERE getting married for as long as I possibly could. She didn't like sudden news—and she didn't much like Ned. Nice Jewish girls weren't supposed to marry artists. My choices were doctor, lawyer, banker. I was upsetting the natural order of things.

"What's the rush?" my mother asked me, over coffee at Bergdorf Goodman. All around us, well-coiffed women with shiny unscuffed handbags were sipping mineral water and picking at their salads. My mother looked like all those women. She had her hair and nails done at Elizabeth Arden, and most of her wardrobe came from the very same department store in which we sat, sipping our coffee. I did not look like the women of Bergdorf's—I had gone out of my way not to. My hair hadn't seen scissors in years; it was curly and long. And for the occasion of my ladies-who-lunch date with my mother, I had worn baggy Levi's and a big men's shirt of Ned's which hid my slightly swelling belly. Years later, I grew to love clothes and to see them as a uniform of sorts, as armor. But back then I was busy trying not to be anything like my mother. I enjoyed seeing the flicker of disapproval dance across her face as I approached her from the escalator. But she was determined to have a pleasant lunch—"pleasant lunch" would have been her term—so she arranged her mouth carefully into a smile and hugged me, ever so briefly, hello.

My mother had an agenda that day. She always did. She spoke in lists.

"*A,* it seems to me you could wait at least until the summer," she said. "The weather's so iffy in the spring. And, *B,* why have the wedding in Massachusetts? *Your* family is from here."

"I know, Mom." I couldn't bear stating the obvious, which was that my family, as she put it, consisted of one person and one person only, and she was sitting right there in front of me in all her powdered glory. My father had died of lung cancer when I was in college. I had no sisters or brothers. Neither of my parents had siblings. There were no cousins, no aunts and uncles, no nobody. Just Phyllis. We were a family of free-floating loners, only children begetting only children. I found it horribly depressing. One of the upsides now, of moving to Hawthorne was the thrill of getting away from it all.

"And, *C,* I want to give the rehearsal dinner at my home," my mother continued.

"Traditionally, the rehearsal dinner is something the groom's family does," I said.

"Since when have you cared about tradition?" She had a small dark speck of lettuce stuck to her pale pink lipstick.

"Jane and Arthur are going to give the rehearsal dinner at their club."

"Oh, of course. Their *club.*"

"What's that supposed to mean?"

"Nothing. Nothing at all."

I saw my mother as infrequently as possible, which still amounted to at least once a week. Being the only daughter of a widowed mother—and, in particular, of *this* widowed mother—was the strangest thing about my life. I couldn't explain it to anybody. None of my friends, in our tender early twenties, had lost a parent. None had a sense of responsibility for a parent. Most of them still had families who took care of *them,* who brought them casseroles and helped them with their taxes. In some dim way, I was aware that I had the duties, if not the emotional life, of a woman twice my age.

"I'm pregnant, Mom," I blurted out.

I hadn't meant to say it. There was no reason for her to know. I was only three months along, and I was still barely showing. So the baby would come suspiciously early in our marriage. Big deal. Nobody cared about stuff like that—at least nobody in my generation. I dug a fingernail into the palm of my hand under the table as I watched my mother's face run through a spectrum of emotions. I knew her well—too well—and I saw her anxiety, anger, fear, and finally, worst of all, a smug and awful satisfaction.

"I knew it," she murmured.

"You knew what—that I was pregnant?"

I felt suddenly vulnerable. Saying it out loud, saying it to my mother made me feel unsafe, as if I had put the baby in jeopardy. I'd trip down the escalator on my way out of the store and miscarry in a painful, bloody mess on the plush carpet, surrounded by Giorgio Armani suits. I'd give birth to a deformed, doomed infant. The key word was *doomed.* How could anything good come out of me, when I came from this angry messed-up woman?

"This is terrible," my mother said softly.

"What did you say?"

"Terrible," she repeated. "You're ruining your life."

I wanted to scrape back my chair, grab my coat, and run from the restaurant, but I couldn't move. I was rooted to the spot, poisoned, numb. I stared at the woman across the table from me. Her lips trembled, and her eyes were wild, pupils jiggling, rippling like tiny stones cast into a calm, shallow pool. Who was she? I felt no love for her, and yet I couldn't leave. A thousand invisible threads bound us together, and when I tried to squirm away they just got tighter. She was my mother. She could say whatever she wanted to me, and no matter how ugly, how hurtful, I couldn't walk away. There was no one else to take my place. Countless times, I had imagined a sister, a brother, someone to pick up the slack. Could you go pick up Mom at the doctor? I'd ask. Or, Mom's acting crazy. Do you think we should call a shrink?

"You have all the time in the world," she was saying. "Why do this now? How are you going to afford grad school? Child care? Have you thought these things through?"

"As a matter of fact, we have," I snapped. I had already started using *we* and *us.* Plural pronouns, words that connoted a family. My new family with Ned.

"We're moving to Hawthorne," I said. I watched my mother's face crumple and become, for an instant, ten years older. It gave me no satisfaction to hurt her. After all, I knew on some level that she was just an unhappy and lonely woman, and she couldn't help the way she treated me. I felt a cold wave of nausea sweep over me. I rested my hands on my belly, feeling the slightest fullness there. Was she right? Was I ruining my life? I was giving up a dream—at least for a little while—but in my mind I was trading it in for another, more vivid one.

"Oh, Rachel." She shook her head. It was a rare moment—she was at a loss for words.

"You'll come visit," I said, as brightly as I could muster. I had a vision of an old house with creaky stairs and lots of nooks and crannies. That's where we'd put my mother: in a nook or cranny, far away from our sunny bedroom. She could stay as long as she liked, and she wouldn't irritate me or make me feel terrible about myself, because she'd be visiting me on my own turf, in my own town. She wouldn't be able to touch me any longer. Ned's parents had sent us Polaroids of the house, and they were trying to help us get it. It was two hundred years old, and every room needed a massive amount of work. "A real fixer-upper" was how Jane described it on the phone. But I didn't focus on the water damage, the crumbling walls, the missing floorboards. It was perfect because we could afford it, and we'd have our baby there, and it would be ours, far away from my mother. And then, after we'd gotten on our feet, we'd come back to New York.

After paying our lunch bill, my mother looked around the café, at the pastry cart, the white-coated waiters; finally she focused on two women at the table next to us, a mother and daughter. They were dressed in almost identical nubby wool jackets with padded shoulders festooned, like army generals, with several heavy gold chains. Their lipstick was the same shade of red, and as they finished their meal, each pulled a Chanel lipstick and compact from her purse. I knew my mother was jealous, wondering why she and I couldn't be like those two women. Where had she gone wrong, to have a hippie-ish graduate-student daughter who was pregnant and moving to Massachusetts?

"Did you even think about me?" she asked.

"Sorry?"

"Did you even think for a second what it would be like for me, for my daughter . . . my only daughter . . . the only reason I even care if I'm alive or dead—"

"Stop it." I closed my eyes.

"Stop what, Rachel? What am I saying that's so hard to hear? It's the truth. If it wasn't for you, after your father died I would have given up. But I told myself, No, I have a daughter. Rachel needs me. What would happen to Rachel if I wasn't around?"

A number of snappy comebacks ricocheted through my mind, and any one of them would have wounded her to the quick, so I said nothing. I had the irrational childlike urge to stick my fingers in my ears and start humming a song. Anything to drown her out as she kept talking. Ned once asked me if my mother had always been this way, or if my father's death had changed her. I wished I could have said that becoming widowed had anything to do with it, but it didn't. She had spent my whole life doing whatever it took to ensure that she would be the center of my existence. It was her career, her reason for being. She had given birth to me so that she would be loved and listened to forever. That was my job. Anything else—husband, children, career—was secondary to being her daughter.

"I am your mother," she was saying. This was her trump card, and I knew where it was going next. "I gave you life," she announced.

"Okay, that's enough." I pushed back my chair. It was the only thing I couldn't sit still for: the I-gave-you-life speech. It was comical, sure, and later when I would tell Ned about it we'd laugh. But this was my mother, and she was dead serious. I swore to myself that I would never even *think,* much less say, anything remotely like that to my child.

"What's the point, Mom?"

"The point is . . . the point is you can't do this."

"I said you're welcome to come visit any time you want," I answered smoothly. I hated her, and I hated myself. I wasn't the miserly, rigid person that I became when I was around my mother. I caught a glimpse of myself in the mirror as I turned to grab my coat, and I looked angry, hard-edged, old.

"Welcome," she spit out. "I'm *welcome* in my own daughter's house."

"Yes," I repeated.

"Like a visitor."

"Uh-huh."

"A *guest.*"

The mother and daughter at the next table were now unabashedly listening to us. Both of them had their heads cocked in our direction, and they were looking at each other as if to say, Thank God that's not us.

"You'll see," my mother said. She stood up. She was still tall then, and she drew herself up to her full regal height. She looked down at my slightly rounded belly, well-hidden under Ned's baggy T-shirt. "You'll have a daughter, and then she'll grow up and be just like you."

I LEAVE THE LITTLE ACORN AND DRIVE SLOWLY BACK through downtown. Sometimes if I circle for a while, Josh falls asleep in his car seat. Main Street is busy with late-afternoon shoppers: I notice a mother from Josh's school walking into

KaBloom, the flower-shop chain that I've boycotted ever since they arrived, displacing Dave Shields's old place that had been started by his father. Only a few of the shops that were here when Ned and I first moved to Hawthorne are left. It was a quaint village then, though there were already signs I didn't know to look for—signs that the wonderful little hardware store, the barbershop, even the local diner would all give way to chain stores and malls on the edge of town. The lure of an easy Boston commute, the prestige of the academy, and the beautiful old houses—some of them pre-revolutionary—made the town appealing to young families who wanted small-town life but still wanted their cappuccino and fresh biscotti. Of course, my in-laws were a big part of that change in Hawthorne, and it had made them rich, so certainly none of the Jensens were complaining. I pass the ivy-covered brick of Jensen Realty and glance at the window of Jane's front office. The shades are drawn.

I keep going, past the turnoff for our street. A couple of miles down the road, I pull my car into the parking lot of the Pine Dunes complex on the edge of the village. Ned has sublet a condo here. The place is an eyesore: a sprawl of two- and three-story stucco buildings with small balconies jutting out. The landmarks council tried to stop it from being built, but there was a variance of some sort, a piece of luck for the developers in what is otherwise a town where you can't build a shed in your own backyard without getting permission. Nothing anybody could do about it. We used to make fun of the place, from the safe smug distance of our marriage. Divorced Dad Dunes. Divorcée Dunes. Pining Dunes. Oh, we'd had a million names for it. Pine Dunes is where people in Hawthorne go when they find themselves alone. At seven or eight o'clock at night, if you drive by the complex, you'll see televisions flickering in all the windows. It isn't hard to imagine the sweatpants, the bad take-out Chinese food eaten straight from the carton. Unlucky folks living in a suspended, dazed equilibrium, waiting for their old lives to be over and their new lives to begin.

I keep the engine running. Josh is asleep in his car seat in back. His head is lolling forward, and his mouth is open, a string of spittle hanging from his lower lip. He is lightly snoring, a beautiful sound, like a kitten's purr. Once Josh goes down, he'll sleep anywhere. I pull my cell phone from my handbag and punch in Ned's number.

"You know what to do, so do it at the beep," is the curt message. What is he, fourteen?

"Hi, it's Rachel," I say. This is our new formality. After a lifetime together, we are back to our proper names. "Are you there?" I pause, waiting. Ned often screens calls. "Hello?"

He doesn't answer. I used to think I had instincts that bordered on clairvoyance about Ned and the kids. I believed I could sense where they were and if they were okay. Like a mother lion, I could sniff them out in the forest. Now, Kate's in that hellhole of a school, and I don't even know which unit of Pine Dunes my husband is living in, much less whether or not he's home. I turn again and look at Joshua, my sweet boy, snoozing in the backseat. *It's five-thirty. Do you know where your children are?* Well, I know where my baby is. Thank God for that.

It's late afternoon and the occupants of Pine Dunes are arriving home, getting out of their cars with their single bags of groceries. All the apartments look exactly alike, with identical windows and dark green doors. In the gray dusk, I squint up at the dozens of tiny balconies, big enough for one chair. Is one of those Ned's? Does he ever sit out there and miss our back porch, the old hammock swinging?

I have not given up hope that somehow Ned and I can go back to the way we were. Well, perhaps not exactly the way we were. Too much has happened. But to a new way of being together, all of us. With Kate home in her room with the Red Sox banners and posters of bare-chested teenybopper movie stars, and Cheese Doodles crumbs under the bed. And Ned home with me, sitting at the kitchen table in the morning, reading the *Globe* and drinking coffee from his favorite mug. And Joshie in his booster seat, flinging his vegetables all over the place and laughing, the adored littlest child of an intact family.

I have to hold on to that. To the degree that I am able to put one foot in front of the other, that's why. If I believe Kate and Ned are lost to me forever, I won't be able to go on. All my life, my mother always told me that denial was her most powerful tool. She said it proudly. "Denial got me through your father's illness," she said, after he finally died. She truly never believed that he had terminal lung cancer, even as he was wasting away before our eyes. But I have spent my life fashioning myself as my mother's opposite. Where she refused to see things, I looked carefully and hard. Where she was in denial, I was the family realist, talking to the doctors, researching the statistics.

What are the statistics here? How many of the occupants of Pine Dunes reunite with their families? How many students at Stone Mountain ever go on to have normal lives? How many women who have watched their world shatter as surely as if it were a glass globe pick themselves up, dust themselves off, and go on?

IT HAS STARTED DRIZZLING, A COLD FREEZING RAIN JUST as the weatherman promised. A storm is coming. The last couple of winters have been unusually mild. Thanks to global warming, we've had almost no snow at all. By now, people have probably stored away their snow blowers and shovels, lugged their huge bags of salt to the corners of their garages.

From the top of the hill I see Ned's car pull into the already-slushy driveway of Pine Dunes. He parks a few spaces away from me, but he hasn't noticed my car. I watch as he unfolds his lanky body, then moves slowly in the rain, goes around to the trunk, and pulls out a few bags. He's been to the video store and the supermarket. He must have been showing houses today. He has on a blazer and that awful brass name tag just like Jane's: NED JENSEN,

JENSEN REALTY. I know I should be grateful that Jane and Arthur were able to give Ned a job at all, once he was fired from the academy. He was pretty much unemployable within thirty miles of Hawthorne, or anywhere people might read the newspaper. But there's no one who knows better than I do how horrible it must be for Ned to have gone to work for his parents. If he could have seen his future self—tired, pale, middle-aged, wearing an ill-fitting blazer and a name tag from his parents' company—would he ever have walked down this road with me? Would he have married me and moved back home?

I give the horn a little tap. He glances over in my direction and I wave, though I'm not sure he can see me. He recognizes the car, though, and walks over, eyebrows raised.

"What are you doing here?" He looks even more tired up close. His eyes are watery, a little bloodshot. I wonder if he's been drinking. He looks through the back window and sees Josh sleeping.

"I talked to the school," I say.

"Couldn't you have called me? I've had my cell on all afternoon. And my mother said—"

"I called Jane because I needed someone to watch Josh tomorrow. They want us to come up there," I say.

"So I've heard. Why? What's up?"

"Can I come in?" I ask. It feels so weird to ask for permission.

"I don't think that's such a good idea," he says quickly, as if he's been anticipating the question.

"Ned, we need to talk."

It's raining harder now, a cold rain, water streaming down the sides of his face.

"Can we go someplace, then? Get a cup of coffee?"

He shakes his head. The doors inside him are closed tight. I can bang my head against them all I want, but he's not going to let me in.

"Why are you here, Rachel? I ask you to call me, and you don't. And then you just show up"—he waves his arms—"on my doorstep."

"I think they're going to ask us to take Kate home," I say. "Things aren't working out up there."

He stares at me with those almond-shaped blue eyes. Jensen eyes. Kate's eyes. I always found them unreadable. I used to ask him the classic wifely question: *What are you thinking?* With equal measures of irony and impunity I would ask, and he would tell me. Or so I thought.

"That's impossible," he says. "They can't just kick her out."

"Hollis didn't actually say there were kicking her out, but I got that impression."

"The guy's an asshole," Ned mutters.

"Nonetheless."

"We should have sent her to Élan."

"You think if we had sent her someplace more hard core, this wouldn't be happening?"

"I don't know. You tell me."

His cheeks are flushed and the tip of his nose is red, the way it gets when he's angry.

"I don't have any answers, Ned."

"Since when?"

I try to take a deep breath, but I seem to have forgotten how. He doesn't mean it; he doesn't mean to be this nasty, I keep thinking to myself.

"Look—it's bad enough, isn't it? Do you have to make it worse?"

Ned takes a step back. "That's what I do. I make things worse—isn't that right? If it wasn't for me, everything would be just fine."

"Oh, stop."

He runs a hand through his wet hair and looks at me beseechingly. "I can't deal with this, Rachel."

I stare straight ahead at the windshield. The wipers swish back and forth like a metronome, hypnotic.

"I'm sorry, okay? I'm really sorry," he says. "We'll talk in the car. We can talk all the way to New Hampshire. Two hours of nonstop talking."

"Fine." I start to roll up the window.

"Wait," Ned says. He wipes the condensation off the back window and looks at Josh for a long moment. I know he wants to wake him up, to smother him with kisses. How can he bear it?

"Ned, please."

I just can't—" He stops, his voice cracking. Then he turns and walks away, up the sloping lawn to the first level of Pine Dunes. He climbs an outside staircase to the second level. He's a stick figure now, a soaking-wet stick figure in khakis and a blazer, stooped over and bent with the weight of the world. He stops in front of a door, turns a key in the latch, and enters his new, secret home.

I NEVER DRANK SCOTCH BEFORE NED LEFT, BUT NOW I FILL a small glass nightly. Neat, or on the rocks, or with a twist, it doesn't much matter. My evening cocktail has become something medicinal now, not the take-it-or-leave-it proposition of my earlier years. Ned's Great-aunt Gloria died a few years back and left us a series of cut crystal decanters, along with every size and shape of cocktail glass known to man. Why us, and not any of the other Jensen relatives, I'll never know. In a family of heavy drinkers, Ned and I were the lightweights.

Tonight, I need the clink of ice cubes in my glass, a sound I have always found comforting, along with baseball on the television and the tumbling of clothes in the dryer. The apartment I grew up in was dead quiet, and when I left I surrounded myself with noise—the more clatter, the better. Kate bringing home friends after school? Fine with me. Music on the stereo, the doorbell ringing, the phone, the dog barking—all of it made me feel happy and safe. Now, my house is as quiet as a library. Only the sound of the ice clinking, the splash of amber liquid from the decanter, and the steady pounding of the rain.

4 1

Josh is asleep in his crib. He was sleeping so deeply that I was able to carry him up the walk, shielded by my raincoat, and into the house without waking him. He stirred slightly as I walked up the creaky stairs, but when I lowered him into his crib and pulled his quilt over him, he flipped over onto his stomach, and I crept out of the room.

The old cracked leather club chair and ottoman in the corner by the window used to be Ned's. I hadn't realized, until he left, the way we had fallen into roles and become stuck there. Ned's chair, my blanket, his dark blue coffee mug, my white-and-yellow striped one. There was even an invisible line dividing our household chores: Ned took out the garbage, I did the laundry. Ned threw out the rancid food in the fridge, I stocked the pantry. He was responsible for getting rid of all the old unwanted stuff, and I kept filling and filling our home with beautiful things: an antique gold-rimmed teapot from a yard sale, lavender water to sprinkle on the sheets, potpourri in a heavy pewter dish. It all seems pretty silly now. I should have a bonfire in the backyard and get rid of it all. It would be the sweetest-smelling bonfire in the history of the world.

I sit in Ned's chair and sip my drink. The warmth of the scotch travels through my chest, unknotting some of the tension there. The wall next to the fireplace is smudged with ash. It would be a nice night for a fire, possibly the last one until fall, but I've never once started a fire in this house. That was Ned's job.

The rain has turned to snow, coming down hard and fast, beating against the curtainless windows. I shiver in the chill and take another sip. *It's a doozy, all right.* I hear Jane's voice in my head. I can picture her lifting her eyes briefly from her martini in her own living room just a mile away, unimpressed. I'm surprised my mother hasn't called from New York. She watches the weather channel; it's her favorite show. *There's a blizzard blanketing New England,* she'd announce in the exact words of the newscaster. Or, *A traveler's advisory is in effect for Boston and the northern suburbs.*

A gust of wind rattles the windows, and Josh shrieks upstairs. I put down my glass and run up and open the door to the nursery. He's standing in his crib, his fists curled around the rails. His face is streaked with tears, his eyes wide and terrified.

"No, Mama!" he screams as I pick him up. "No, me-me-me-me." How close the words are in his toddler mind. We are one and the same. I hold him against my chest, feel his wet cheek against my neck. His little heart is thrumming, pounding fast against my own.

"It's just weather, Joshie," I whisper into the top of his dark curls. "Just a storm. You're safe inside." I don't know how much he understands, and he can't tell me. The words are trapped inside of him, forming and dissolving before he can manage to get them out.

"Mama's here," I murmur.

He looks up at me, snot running out of his nose, and his face breaks into a sunny smile.

"Mama," he says. "Mama, bed."

"You want to go back to bed?" I ask. I wonder if he can smell the scotch on my breath, if, as a grown man, he'll have a memory of his mother holding him and smelling of liquor.

I start to lower him back into his crib, but his back arches and he screams again.

"No, no, no!" he yells. "Mama bed!"

"Oh, you want to come into *Mama's* bed."

He nods furiously. I know I'm not supposed to do this. All the books say not to take your baby into bed with you. They have to learn to go to sleep by themselves. They'll never break the habit. It's not good for their sense of independence. But as I carry Josh down the hall, his head heavy on my shoulder, all I can think is that he's only two. What possible harm could there be in giving a two-year-old what he needs?

When I walk into the bedroom, the television is still on. Kate is frozen on the video, which I had paused on the VCR before running out of the house. She has been trapped there, looking into her parents' room—her mother's room now—from the distant land of age thirteen. I keep Josh's face turned away from the screen. I don't want him to see her. The confusion, the little furrow in his brow when he sees somebody he knows is familiar but he can't quite place—seeing that would break my heart. I lie down with him and bury us under three quilts. He turns on his side, snuggles up against my rib cage, and flings one arm across my stomach. Instantly, he is back asleep, his eyelashes wet with tears. I watch my baby. Our skin is the exact same color. The light from the television bleaches his face, turning it ghostly white, and the house creaks and groans in the wind, but now he doesn't stir. His mother is his safe haven. I never felt this way about my mother. All I wanted in the world was for Kate to feel this way about me.

I CAN STILL SEE KATE CLIMBING INTO OUR CAR THAT MORNING she returned from camp, barely saying hello. When she stretched across the backseat, her T-shirt hiked up and I saw a tiny silver ring in her belly.

"Oh my God, Kate," I blurted out. "A belly ring?"

"What?" she mumbled, pretending to be casual. "Everybody has one." She kept her eyes averted. Ned and I exchanged a glance, but we didn't push it. That was what it was all about, I tried to reason—being a teenager. She was supposed to do everything possible to unsettle us. I wanted pierced ears when I was her age; this was just the next generation taking it to the next step. After all, what could she do to shock us? Ned and I had grown up smoking pot, drinking. I dabbled in cocaine, and Ned did psychedelics. We never talked about it, but on some level she must have had some idea that her parents had had their own rebellion. Ned threw her duffel bags filled with dirty laundry into the trunk, and we took off for home. The three of us drove for a while in an uncomfortable silence. Finally I couldn't stand it anymore.

"So how was camp, sweetie?" I turned around and looked at her in the backseat. She had her face pressed against the window, and in her frayed denim shorts and tank top her whole body looked different to me. Her strong thighs, her long skinny arms—it was her own body now, and I no longer had any right to it. She could twist it, turn it, pierce it any which way she wanted.

She didn't move her head.

"Fine," she said.

"Did you make new friends?"

"Uh-huh."

"Do any of them live around here?"

"No." She snorted.

"So what was your favorite part?"

She shrugged, her eyes widening in a display of barely contained sarcasm. The gesture unsettled me, like a piece of a bad dream. As I watched her, it slowly dawned on me that I had become the enemy. I had sworn this would never happen to us. If I was as good a mother as I knew how to be, if I gave her space and respected her all her childhood, she wouldn't need to rebel against me. Oh, I knew all about mothers and daughters; there was no escaping the friction, the anger and competitiveness. I had read the books, talked to other mothers of teenage girls. But I believed Kate and I were different. She could talk to me about anything. She knew I would never judge her, would never manipulate or betray her—the things my own mother had done to me. It was as if I had an internal rule book for the kind of mother *not* to be, and I followed it to the letter. And yet it seemed that history was bound to repeat itself. We were just following a blueprint, as in control of our own destinies as rats in a maze.

Kate's cheeks were a splotchy pink. She was fair, like Ned, and her face and neck were a road map to her feelings; ever since she was a little girl, I had always known when she was upset by her ruby necklace, as we called it.

"What's going on, sweetie? Did something happen at camp?"

She lifted her head then and flashed me an angry look.

"I don't know what you're talking about," she said scornfully.

Ned was staring straight ahead at the road. He gripped the steering wheel with both hands, and a muscle along the side of his jaw throbbed like a heartbeat. Ned didn't often lose his temper, but when he did it was scary. The few times it had happened, the force of it made me wonder if that kind of rage was always there, lurking beneath the surface, just waiting to explode when he was pushed.

"Why don't you try talking to us, Katie," he said. I could tell that he was straining to keep his tone jovial. We had missed her so much, after all—and now here she was, a strange sullen creature.

She didn't answer. Just pressed her nose back up against the window, a curtain of hair—that hideous orange color she had dyed it—obscuring most of her face. I thought about the silver ring in her belly and wondered if it hurt. I could feel the air thickening inside the car, the heat of Ned's anger starting to build. I tried to combat it with chatter.

"We saw Tommy and Liza last week," I told her. "Sophie's back from riding camp. Riding camp! Can you imagine? Anyway, I thought maybe we could visit them in Nantucket next weekend, before school starts. If we can even get onto the ferry. What do you think, Ned? Do you think we're too late? It *is* Labor Day weekend."

"Too late," he said tersely.

I put my hand over Ned's on the gearshift.

"Well, maybe if we—"

"I don't want to go," Kate said.

This was a surprise. Kate loved visiting the Mendels, especially in Nantucket. They had a huge old shingled house on the beach, and there were always lots of families around with kids her age. She had a crush on Tommy and Liza. Who wouldn't?

"How about if you tell us what's going on," said Ned.

"Nothing's going on."

"Obviously something's bothering you," Ned continued.

She said nothing, just kept her nose pressed against the window, staring out at the blurry landscape whizzing by.

"Kate—you'd better start talking to us," he said.

I rubbed his hand, gave it a squeeze. Maybe it would just take some time.

"Why don't we stop at Friendly's for ice cream?" I carried on nervously. "I'll bet you haven't had decent—"

"Shut up," Kate muttered.

I felt like I had been socked in the stomach. I turned around and looked at her. Her forehead was creased above a spray of pimples.

"What did you say?"

"You heard me."

"Kate, please don't—"

"Leave me alone!" she said loudly.

"Apologize to your mother this instant," said Ned. The muscle along his jaw was now pulsing nonstop.

"Don't tell me what to do!" Kate yelled from the backseat.

Ned swerved into the empty parking lot of a bowling alley, then slammed on the brakes. The old Volvo rocked to a stop. He turned around and glared at her.

She didn't move.

"I mean it, Kate. Get out of the car this instant."

I no longer recognized my own family.

Ned jumped out, swung open the back door, and pulled Kate out by the upper arm. Neither of us had ever raised a hand to her. When he let go of her, I could see a faint fading handprint around her arm. She took a couple of steps back, away from him. Then she just stood there, in the middle of the parking lot, staring into the distance. A hot wind blew her hair across her face. My mind raced. Was it drugs? Was she stoned? I looked hard at her and decided no, that wasn't it. Her eyes weren't red, and she didn't look at all spacey. If anything, she seemed sharp and clearheaded.

"All I said was that I wanted to be left alone," she said. "Is that a crime?"

"You can't just—"

"No, *you* can't just."

"Rachel?" Ned turned to me. "Are you going to say anything here?"

I had gotten out of the car and was leaning against the door. The air smelled of asphalt, and everything had slowed down. It was as if a layer had been peeled back from what I had thought of as my life, and now there was a deeper, more tender layer underneath. I knew I was seeing some sort of truth, but I had no idea what it was.

"We missed you, Katie." I was hoarse, and it came out in a croak. "Why are you being like this?"

She wouldn't look at me. She crossed her arms and bowed her head.

"We're going home," said Ned. He got back into the driver's seat and slammed the door. Kate climbed in back and curled up into a ball, burying her head in her knees.

3

IT WAS SEPTEMBER. THE WEATHER HAD STARTED TO COOL, and my favorite flowers in the back garden, tall proud purple stalks of atropurpureum, had begun to bow over in deference to the chill. Kate was back at school. Ned was keeping an eye on her at the academy, and he said she seemed to be doing fine. Certainly on the surface she was thriving in her usual manner; she had just been named captain of the middle school field hockey team, and she was getting 95s and 98s on eighth-grade quizzes. She came home with her girlfriends after school, and they spent hours behind the closed door of her room, punctuated by muffled bursts of laughter. I tried to tell myself that she was all right, but call it a mother's instinct: I watched Kate carefully—perhaps too carefully—and what I saw disturbed me.

One afternoon I drove to the academy to take her to a dentist appointment, parked near the quad, and waited for her to get out of her two o'clock class. She wasn't expecting me. I had very nearly forgotten about the appointment and only remembered hours earlier when I checked the calendar. I watched as she crossed the lawn with a few other kids. She was wearing jeans, a blue cardigan, unlaced high-tops, and she looked like an ordinary pretty girl. So what was it that made my heart sink when I saw her? The angle of her neck as she stared at the ground? The tense cast of her shoulders, as if she were trying to hold herself together? She looked older than the other kids, less innocent, as if she knew things they were years away from knowing.

She stopped when she was a few feet away from my car.

"What are you doing here?"

"You have an appointment with Dr. Klinger," I said.

"Shit." She kicked the ground. Two girls behind her giggled uncomfortably and shot me sideways looks to see how I was going to respond to my daughter's cursing.

"Let's go, Kate."

She climbed in reluctantly and closed the door hard.

"See you guys later," she called to her friends. They weren't girls I knew.

As we pulled away from the curb, she turned away from me and leaned against the passenger door. I flipped the car locks to make sure she wouldn't fall out. We drove in silence for a few blocks, but finally I couldn't stand it.

"So how was school today?" I asked. I hated the falseness in my own tone of voice.

She shrugged.

"Come on, Kate, can't you be civil?"

"Could you just stop bugging me?"

"Kate—don't talk to me like that. Please."

Were all teenagers so sullen and withdrawn? I couldn't go by my own history, so I started polling everyone I knew. I talked with other mothers around town, and they all said the same thing: their kids were gone, *gone;* they shook their heads in wonderment. Just yesterday they were babies. It's a stage, they said. Don't worry, she'll grow out of it; you'll be friends again when she's thirty. They laughed and I laughed too, although it was anything but funny to me. Twenty dollars was missing from Ned's nightstand. Had Kate taken it? And if so, was that normal? I had a feeling that she lied to me about where she went, which friends she was spending time with. Was that normal? There was a fine line between worry and paranoia—just as there was between respecting her privacy and remembering that she was only thirteen—and I wasn't sure where that line was. I was afraid that if I pushed things I'd drive Kate even farther away. I had spoken with Joanne Owen, the head of Kate's camp, to see if she had any thoughts as to what had happened over the summer, but Joanne didn't seem to feel anything was too terribly wrong. *These girls,* she said, *all go through changes. By next summer she'll be a different person.*

I tried to talk to Liza about it; after all, she was my best friend, and her daughter Sophie was only a year younger than Kate. But I could tell that Liza thought I was overreacting.

"It happens," she said to me, during a late-night phone conversation. "They're growing up. We just have to find ways to get used to it."

"But Liza—" I stopped. That was precisely it: I was afraid that Kate *wasn't* growing up but, rather, was growing inward, her insides becoming all tangled and distorted. I wasn't sure when to intervene—after all, nothing had actually happened. *She's okay,* I reassured myself. *She's going to be okay.*

WORK WAS GOING WELL. I HAD A PRIVATE COMMISSION from a couple in Boston: a small Alice Neel canvas that had water damage after a fire. It was a painting I particularly loved: a stark, shadowy oil of a young mother holding her naked baby boy. The mother had long dark hair hanging over her face and enormous exhausted green eyes. The baby had a pudgy belly, and he sucked his thumb as he nestled into his mother's bony lap. It was a great opportunity for me, restoring a valuable work by a great painter. My private commissions tended to be less interesting: bad copies of Chagalls left too long in New England attics, the occasional minor nineteenth-century ancestral portrait. Liza had recommended me to this couple, who it turned out had one of the best art collections in Boston. Liza was the lawyer for the wife's family trust, and when she found out that the wife was planning to take the Neel to the Museum of Fine Art for restoration, she suggested me instead.

My hands shook each morning as I set to work. Technically, it was a challenging job, and it had been a long time since I had worked on a great painting. A whole corner of the canvas had been destroyed. Every afternoon, I blared opera on the boom box in my top-floor studio, laid out my tool roll, and breathed deeply, steadying myself. The painting was warped, and I was using moist heat to coax it back into shape. I applied the water through a thin layer of tissue and plastic, then slowly moved across the area with a hot spatula, constantly adjusting the temperature. I worked from noon until three, when I began to think about when Kate would be getting home from school. I no longer knew her exact schedule. She might show up at three, slamming her way up the stairs and into her room. Or she might not come home until dinnertime.

"What do you want for dinner, honey?"

"I'm not hungry."

"Kate—you have to eat something."

"You can't make me."

"Goodness, Kate, I wasn't trying to force you to do anything, I just—"

"Leave me alone!"

I stared endlessly at the Neel and tried to banish thoughts of Kate from my mind. The woman was skinny, almost sickly looking. But she was also beautiful, and somehow seemed rendered stronger by motherhood. Her gaze was direct: her eyes seemed to follow me as I moved about my studio. I knew her name; the painting was titled *Betty Homitsky and Jevin.* I wondered what had happened to Betty Homitsky since she had sat for a portrait in 1968. Did she have more children? Was she happier than she looked? Did she soften or harden with age?

As I worked on the Neel that fall, I began to feel changes in my own body. My breasts were distinctly sore and heavy, painful to the touch. I felt fuller all over, bloated and slightly sick. It wasn't a complete surprise—over the summer, with Kate gone, Ned and I had decided to try one last time to conceive another child—but still I found it shocking. For years after Kate's birth, we'd tried with no success to have a second one. I desperately didn't want her to be an only child, but after three early miscarriages I had given up. If it just wasn't meant to be, I didn't want to push the issue. It was very disappointing, but also somehow unsurprising. Ned and I would get on with our careers and devote all of our parenting energy to Kate. There were worse things in the world.

ONE NIGHT I NUDGED NED.

"Honey?"

He leaned up on an elbow and looked at me sleepily.

"I'm pregnant," I whispered.

He blinked a few times.

"Are you awake?" I asked.

"I am now," he said. "Are you sure?"

"Pretty sure."

And then—I attributed this to hormones—I started to weep. I was unable to go on, surprising both of us. I didn't know how to tell him what I was feeling. Ned wrapped his arms around me and held me close. He raked his fingers through my hair, murmuring *ssshhh.* "Talk to me," said Ned. "Baby, what's going on?"

Ned put his hand on my stomach and held me close. Down the hall, I heard Kate's door open and close. I could picture her in her oversized T-shirt, going downstairs and getting some ice cream from the freezer.

"Talk to me, Rach," Ned said again. He was studying me from inches away, his eyes warm and loving.

I sat up and pushed my pillow behind me.

"I guess I just really wanted this," I said. "More than I realized."

Ned nodded, as if this was something he had already known.

"But—it also changes everything," I said.

"Yes."

"And that's scary. And—what if this doesn't—"

Ned put a finger to my lips, then kissed me.

"Don't even go there," he said.

We fell silent, both of us watching the shadow of the swaying poplar out front play against the cracked plaster of the bedroom ceiling.

"When should we tell Kate?" I finally asked.

"I don't know," Ned said. "Do you think we should tell her now?"

"No," I said quickly, vehemently—surprising both of us.

"You're right. It would be a big deal for any kid."

Another long pause. I was anxious, my thoughts coming too fast.

"And she's not any kid," I said quietly.

Our eyes met, and Ned held my gaze. So much was unsaid between us on the subject of Kate. But on that night, I could see that he was as worried about her as I was.

"So we won't tell her for a while," he said.

"Right." I nodded.

I snuggled next to Ned and allowed his warmth to comfort me. Generally, he wasn't a worrier. He figured things sorted themselves out, and even if they didn't there was no point making yourself nuts about them. He was a happier person than I had ever been. Whatever Jane and Arthur's failings were as parents, they weren't crazy—*malicious* crazy—like Phyllis. It was amazing to me, actually, that I had come as far as I had in life. I had a semblance of a normal family. I lived in a home with food in the fridge, curtains on the windows, quilts on the beds. Martha Stewart on a budget. I even had a career, for better or worse. And now, with a little bit of good fortune, I was going to have another baby. I thought of the painting upstairs in my studio. I was lucky. Blessed.

PHYLLIS MADE HER ANNUAL PILGRIMAGE TO HAWTHORNE that October. She came at the same time every year—leaf season—and having traveled all the way from the Upper West Side of Manhattan, she often stayed a week or even longer. I prepared for these visits in the only way I knew how: I tried to protect myself. Days before she arrived, I started to do yoga. I pulled out the dusty meditation tapes from the drawer under the VCR and sat on my bedroom floor, cross-legged, learning to breathe. I cleaned my house from top to bottom, waxing the floors until they gleamed in the sun. I saw my house the way Phyllis would see it, with an immensely critical eye. The rugs had threadbare patches, and the door frames were chipped. The fireplace mantel was darkened with soot. Things I never noticed, or even found charming, were now ugly to me. I tried to fix it all, make everything perfect—make myself perfect—so that my mother would be able to find no fault. I had panic attacks around my mother, and so did Ned. One year, after dropping her off at Logan after a particularly difficult visit, we got stuck in a traffic jam in the tunnel as we were leaving the airport. I started hyperventilating, and Ned threw out his back. We hobbled home, the two of us, crippled by a seventy-five-year-old woman.

Usually, I fortified myself with alcohol when my mother was around, but this year that was out of the question. Pregnant, I took daily doses of folic acid, prenatal vitamins. I eschewed sushi, unpasteurized cheese, lunch meats. I made myself big salads, bowls of whole-grain pasta, fresh steamed vegetables. How was I going to get through a visit with Phyllis fully conscious? To top it off, I had morning sickness, which I had decided was a misnomer. It was all-day-long sickness, hitting me at odd moments. The only sure thing was that at some point during the day, I'd find myself with my head in the toilet. I wasn't showing yet, and Ned and I hadn't told a soul.

We were afraid that, if anyone knew, Kate might find out. I figured I had until I was about five months along. I could get away with wearing loose clothes, Ned's shirts. I had a very strong feeling that Kate shouldn't know until it was absolutely necessary.

I was in my studio retouching the Neel when I heard a car door slam outside and the sound of Phyllis's voice penetrating the walls and glass three floors up. She was early. I stopped what I was doing, stood, and looked out the window. There she was, directing the cabdriver, a heavyset Ethiopian man in his sixties, up our front walk with her three huge suitcases. She was wearing her traveling clothes: a gray pants suit with gold buttons that glinted in the autumn sun. I could see that she had highlighted her hair a deep russet. Her small head blended with the fallen leaves, the carpet of red, yellow, and gold that covered our lawn. She stopped and looked up at our house before following the driver up the walk. I could see her nostrils flaring from where I stood, the thoughts that gathered in her mind like storm clouds. *Why would my daughter live like this?* She was wondering. *She could have married that nice Sidney Greenbaum and had an apartment on Central Park West.*

She knocked sharply, a military *rat-tat-tat,* and then opened the door. I heard her voice drifting up the stairs.

"Hello-o-o-o!" A long pause. "Is anybody home?"

I closed my eyes and tried to visualize a setting sun, waves on the ocean, new sprouts pushing themselves up from the soft earth—everything the meditation tape had suggested. I did the breath-of-fire, short shallow breaths meant to release toxins and calm the mind. None of it worked. My heart was pounding, and I couldn't breathe all the way in. The yogis obviously hadn't had Phyllis for a mother. I hated the fact that she could still get to me. We weren't even in the same room, and already I was becoming the person I always turned into around my mother: tense, unforgiving, ready to be hurt. I was nearly forty years old—surely old enough to have gotten over this. But there *was* no getting over it.

"Be right down!" I called. I had to wrap things up, put away the raw pigments and solvents before I left the studio. It was a rule of mine never to walk out of the room with materials exposed. I had almost finished putting the paintbrushes on the shelves when I heard her climbing up the stairs.

"Hold on!" I yelled.

"If the Mohammed won't come to the mountain, then the mountain will come to the Mohammed." She huffed and puffed. This was one of Phyllis's favorite phrases, along with "Caesar's wife is above reproach." I guess she liked to think of herself as a mountain—or as Caesar's wife—important, immutable, towering, royal.

"There you are." She stood in the doorway.

It had been six months since I'd seen my mother. She walked into my studio and looked around, running a veiny hand over my desk, the windowsill, an easel propped in the corner. She picked up two framed photos of Kate and Ned and stared at them, frowning. She didn't exactly say hello to me, but instead she laid claim to me, touching all that was mine. She had no thought that this might be my private space. There was no such thing as privacy between mother and daughter. Her skinny heels clicked against the wide, uneven floorboards. There were a few holes in the floor I had never bothered to patch, and I pictured a heel sinking, stuck, my mother pitching forward onto her face.

"How was your trip?" I asked weakly.

"I sat on the plane with a delightful woman. Just delightful," said Phyllis, pacing the room. She stopped and rearranged some tulips on the side of my desk, pulling off a dangling petal.

"That's nice." I was barely listening. My mother described people only in superlatives. They were delightful or dreadful, brilliant or complete idiots.

"She's also here visiting her daughter and son-in-law—in Cambridge, I think—and when we got off the plane there was her son-in-law, waiting for her." She paused, rubbing the pink petal between two manicured fingers.

"Uh-huh." I nodded slowly. It was obvious where this was going.

"What do you think of that?" she asked.

"Of what?"

"The fact that her son-in-law cared enough to show up at the airport," said Phyllis.

"Ned is at work, Mom," I said.

"He couldn't have taken the afternoon off?"

"No, he really couldn't," I said. "Please don't start this, Mom. You just got here."

"Start what? I'm not starting anything. I'm just asking a simple—"

"You're trying to start a fight."

"You always think the worst of me, Rachel. Why do you feel the need to attribute the worst possible motives to me?"

I took a shallow breath. "Do you want some tea? Let's go downstairs." I was desperate to get her out of my studio.

"What about you?" Phyllis went on. "Couldn't you have picked me up? 'Where is your family?' the taxi driver said. Imagine my embarrassment!"

"Do you remember that we suggested you take an evening shuttle? We would have happily come to get you at night," I said.

"This woman's son-in-law," Phyllis said, "is an investment banker."

"How nice for her."

"He took the afternoon off from work at Morgan Stanley."

"Well, I guess he's a better son-in-law than Ned," I said.

Dammit, it was starting. I was getting sucked in. Surely there was some way to avoid getting into this. But if there was, I hadn't figured it out.

"What's this?" she asked, turning her attention to the Neel painting.

"Just something I'm working on."

"So you're still working," she said. Finally she stopped and looked at me. "That's . . . terrific." Her mouth stretched into a smile, revealing a row of laminated teeth. Why did it seem to me that she was really saying it was terrible that I worked, that I had to work? I knew she felt sorry for me. I had married a man who hadn't *done well.* I didn't have a good haircut, and my face had never once appeared in a society page of any kind. I could only imagine what she said about me. The phrase *Poor Rachel* had no doubt been uttered frequently, with a sad shake of her head.

"Let's start over again," she said.

She grasped my shoulders at arm's length. She stared into my eyes with an intensity, a ferocity, that made my own gaze slide away. I couldn't help it. I felt like she could see all the way inside me. Even though I knew she saw nothing—knew nothing—about me and my life, I felt penetrated by her. It had taken no more than five minutes for her to worm her way inside me once again. What was the point of therapy, yoga, meditation tapes, or even the self-help books I had occasionally tried to read? *When You and Your Mother Can't Be Friends. My Mother, Myself. The Mother Within.* Nothing stuck. Nothing except for Phyllis.

"You look good," she finally said.

You look like shit.

"Have you done something to your eyebrows?"

You need a visit to the salon.

I took a step away from her and busied myself with covering the canvas. Betty Homitsky looked different to me with Phyllis in the room. The baby—how had I not noticed how frail he seemed? And Betty herself—she wasn't the picture of maternal strength at all. What had I been thinking? She looked shell-shocked. My life closed around me. Everything I looked at was as changeable as a Rorschach inkblot.

"Where's my beautiful granddaughter?" Phyllis asked.

"School," I answered faintly. It was the middle of the afternoon. Where the hell did she think Kate was? I sent a silent scream in Ned's direction, just a half mile down the road. I liked the idea that maybe he would sense my panic and come running home. The way I was feeling inside couldn't possibly be good for the baby. It was a war zone in there, full of pulsing, pounding blood. I was hopped up, terribly anxious. I should have canceled the visit. I wasn't up to it.

I started walking downstairs, hoping that Phyllis would follow me. I heard her behind me, the sharp little click of her heels. The banister had fingerprints on it, and the skylight was dusty. I was on the landing when it hit me—a powerful wave of nausea—and I ran down the rest of the stairs to the bathroom, kicking the door shut behind me as I retched into the sink. All I had eaten was a few saltines. How could saltines do this? My forehead was cold and sweaty, and I held on to the rim of the sink as I tried to steady myself. I wanted to curl up into a little ball, right there on the bathroom floor.

"Rachel?" My mother's voice was too close, just on the other side of the door. "Are you all right?"

"Fine," I croaked. "Be out in a minute."

I straightened up and examined myself in the mirror. You really couldn't tell by looking at me. My cheeks were maybe a little fuller, that was all. *She can't see inside you, she can't see inside you,* I kept repeating to myself.

"What's going on in there? Are you sick?"

I ran my fingers through my hair and splashed some cold water on my face. Then I opened the door.

"Let's have that cup of tea," I said, walking quickly past my mother into the kitchen.

I LEFT HER ALONE. THAT WAS MY MISTAKE. I SHOULD NEVER have left Phyllis to her own devices, unsupervised. But that afternoon, after a restorative cup of tea—chamomile, good for the baby—I went back up to my studio. I had left it in a state of disarray and, besides, I needed to get away from her.

"Make yourself comfortable, Mom," I said, carrying her suitcases upstairs.

"Don't mind me," she sang out. "I'll settle in, maybe take a bath."

Her cheerfulness should have tipped me off. How could I possibly not have realized that, given the opportunity, she would open every drawer, every door; she would scrounge for keys and fit them into locks, blindly searching for something. If asked, she would have denied that she was snooping. *My own daughter's house!* Upstairs, in my studio, I listened to the first act of *Aida* and packed away my tool roll. I composed a letter about a private commission I was hoping to get; then I called Ned at his office. It was after four; he was finished with his last class of the day and was probably meeting with students.

"Ned Jensen," he answered. His professional voice.

"Hey," I said softly.

"Oh, hi, honey. I was about to call you."

I sighed into the phone.

"Has the eagle landed?" He laughed.

"The eagle had crashed into our fucking roof."

"I'm sorry I'm not there," he said.

"No, you're not."

"Are you mad at me?"

"No . . . I'm just going crazy."

"Where is she now?"

"Downstairs, hopefully drowning herself in the bathtub."

I felt a sick little twinge, the way I always did when I said something that awful. What kind of monster was I, to say such a thing about my own mother? I wished her dead. It was true. Countless times, I had searched my soul for the slightest bit of warmth toward her, an iota of love, and had come up empty. I walked across the room and gently lifted the plastic from *Betty Homitsky and Jevin.* I stared at the painting. Phyllis had never held me like that. I was sure of it. I had never felt the warmth of her body as she held me close. When Kate was one day old, Phyllis picked her up out of her hospital bassinet for the first time without supporting the weight of her head. I shrieked as Kate's head lolled back on her fragile string of a neck, *Hold her head!* I yelled. Ned jumped out of his chair and snatched Kate from Phyllis's arms. And then I saw the faintest shadow of hurt in my mother's eyes before she stiffened, her posture perfect as she stood in my hospital room, surrounded by wilting bouquets of flowers and IT'S A GIRL balloons. *I know perfectly well how to hold a baby,* she said. *I held you all those years, didn't I?*

"I'll be there as soon as I can," said Ned. "Is Kate back yet?"

"Of course not."

"I saw her leave campus a while ago," he said. "I thought she'd be home by now."

I felt myself stiffen, but I didn't say anything.

"I'm sure she's fine," said Ned. "She probably stopped at a friend's house."

I pictured myself at Kate's age, in Nancy Perlmutter's brownstone apartment, her parents both working. We sat cross-legged on the floor of Nancy's room, a quarter ounce of pot spread on the newspaper between us, separating the seeds and twigs, expertly rolling joints and storing them in our empty Marlboro boxes. We walked to Central Park and met a couple of eleventh-grade boys in Sheep Meadow, spread a blanket on the grass, and got stoned out of our minds, watching the clouds float by overhead. Everything seemed so much more dangerous to me now—even my own memory of my younger self. I could have been killed in Central Park. I could have smoked pot laced with angel dust and lost my mind.

"Right," I said. Downstairs I heard the water being let out of the tub. Phyllis hadn't drowned after all. I hung up the phone and went down to the kitchen, tiptoeing past the guest room. I had a nice dinner planned: lamb chops, green beans with slivered almonds, a new potato casserole. I still had the notion that we might be able to have a pleasant meal. Three generations at table. Good food, a bottle of wine, easy conversation. I took the lamb chops out of the fridge and laid them on the counter for seasoning. As I rooted around for some rosemary in the spice rack, I looked out the window and saw a lone squirrel burying his nuts in the backyard, his little front paws frantically digging. Ned was convinced that the same squirrel visited us every year, burying his nuts in the fall, digging them up in the spring.

"What's this?"

My mother appeared in the doorway. I hadn't heard her coming. She had a terry-cloth robe wrapped around her, the belt cinched tightly at her waist, and she had scrubbed all her makeup off. Her face was pale and wrinkled, without definition. Her lips and eyebrows had disappeared.

"Rachel, what's this?" she asked again.

She reached out a hand. She was holding a bottle of my prenatal vitamins. I thought quickly. Had I left them out? No, I knew I hadn't. They were on the middle shelf of the bathroom medicine cabinet, along with my other prescriptions. The medicine chest doesn't even have a knob or handle; it's an old wooden cabinet that came with the house. She would have had to jiggle the door ajar, then pry it open with her fingernails.

"Where did you find that?" I asked.

"The medicine cabinet door just swung open," she said. "It almost hit me on the head. And then I glanced inside—I couldn't help it!—and there was this odd-looking bottle. I admit, I was curious. I looked. So sue me."

"What were you even doing in our bathroom?" I asked.

"Looking for a washcloth," she answered smoothly. I had left a stack of washcloths in the guest bathroom for her.

"That's bullshit," I said quietly. I was either going to whisper or scream. "You've got no business snooping into my life."

Her pupils started to jiggle. This was the sign I always looked for, the way I knew she was starting to lose it, shaking and trembling from the inside out. The seismic shifts of volcano Phyllis.

"You are my business!" she screamed.

I tried to leave the room, but she was blocking my way. I pushed past her, nearly knocking her over. I didn't care. I was trapped in my own house, and I had to get out of there. I remembered how I had felt, almost fourteen years earlier, when I had stupidly told Phyllis that I was pregnant with Kate. It was the same thing, all over again, only this time it was worse because I was older and she was older and nothing had changed. We were still knotted together, all tangled up.

"Stop!" she yelled at me. "Stop right now!"

I threw on a jacket and jammed my feet into the clogs by the front door.

"Where do you think you're going?"

I turned around and looked at her. Without her face painted on, she looked old and faded. Her hair was thinning, and through the expensive reddish highlights I could see patches of scalp.

"I'm thirty-eight years old," I said. "This is my house."

"Are you pregnant, Rachel?"

I didn't answer. Blood was pounding in my temples, my fingers were tingling.

"Well, are you?"

"Like it or not, I'm a grown woman," I said. My voice was shaking, and I hated myself for it. "You're being intrusive, and I won't stand for it."

"It's a simple question."

"Nothing's simple with you."

"Well," said Phyllis, "obviously I know the answer." She walked into the kitchen and sat down at the table. She shook her head. "Do you know what, Rachel? I feel sorry for you."

"Get out of my house!" I screamed, following her into the kitchen. I towered over her chair, a smoking column of rage.

She sat frozen. She wasn't used to me losing my temper. Usually, I got smaller and smaller around my mother. Quieter and more numb. I never yelled.

"I mean it. Get out!"

"What's going on?" Kate had come through the front door, wearing jeans and a midriff-baring top. I hadn't heard or seen her. Usually she made a big clatter, dumping her knapsack, an avalanche of keys and coins. Her eyes were wide.

"Nothing," I said quickly. I shot my mother a warning look.

"Hi, sweetheart," said Phyllis, rising to give her a kiss like nothing had happened at all. "You've got something in your—" She bent down, noticing Kate's navel ring glinting in the light. "Oh my God, what is that?"

Please, please, please, I was thinking.

"Hi, Grandma," said Kate. "A lot of kids have them."

Phyllis sniffed and turned to me. "You let her do that?"

"Kate's a big girl," I said lightly. "She makes her own choices."

"Well, I think it's—"

"There's some of that yogurt you like in the fridge," I said to Kate. "Do you want a snack before dinner, honey?"

Kate shot me a look, as if to say *Who died and made you June Cleaver?* except that she wouldn't even know who June Cleaver was. Then she turned to her grandmother. "Why were you guys yelling?"

"It was your mother who was yelling," said Phyllis.

"Mom," I said. "Don't even—"

"Hi, Phyllis." Ned came in, his hair ruffled from the early evening breeze. He was wearing a gray Hawthorne sweatshirt and sweatpants, straight from coaching JV soccer. He looked warily around the kitchen at all of us.

"Boy, it's getting nippy out there." He shrugged off his jacket and hung it over the kitchen chair. "Anybody want a beer?"

"Perhaps we should make it champagne, since I gather that congratulations are in order," said Phyllis.

"Sorry?"

"You have some happy news, do you not?"

"Shut up," I said, deadly quiet. "You don't know what you're doing."

"Rachel?" Ned turned to me.

Kate was watching us carefully, and she reminded me of the way she had looked as a toddler. Absorbing everything, watching behavior, never missing a trick.

"Ned, why don't you take Kate—"

"A brand-new baby," Phyllis interrupted. Her eyeballs were bouncing now, swirling like a comic-book character's. "Isn't that wonderful?"

"Mom?" Kate's eyes were glued to me. "What's Grandma talking about?"

"You're going to have a little brother or sister," said Phyllis.

The room tilted. I was in my own kitchen, surrounded by my family, and suddenly it felt like the most dangerous place in the world. All my blood seemed to rush to my throat, pooling there, blocking my breath.

"Mom?"

Kate was standing with her back against the wall.

"Honey, I—"

I reached for my daughter and she shrank from me. She looked at me as if she had no idea who I was.

"We were going to tell you after—"

"You're having another baby?" Her mouth curled around the word *baby,* spit it out. "Aren't you too old?"

"Lots of people—"

Ned came over to me and put a hand on the small of my back. I wasn't feeling too steady, and he knew it.

"We were waiting until after the amnio," he said. "Honey, we weren't trying to hide anything from you."

"It doesn't matter," she said. "I don't care."

Kate's expression was blank. I couldn't imagine how much effort it must have taken to maintain such absolute impassivity.

Phyllis cleared her throat. "I'm sorry. Did I let the cat out of the bag?" Her features were arranged in a parody of concern. I had never felt such a murderous rage. I wanted to kill her. How was it possible that she could still ruin everything for me? My husband, my daughter, my house, the life growing inside of me—nothing offered the slightest bit of protection. And the worst of it was, I could tell she was happy. She'd had an impact. Once again, she had placed herself at the center of the universe.

"Phyllis?" Ned said. "What the hell is wrong with you?"

"Ned? Would you please call a taxi for my mother?" I asked.

"What are you doing?" asked Phyllis.

"You're leaving," I replied.

"I'll drive her to the airport," said Ned.

"Fine," I said. "See, Mom? He's a good son-in-law after all."

My mother stood up as regally as she could in no makeup and a bathrobe.

"Caesar's wife is above reproach," she said, and walked out of the kitchen.

"You're a horrible person, Phyllis," said Ned, to her receding back. Each word was bitten off with something like pleasure. He had wanted to say that for fourteen years.

"Oh, God." I sank into a chair. I felt sick, not just nauseated but poisoned, as if a toxic gas had seeped inside of me. I buried my head in my hands and cried quietly.

"Mom?" said Kate.

She came over to me and put her arms around me. It was the first time she had touched me in months. She smelled of cigarette smoke. Up close, she looked like she had just woken up from a long and fitful sleep.

"Ssshhh," she whispered. Her hair fell across my face, and I felt her breath on my cheek, sweet and warm. "Don't cry. It's not good for the baby."

4

"IT WOULD HAVE TO BE A BLIZZARD TODAY," SAYS NED. "Like this isn't bad enough." His hands are tight around the steering wheel as he pulls onto 93. We've taken my Volvo, because it's better on icy roads than the seven-year-old Honda that Ned bought when we separated. And he's driving because that's the way we've always done it. Seventeen years of habits die hard.

"Can you see?" I look nervously out the window. The snow, the road, the sky are all the same shade of white.

"Rachel, I grew up on these roads," says Ned. "Relax."

"You're the one who said something about the weather."

"Fine," Ned says evenly. Like he's humoring me. So I decide to humor him back. I change the subject.

"How long do you think it'll take to get there? Hollis expects us at noon. You know how that place is—they take their appointments seriously."

"There's nothing we can do about it. We'll get there when we get there."

I steal a glance at Ned. He's taken off his parka and thrown it in back next to Josh's car seat. His sweater is pushed up around his elbows, exposing his strong forearms. I fell in love with those forearms, along with his elegant hands, his delicate, tapered fingers. An artist's hands. An artist who now sells houses for his parents' company, pointing out granite counters and Italian-tile shower stalls to Boston bankers ten years younger than himself.

We settle into a slow crawl north. There aren't many cars on the highway. Only people with pressing business would be out on a day like today. Schools are closed, and most workplaces. Jane and Arthur even closed Jensen Realty today, and they almost never give in to the weather, with their Yankee can-do spirit. They're home with Josh, who is probably tearing up their living room. I imagine that the cars and vans surrounding us are full of people on their way to hospitals and institutions, people whose lives aren't affected by something as ordinary as weather.

"So how are we going to deal with this?" I ask.

"What do you mean?"

"If they're kicking her out."

"Why don't we cross that bridge—"

"We have to at least think about it, Ned."

"No, we don't have to think about it," he snaps. "Let's just see what they say."

I know where his anger is coming from, but still it surprises me. For so many years, Ned was my best friend. This angry side of him was reserved for other people. I was almost never on the receiving end of it.

"I just don't know if she'll be safe at home," I say softly. "And I have Josh to look after."

"Well, maybe you should have thought of that before . . ." He trails off, as if he knows he's about to go too far.

"Before what?"

He doesn't answer.

"Before what?" I repeat.

He sighs. "I don't want to get into this, Rachel."

"No." I press on. "I want to hear what you were going to say."

Each word is as heavy as stone. "We had no business having—"

"Oh, don't. Please don't," I interrupt.

"Why? It's the truth, isn't it?"

Ned closes his mouth, presses his lips together. A small muscle flutters in his jaw. He's lost so much weight since we split up that it has sharpened the angles of his face. He looks hard, raw-boned and mean. He has lines in his face now, vertical creases in his cheeks where his dimples used to be.

"Are you saying I was the only one who wanted another baby?" I can't help it, I know I should be more mature. I should just keep my mouth shut and not blurt out every little thing I feel. But Ned has barred me from his life, and this is the first time in ages that I've been alone with him for more than a few minutes. Our conversations have consisted of logistics only: bills, insurance, taxes. The only stuff, outside of our children, that binds us together.

"I would have been happy the way things were," he says. "I didn't think it was such a bad thing—Kate's being an only child."

"That's easy for you to say now."

"We should have realized—it was a terrible time to have another one."

"We didn't know."

"We should have sensed it. We just piled trouble on top of trouble."

"Are you calling Joshua trouble?" I asked.

"Rachel, I love that child every bit as much as you do"—Ned's voice was strained—"so don't you fucking dare take what I'm saying out of context."

The air inside the car is hot and thick between us. I lean over and turn down the defroster.

"You were the one who kept telling me not to worry about Kate!" I could feel my face twisting into an ugly sneer. *"She'll be fine. Just typical teenage stuff."*

"Well it *was* typical teenage stuff," said Ned. "It didn't get worse until—"

"Ned, don't." I leaned my head back. "Please don't imply that—"

"I'm not implying anything. I'm just telling you the truth."

"Which is what? That having Josh started all the problems?"

"You said it, not me."

"What's wrong with wanting a baby?" I ask. "At least I didn't just give up on life."

"What, you mean like me?"

"You quit," I say.

"Oh, now we're really getting someplace."

"Well, it's true, isn't it? You just stopped painting—stopped, without ever thinking what it might do to you. Or to us."

I'm breathless, almost sick from saying things that have been buried inside of me for years. Even during the best of times, the subject of Ned's work was the no-man's-land of our marriage.

He's quiet for a long time.

"I know exactly what it did to me," he finally says.

He's driving faster now. The speedometer reads 50 mph, which is much too fast for this weather.

"Slow down," I say.

"Don't tell me how to drive."

"Dammit, Ned, slow down or let me out," I say. My heart is racing. I can see our senseless deaths open like a door in the whiteness. "You have two children. Don't drive like an idiot."

The mention of Kate and Josh does its job. Ned slows to a more reasonable speed. We drive along in silence for a few exits. I start to cry, though I don't think he notices. I keep my face turned toward the window, and I wipe my cheeks with the back of my hand.

"Sorry," he says, after a while.

I don't say anything because I don't trust my voice. The last thing I want is for Ned to see me this upset. It's not going to do us any good today. We need to hold it together, to prepare ourselves for whatever we're going to find at Stone Mountain.

He reaches across the gearshift and pats my hand. It's a tentative pat, and his touch feels alien. Still, I grab his fingers reflexively. He pulls away and puts his hand back on the steering wheel.

"So . . . that was all Hollis said? Just that he wants to meet with us?"

"Pretty much," I say. "That, and he seemed pretty upset about the pill they found in her pocket."

"Well, yeah. Especially with the drugs they're giving her. Who knows what the contraindications might be."

"I hadn't even thought of that," I say.

"Look, the important thing now is that it never should have happened," says Ned. "Not at a reform school."

"It's not a—"

"I know, I know. What's that bullshit politically correct term they use?"

"Therapeutic community," I say.

"Right. Well, you'd think in a therapeutic community, they'd be a little more careful."

"Hollis also said something about a fight with another girl, but I don't believe it," I say. "That's not Kate."

"We don't know who the hell Kate is anymore."

Ned's words hang in the air as we crawl through the blizzard. He's spoken the truth. We don't know our daughter. How is it possible? I could find her if I were blindfolded in a room of a hundred girls, but I don't know what's going on inside her.

"Do you think we should talk about it?" I venture. It feels like an opening to me, a way into a discussion we have successfully avoided for many months.

His jaw tightens.

"About what, exactly?"

"You know."

"No, I don't know."

Ned's playing games with me now. But I've learned to play too, so I fall silent, listening only to the swish of the windshield wipers, the howling wind.

"There's nothing to talk about, Rachel," he finally says.

"One way or another, we're going to have to deal with it," I say. "You can bury your head in the sand—"

"Now you sound like your mother," he says. "Isn't that one of her favorite clichés?"

"Don't you dare," I say quietly.

"You're right. I'm sorry," says Ned. "How is she, by the way?"

"She's the same."

"Does she know what's going on?" asks Ned.

"Are you kidding?"

I have gone to great lengths to keep Phyllis from knowing anything about my current situation. If she wonders why Kate never answers the phone, or why Ned never seems to be at home, she hasn't said a word. The truth is, she probably doesn't think about it.

"What are you going to do when she wants to come visit?" asks Ned.

"I've been putting it off. I guess I've been hoping that maybe things would change."

He doesn't respond. Not a blink, not a word.

"Please, Ned. Is this ever going to stop?"

"You never know. With the right medication, a good therapist—"

"I meant with you and me," I say.

His eyes flicker over to me, then back to the road.

"Are you seeing anybody?" I ask.

"You mean a shrink?"

"No, I mean a woman. Are you dating?"

My forehead is pressed against the cold of the window. *Are you dating?* is not a question you should ever have to ask your husband.

"No," he says softly. "There isn't anybody else."

"So why can't we—"

He shakes his head. "You just don't get it, Rachel. You don't realize what—"

He breaks off. I feel for him, I really do. Ned wasn't raised to be a man who expresses his feelings. I can only imagine what Jane was like when he was a little boy. If the way she treats Josh is any indication, Ned must have eaten lots of peas and sat up straight in his high chair. No whining, no tantrums. No grabbing his mommy around the knees and holding on tight.

"Please?" I turn to him and reach over, lightly touching the back of his neck. "There's no hope if we don't talk about it."

"I'm supposed to show a house in North Hawthorne at the end of the day," he says. His voice is strangled. "They'll probably cancel on account of the weather. Seven hundred and fifty grand for three acres."

"Ned?"

"Did you know that my parents are talking about making me a partner? I've already sold six houses in Appaloosa Court this quarter."

"Oh, Ned."

"Goddammit!" he cries. He shrugs off my hand. "Don't do this, Rachel. I need—"

He gulps for air. I've never seen Ned like this.

"It's okay," I murmur. "Take it easy."

"Do you have any idea how horrible my life is?"

"I think I do," I say.

"Selling houses. Living in Pine Dunes. Never seeing my children. And everybody thinks—"

"Oh, honey, it doesn't matter what everybody thinks," I say. "Is that what this is about?"

"It matters! This is my hometown! This is where I'm from!"

He suddenly pulls the car onto the shoulder of the interstate and stops next to a guardrail. His shoulders are shaking. I lean across the dashboard and flick on the hazards. They light up the snow all around us like the strobe of an ambulance, a red flashing sign of danger. Trucks and cars whiz by, spitting up slush.

I stroke his hair, wipe his hot forehead.

"Don't," he says.

"Let me help."

"I can't."

"I love you."

He lifts his head and looks at me through glazed eyes.

"That used to matter," he says. "I used to think that if you loved me, I could do anything."

"You still can."

"No," he says. "That time is over."

"It doesn't have to be."

"That's not how it works, Rachel."

He takes a deep, shuddering breath. Slowly, with the grim determination of a sick old man, he turns off the hazards, checks the rearview mirror, and pulls back onto the highway.

THE DIGITAL CLOCK IN THE CAR READS 12:43 BY THE TIME we see the sign for Stone Mountain. It is emblazoned with a small monarch butterfly, which is the school's logo. Girls come in crawling on their bellies and emerge with their wings spread, colorful and free. Or at least that's what we're supposed to think. We turn up the long driveway leading to the Tudor buildings of the campus. There are only fifty or sixty girls in residence, but the grounds are sprawling, parklike, as if all that space is needed to contain so much emotional trouble. There must be two feet of untrammeled snow. At a regular school, there would be evidence of a snowball fight or some half-finished snowmen. But here there is nothing but smooth whiteness, as if nature itself can be brought to order.

Ned swings the car into a parking lot next to the largest house, where Hollis and Esposito have their offices. When we dropped Kate off here, this is where we came. I shake my head, trying to stop the flood of images: the dark campus at dusk, the single yellow light hanging from the porch where Hollis stood waiting for us. Kate's tearstained face as we led her up the front walk. Her eyes wild as a trapped animal's, legs kicking. *Mommy, no!*

"Ready?" Ned's face is composed, back to normal.

"No," I say. "Not remotely."

But we walk toward the main house, Ned and I, in single file. Snow is banked high on either side of us. What else is there to do? We look for all the world like parents on visiting day. Ned is in a proper tweed blazer and khakis, dressed like an aging preppy. And I am doing Phyllis proud in my one good cashmere sweater, knee-length skirt, and boots. Each of us made the same choice, in the loneliness of our own bedrooms this morning, to dress the part.

Ned holds the front door open for me, and as we wander into the waiting area, I have the strange sense of having walked onto a stage set. These polished parquet floors, the tapestries hanging on the walls, leather sofas and chairs arranged in clublike groupings around low coffee tables fanned with recent copies of *The New Yorker* and *The Atlantic,* these all appear to have been designed to make parents comfortable about leaving their girls in a place where they'll have no direct contact, not so much as a letter, for many months. An older woman is stationed behind a gleaming wood desk to the far left of the waiting room.

"May I help you?" She looks up, a pencil tucked behind her ear.

"We have an appointment with Frank Hollis. Rachel and Ned Jensen," I say.

She glances down at an open calendar, then picks up the phone. "The Jensens are here," she announces.

She gestures to the deep leather sofa.

"He'll be a few minutes. Have a seat," she says.

Ned and I sink into the sofa. Instantly I feel tiny; my feet barely touch the floor. He reaches for my hand and holds it, squeezing tight. I pick up a *New Yorker* and start thumbing through it. I can't concentrate, so I look at the cartoons of attenuated city people holding martini glasses and speaking in bon mots that I don't even understand. I suppose if we had stayed in the city, we would have been closer to all that. I was always so sure that we made the right decision to leave, to bring up Kate in a small town with small-town values. Now, all my great ideas and plans seem like a huge joke on me.

"Mr. and Mrs. Jensen?" Frank Hollis pokes his gray head out from his huge mahogany office door. "Please, come in."

Ned and I jump to our feet like people in a courtroom. The judge is entering the chamber. All rise. We hurriedly cross the room to where Hollis is standing. He offers us each a quick handshake, then holds his door open for us. His enormous office is furnished like a statesman's or politician's, down to the framed quilt of the American flag behind his desk. This was the last place I saw my daughter. Spitting, screaming, cursing at me. *You bitch! How can you do this to me? I'm never going to fucking speak to you again!* And then Dr. Esposito led her away. I watched as she shrugged off his arm and followed him out of the building as proudly as a fashion model on a catwalk, tall and regal in her yellow flannel pajamas. She turned once and looked at Ned and me, and the expression on her face can only be described as triumphant. *I don't need you. I don't need anybody.*

Now she is standing with her back to us, looking out the window. I wasn't sure she'd be here, and my heart leaps with as much fear as love. She is skinny as always in her jeans, hiking boots, a baggy old sweater. Her hair is longer, falling halfway down her back.

"Kate?" Hollis says.

She doesn't move. The blizzard is slowing down. She is silhouetted by the arched picture window like a figure inside a snow globe.

"Your parents are here."

I wish Hollis would just shut up. I wish he'd leave the room and let us have some privacy. I want to hold my daughter, shower her head with kisses.

"Kate?"

With a small shrug of her shoulders, she turns around and looks at us. Her left cheek is bruised and swollen, her eye black-and-blue.

"Oh, my God," I whisper.

"I told you there had been an altercation," says Hollis. His voice seems to be coming from far away.

"Katie, Katie—"

I rush across the room and wrap my arms around her. Neither of us speaks. I just hug her close, and she buries her head against my shoulder.

"Please, won't you sit down," says Hollis.

None of us move.

"Really, I think it would be best. . . ."

I look at Hollis over the top of Kate's head.

"Best?" I say softly. "You think it would be best if what?"

"Katie?" Ned tentatively moves toward the two of us. I am rocking her slightly, swaying as if to music.

"Daddy?" She reaches an arm out to him, so skinny I could wrap my whole hand around it.

"We're leaving," Ned says to Hollis. "Where is my daughter's room? I'm going to get her things."

Hollis presses a button on his desk, and almost instantly his office door opens and in walks Bob Esposito, the head psychiatrist at Stone Mountain and the one person with whom I've regularly spoken about Kate.

"I've asked Dr. Esposito to join us," says Hollis.

"Didn't you hear me?" asks Ned. "We're leaving."

I just look at Esposito. *How could you?* I want to say—but I refrain, for now. I've liked him during our conversations, and I have truly believed he cares about Kate.

"Mr. Jensen, we should talk about this," says Esposito. "I don't think you realize what's—"

"We walk in here. And my daughter"—Ned voice catches—"my daughter has been beaten up. While under the care of your institution."

"That's not exactly—"

"Mommy?" Kate sounds the way she did as a little girl. Her voice is thin and sweet. "Can we go now?"

"Don't you see what she's doing?" says Hollis. "She's playing on your guilt."

"Give me a break!" I burst out. I gently touch Kate's swollen cheek. "She's black-and-blue!"

The three of us are huddled in the middle of the vast room, with Hollis and Esposito flanking us like stately bookends keeping together an unruly mess.

"She did this to herself, Mrs. Jensen," says Esposito.

"What's that supposed to mean?"

"Why don't you tell them, Kate?"

She looks at him blankly.

"Do you remember what we discussed? About honesty? Full disclosure?"

"I don't know what you're talking about." Her eyes flash at him.

"We're leaving," Ned says again.

"Please, Mr. and Mrs. Jensen. I understand completely—of course you're upset. But you don't actually have the whole picture here. You think you do, but—"

"Don't treat me like an idiot," says Ned.

"Believe me, that's not my intention."

I feel myself beginning to calm down in Esposito's presence. He's a small man with a big head, and his dark brown eyes—magnified by wire-rimmed glasses—are focused on me.

"What happened?" I ask him. "And why wasn't there any warning—any idea at all that something like this could have happened? You told me she was improving."

"Please, sit down," says Esposito, gesturing to a seating area next to a huge stone fireplace. "Let me fill you in."

Hollis has retreated to the other side of his desk.

"I want to go now," says Kate. "Don't listen to them. They're lying to you—don't you get it? They're just trying to cover their asses. They're probably afraid you're going to sue them."

"Five minutes," I say. Ned and I sit down on a small sofa, and Esposito perches on the edge of a chair, facing us. Kate drifts back over to the window.

"Kate? I think you should be part of this conversation," Esposito calls out to her.

She doesn't budge.

"Excuse me for a minute."

He hops up and goes over to Kate, standing close to her and speaking softly into her ear. She listens, then shakes her head hard.

"Okay." He comes back over to us. "I'd rather say this in front of Kate, but she's acting out now, and I can't capitulate to that kind of behavior. It's not helpful. I think she actually would like to be a part of—"

"Please," I blurt out. "Could we just get to the point?"

He pauses and looks at me with those big sad brown eyes. How many tearful mothers have sat on this sofa? A box of Kleenex is on the table in front of me.

"I have something to say that's going to be tough for you to hear," Esposito finally says.

"All of this is tough," Ned says.

Esposito tents his hands under his chin.

"As you know, when Kate was first admitted to Stone Mountain, her diagnosis was Adolescent Adjustment Disorder. But as time has gone on, we've begun to look at other possibilities that we simply can't rule out."

"Like what?"

"Look, Mrs. Jensen. Kate did this to herself," he says.

"What did she do?" I ask. My brain is clearing, the shock is wearing off, and there's room inside of me—not much but just enough—to take in the possibility that Kate harmed herself.

"She had a fight with a Level One girl," says Esposito. "We're still trying to get to the root cause of the fight itself. But she beat that girl pretty badly—she wound up in the infirmary, needing stitches in her cheek."

Kate is standing still. I don't know if she can hear us from all the way over by the window. Her silky hair spills over her back, glowing in the yellow light. Somewhere, I have snippings of her first haircut. In a Ziploc, in the bottom of a drawer. Stitches, infirmaries, drugs, fights—what has happened to my child?

"It looks like that girl did a pretty good number on Kate," says Ned.

"No." Esposito shakes his head. "Kate managed to close herself off in a bathroom afterward. She pulled in a chair and wedged it against the doorknob inside, so it was a good few minutes before we were able to get to her."

He swallows, then leans toward us.

"She bashed her face into the radiator," he says. "Over and over again. We had to pry her off. Her fingers are burned."

I glance over at Kate's hands. Sure enough, there are bandages around each fingertip. Esposito stops speaking, sits back, and watches us. Having said his piece, he's waiting for a reaction. I feel the heat of Ned's body next to mine and wonder if he's feeling the same sickening shame. It must be our fault. Some fault in our combined biochemistries, our histories, the way we raised her. It's the only way I can possibly explain Kate's behavior. All those years of play dates with other families—dozens upon dozens of birthday parties, summer picnics, winter skiing trips—I thought we were all living similar lives. But those families are not the ones sitting here in this godforsaken institution listening to a psychiatrist tell them that their daughter is sick. No, those families are home, north of Boston, doing laundry, making sandwiches, watching videos.

"What are you saying?" My voice is barely audible. It's hard to move my lips, to form words.

"We can't rule out the possibility that she's preschizophrenic," says Esposito, "though she's too young for us to know for sure. And then there are various personality disorders that would explain this kind of self-mutilating behavior—"

"Oh, God," I hear myself moan. "What are you telling us?"

"She needs to stay here, that's for certain," says Esposito. "Under what essentially amounts to house arrest. No academics for now. She needs to be in intensive therapy—perhaps even hospitalized while we try to stabilize her meds."

"What if we took her home?" I blurt out. "Get her into daily therapy. And I can watch her, keep an eye on her all the time—"

Esposito waves his hands in the air, graceful as a conductor.

"Simply put, she's too sick, Mrs. Jensen," he says. His big brown eyes blink at me. "And I can't stress strongly enough that she cannot—must not—have access to drugs. The ecstasy that was found in her pocket—hallucinogenic drugs are a catastrophe for someone in her condition and on her meds."

"But she got the ecstasy here," Ned says. "How do you explain that?"

"I hate to say this, but it happens," says Esposito, "and not just at Stone Mountain. It's a risk at any of these schools. I'm just being honest with you. One of the kids probably snuck it in." Esposito pauses. "But if she's kept isolated, believe me—it won't happen again."

"That's not good enough," Ned says. His voice is hoarse, and when I look at him I see how shaken he is by all this new information. "How can you guarantee us that—"

"We can't guarantee anything. But I promise you that she's safer here than she'll be anywhere else."

Kate turns away from the window. I can hardly bear to look at her. One whole side of her face—that beautiful face—is swollen and bruised. I don't know which is worse: to imagine that another girl did this to her or that she did it to herself.

"We've prepared some documents for you to sign," says Esposito, leading us to Hollis's desk. "Of course, this level of care is quite a bit more expensive."

"Can we go now?" Kate walks toward us.

I shake my head. "No, baby," I say quietly. Deep inside me, I know Esposito is right. I can't stand it—the idea that I can't protect my own daughter—but it's true. I'd have to lock her in her room, chain her to her bed.

"I'm all packed up. I don't want to stay here," she says. "Please, Mommy—I want to go home."

"I'm sorry, Kate," says Ned. "Dr. Esposito thinks—"

"Fuck Dr. Esposito!"

"Kate!"

"He's lying to you! Don't you get it? They just want your money. They don't give a shit about me."

How does she know exactly what to say? She's either a brilliant liar or I'm living in a universe in which nothing is as it seems. Could this well-educated and well-meaning doctor really be some sort of monster? *He's lying to you!*

But this is not the first time I've heard those words from Kate. I stiffen, then slowly stand.

"We think you're in trouble, and we're going to keep you here until you're safe."

I look at Ned, silently pleading with him for help. He's still sitting on the sofa, head bent down, reading the papers that Hollis handed him.

"Your mother and I are in agreement, Kate," he says, without looking at her.

"You'll be sorry," she says.

"What's that supposed to mean?"

"Nothing."

"Kate?" Esposito walks over to her. "It's almost two. Time for group."

"Screw group!" she screams. "You can't make me!" She falls to her knees the way she did when she was Josh's age. We used to joke about it. We called it "civil disobedience." Kate, making her body limp and heavy, harder to drag away.

"Let's go." Esposito reaches a hand down to her. "Say goodbye to your parents."

I walk over to Kate, then crouch down and try to look her in the eye. She's rocking back and forth on her knees, keening like an old mourner. I remember when she was little, the way her mood would shift in an instant. She'd be screaming one minute, her face purple with fury, and then with the right touch—a tickle, a joke—she'd dissolve into helpless laughter.

"Honey, listen to me."

She doesn't respond.

"Listen."

My voice is shaking, and tears are spilling from my eyes.

"We have to go now," I say.

She cries louder, but she doesn't look up. I lean over and kiss the top of her head, breathing her in.

"I love you," I whisper in her ear. "Never forget that."

Then I walk out the door, leaving them all in there: Ned, still signing the papers; Esposito, waiting to take her away; Hollis, who hasn't said a word since Esposito took over. I pass the receptionist, nearly tripping over the fringe of the rug. I push the heavy doors open and am hit with a blast of freezing air. I step outside, gasping for breath. The snow has finally stopped. All I want to do is run down the long driveway of Stone Mountain, run as far and as fast as I can away from my own child, away from her terrible face and shining guileless eyes. I'm glad—glad to be leaving her in the care of doctors. I can't handle her. The truth is, I don't even want to handle her.

Ned comes out, holding our two coats. He places mine around my shoulders, wrapping it tight around me the way he used to. I sag against him. He holds me close, and I smell his sweat mixed with spearmint-scented deodorant.

"I signed the papers," he whispers.

We both stand there on the stone steps of Stone Mountain, listening to the wind, to a heavy door creaking open on the other side of the building, and to our daughter's muffled cries. We sway back and forth, neither of us moving until finally we can no longer hear her voice.

5

"I THINK I CAN HEAR HIS HEARTBEAT," KATE WHISPERED. I was sprawled across my bed, watching the evening news, and she was curled up with her ear pressed against my big belly. It was early June; a heat wave had settled over southern New England, and for days I had been lying around, just trying to stay cool. We had the door closed and the shades drawn, all in an effort to keep me from overheating. I was a huge, red, sweaty mess.

Kate lifted her head up, eyes startled, laughing.

"He just kicked me!"

We knew it was a boy. Then the amnio confirmed it. And even though I had claimed not to care about the sex of the baby, when we got the amnio results I was relieved. It was going to be easier to have a boy. I had less concern about Kate being jealous. In fact, she seemed anything but. Over the course of my pregnancy her mood had improved. She wasn't exactly the old Kate—there were still tense moments of slammed doors and sullen retreats into silence—but she was happier than she'd been. That spring, we'd been spending most weekends at Tommy and Liza's beach house, where I sat on the back porch, wrapped in a blanket in the ocean breeze while Kate and Sophie wandered the Nantucket shore together, collecting shells, looking for all the world like two normal healthy teenage girls.

"See?" Liza asked me, as she squinted out at them. "What did I tell you?"

I rested my hands on my belly and looked at Kate, strong and already tanned in her tiny cutoffs. She was laughing at something Sophie said to her.

"Maybe you were right," I said.

"Of course I was right. You worry too much," said Liza.

A BLACK FLY BUZZED AGAINST THE BEDROOM WINDOW, keeping me from dozing. The baby turned, and I felt a sharp pain below my rib cage. Kate had fallen asleep with one hand resting on my stomach, her pale, almost platinum hair spilling over the rumpled sheets. I loved to watch her sleep. I could examine her voraciously, without worrying about making her self-conscious. Her eyelids fluttered, as if she were trying to sort something out in her dreams. She had the finest down across her upper lip and cheek, but her eyebrows and eyelashes were dark. I ran a hand along her smooth, skinny arm.

Ned was at the academy that evening, at a meeting he couldn't miss. The end of the semester was always a busy time. Ned's star had been rising at the academy over the last couple of years. There was talk of his becoming the head of the department or maybe even assistant headmaster. Funny—he didn't even want that kind of success in academia, and yet it came so easily to him. Ned still painted in the barn out back, but all of his early ambition had turned into a middle-aged hobby. We didn't discuss it anymore—the art dealers who might be interested in his work, or his book of slides left with some Newbury Street gallery. It had faded away slowly, the way a painting itself fades when left too long in the sun. One day the image of Ned-the-artist was impossible to make out, and in his place was a high school teacher.

I was looking at an early painting of Ned's, a pale blue series of square shapes covered with squiggles of script, indecipherable words that hung above the fireplace in our bedroom, when I felt a gush between my legs. It was sudden, torrential. With Kate, my water had never broken, so the feeling was unfamiliar and for a moment I thought I had become incontinent.

Kate woke up, the side of her T-shirt soaked in the clear warm fluid.

"Oh my God!" she said, breathless.

"My water broke," I said calmly. "Call your father."

"Where is—"

"Call his mobile."

Kate ran around my bedroom gathering up things I'd need in the hospital, even though my bag had been packed and ready to go for days. It was a week before I was due, but I'd had the sense that the baby would come early. There was a pressure when I walked, his head banging low against my pelvis. I stood up, dizzy. The contractions started right away, and they were fierce. I walked to the closet to change my clothes, but when I got there I grabbed the edge of the door frame, hunched over in intense, throbbing pain.

"Are you okay?"

"I'm fine, honey," I managed to say.

She had the phone in her hand, and she had stripped off her T-shirt and was throwing on one of Ned's huge button-downs.

"Dad?" she spoke into the phone. "It's happening."

WE DROVE TO BOSTON SOON AFTER MIDNIGHT. I WAS splayed in the backseat of the Volvo. Ned was driving, and Kate was in the front passenger seat, her legs crossed in some elaborate twist she had learned in yoga class. It looked painful, but her face, when I caught glimpses of it, was serene. She put a hand up to her nose and closed off one nostril, then the other, doing a breathing exercise.

"You ready for this, Katie?" Ned asked.

"Uh-huh."

"Because if you don't want to stay for the whole thing, I'm sure there's a waiting room," I said before doubling over with another contraction.

"No, I want to," she said. Her voice sounded tiny in the darkness.

We had decided, after much discussion, to have Kate with us in the delivery room. Ned had balked at first, thinking that it might be too frightening for a fourteen-year-old. But I really felt it was the right thing to do. I wanted Kate to be able to connect to this baby from the very beginning. I didn't want her to feel displaced, not even for a minute. But maybe it was a crazy idea. Even though she was mature for her age, she was just a kid.

"Are you sure? Because if—"

"I'm sure."

Ned met my eyes in the rearview mirror. *Great timing, Rachel,* I could almost hear him thinking. *Now that we're halfway to Boston, you're having second thoughts.*

The contractions were five minutes apart when we were finally admitted to Beth Israel. The room in the maternity ward was small and white. The window overlooked the inner courtyard of the hospital, where there was a scattering of light from other windows on other floors. I thought of my father, dead at fifty-eight. Strange to think I was only a few years older than Kate when he died. In those final weeks of my father's life, I grew to despise hospitals. I never imagined, not for a minute, that someday I would be in a hospital for a happy reason—that I would be strong and well and able enough to bring a child into the world. I thought only of doom and gloom. Someday it would be me lying there, a gray and wasted shadow. *Hey, Dad,* I said quietly to myself. *Hey, you're having another grandchild.*

I put on a printed hospital gown and climbed onto the bed, just as another contraction hit.

"Ned!" I groaned.

He was bent over the small suitcase, and when he stood up he was holding the camcorder.

"Oh, come on," I said.

"I promise I won't film the birth," he said.

"I don't even think they let you."

"Why?"

"Afraid of lawsuits, I guess."

Ned pointed the video camera out the window. He fiddled with the zoom.

"Do you think you could help me here, instead of playing Truffaut?" I asked.

"More like Fellini," he said, training the camera on me.

"Thanks a lot."

I turned on my side, and Kate pressed her small fists into my lower back as I gritted my teeth through the contractions. Kate and I hadn't been this physically close in years. She was seeing my bare back, my hairy armpits, my less-than-perfect butt hanging out of the flimsy hospital gown. I wondered what she thought: probably that she'd never be this old.

"Did it hurt so much with me?" she asked.

"You were easier," I said.

"Really?" She seemed pleased by this.

"Yeah."

"Oh, you just don't remember," says Ned.

I shot him a look.

"She was easier," I said.

"Breathe," said Ned, which was the only piece of information he had retained from our Lamaze refresher class.

"Shut up," I moaned.

I didn't notice that I seemed to be getting hooked up to more and more machines as the hours passed. A fetal monitor, then an oxygen mask. A nurse came by every fifteen minutes and read a long sheet of paper that the fetal monitor was spitting out. Ned filmed that too, the paper scrolling like ticker tape onto the floor.

"What are you doing?" I asked.

"It's all in the details," he said.

"Film me!" Kate wheedled. She grabbed a rubber glove, blew it full of air like a balloon, and then released it, and it swished around the room. She was giddy with exhaustion.

A television hanging in the upper corner of the room was broadcasting a soap opera I was pretty sure was a rerun of *All My Children.* The volume was turned down, but still I focused on the screen. They had said something in Lamaze about finding a focal point. Of course, they meant you should focus on some soothing image: a family photo, a flower, a favorite painting. I watched intently as one big-haired blonde slapped another.

"Do you want some ice chips?" asked Ned.

"Sour candy?" offered Kate.

I shook my head. It was getting pretty bad, but I didn't want to scare Kate. I was trying to stay calm when the doctor came in, a white coat tossed over her sweater and jeans. Her name was Lisa Sorenson, and she had asked us to call her Lisa, which both put me at ease and made me uncomfortable. She was a young woman—younger than I was, which was something I couldn't get used to—and she was holding a clipboard, looking down at it, frowning. She tucked her long brown hair behind her ears.

"We need to do a little test," she said. "Nothing to worry about."

"What kind of test?" Ned asked.

"We take a very fine needle and insert it into the baby's scalp."

Kate shot up in her orange plastic chair, her back rigid.

"What's wrong?" I asked quickly.

"Probably nothing," Lisa said. "We just want to be sure he's getting enough oxygen."

She ripped open a plastic kit and instructed me to lie back. I couldn't imagine a needle going into my baby's head—what was she doing? I was suddenly frightened, but I didn't dare show it. Ned came over to the side of the bed and held my hand. He was pale, his fingers ice-cold.

Everything got very quiet after Lisa left the room with the kit in hand. I was just trying to breathe into the oxygen mask strapped around my nose and mouth. Kate was staring at the television. And Ned had his head bowed. I wondered if he was praying. I could feel the baby moving around inside of me. He just wasn't ready to come out yet, that was all. Inhale, exhale. My heart was skipping beats in my chest. Could I have a heart attack during childbirth?

I heard the announcement over the PA system and registered what it meant before Ned or Kate did: *Anesthesia to room ten, anesthesia to room ten stat,* broadcast through the maternity ward.

I turned to Ned and lifted up my oxygen mask.

"That's us," I said, only a second before Lisa rushed back in the door.

"The test results were not reassuring," she said. It sounded like something they had taught her to say in medical school. Don't say *bad,* say *not reassuring.*

"We're going to be doing a C-section," she said, as she handed Ned some green scrubs, along with a green shower cap. Ned sat down and struggled to pull the scrubs on over his shoes.

"What about me?" Kate reached out her arms. "Where are mine?"

"You can't come in, honey," said Lisa.

"I have to come in!"

"I'm sorry. It's not allowed."

"Mommy?" Kate grabbed my hand. "What's going on?"

I pulled her head down for a kiss. Two orderlies had materialized, and one of them held my IV pole as they started to wheel me out of the room.

"Everything will be fine, Katie," I said.

"I want to be with you!"

"I know, baby. But it's the rules." I stroked her hand.

Her eyes were huge. I had only myself to blame. What the hell had I been thinking? How could I have let this happen? There was a decent enough chance of something going wrong. I was thirty-eight—a geriatric pregnancy, they called it. I never should have allowed Kate anywhere near the hospital. She should have stayed with her grandparents, waiting for the phone call. Ned should have put his foot down. He was right, I was wrong. I had been asking for trouble, tempting fate.

Ned handed Kate the video camera. "Listen—take this, and as soon as the baby is born, you can be the official photographer."

Kate was running alongside the stretcher as I was wheeled toward the operating room.

"Mom, I'm scared," she cried.

I reached up and touched her cheek. "I promise you, I'm going to be fine. And the baby's going to be fine. You're going to have a little brother in no time at all."

"I'm coming in!" she shouted. But two orderlies held her back as the doors swung open and I was pushed inside.

"I love you," I called out, but the doors had already swung shut.

Everything had gone from calm to chaos with a single drop of blood from my baby's scalp; we had switched channels from *Little House on the Prairie* to *ER.* No stenciled teddy bears in the operating room, only enormous bright lights and steel counters, gleaming white machinery. I was shaking, holding on to the sides of the gurney so hard that, later, my whole chest would ache from the effort. A needle in my spine, then a dull, almost impossible numbness seeping across my middle. There were people in the room, a dozen of them, all moving purposefully. I wanted to move too. To do something, anything other than lie there helplessly.

"Can you feel this?" A pressure, nothing more. "And this?"

Ned was sitting behind me in his scrubs and shower cap, holding my hand. A curtain went up above my stomach.

"Is Kate okay?" I asked Ned.

"Yes," he said tersely.

"She never should have been here," I panted.

"Don't think about that now."

"I wish somebody could be with her," I said. My teeth were chattering. "Can we call someone?"

"There's no time."

Ned's fingers were still freezing cold. I was bisected. Half of me was shaking and digging my nails into my husband's hand, and the other half was being cut open. Lisa swung her head around the side of the partition to ask one of the nurses something. She looked too young, her face unlined in the fluorescent light.

"How's it going, Lisa?" Ned asked. *How's it going.* Casual, like he was checking on the score of a game.

"Everything's fine," she said, her voice muffled from behind the curtain.

I tried to calm down. I concentrated on my breathing. The baby—he, Joshua; we had already named him after my father—was still inside me. I tried to communicate with him, to send him waves of love and strength.

"We're almost there," said Lisa. The anesthesiologist rested a gloved hand on my shoulder.

Ned bent his head down so that his cheek was touching my own. Our tears were mingled.

"I love you no matter what," I whispered.

And then, piercing through everything in that room, a baby's cry. A healthy, furious little wail that brought tears instantly to my eyes as Ned jumped to his feet. All I heard was Lisa saying, "He's beautiful," and the sound of that cry.

"Look." Ned was by my side, holding our tiny perfect son.

I couldn't stop trembling. All my life I had lived on the precipice, a step away from a bottomless black pit. Ned stood between me and the precipice. Then we had Kate, and she stood there too. My little family! And now, with this new baby, the space between me and the free fall stretched, became wider. With Joshua Jensen's ragged first cry, the spell was broken. The cycle of onliness, of loneliness, that had been passed down from my mother to me like a torch was finally over. I was the mother of two. It had taken me fourteen years. And nothing dreadful had happened; everything had turned out fine. Tears rolled from my eyes down the sides of my face, into my hair.

They took Josh to the other side of the operating room to weigh and measure him and put drops in his eyes. He was still crying lustily, his face red and wrinkled like an old man's. I turned my head to watch as they hovered over him in their surgical greens. I could tell he had my coloring: a thatch of dark hair and olive skin.

"Honey, bring Kate in," I called over to Ned.

"She can't come into the OR," said Lisa. "Sorry. We'll have you out in just a few minutes."

The nurse put Josh on top of my chest, swaddled in a tiny blue blanket. *Thank you, thank you,* I kept repeating, even though I wasn't sure who I was thanking. God? Lisa? Ned, for going along with this? Or even tiny Josh himself?

"I've finished stitching you up," said Lisa. "It'll be a small scar. You'll be able to wear a bikini." She brushed a strand of dark hair off her sweaty forehead.

"As if," I said. We all laughed, giddy with relief. A near miss, is what we were all thinking—it didn't even bear saying. One minute we were looking at a catastrophe and the next, a healthy baby boy.

The anesthesiologist wheeled me out of the OR and down the hall toward recovery.

"We have to call Phyllis," I said groggily. "And Jane and Arthur. And—"

"I gave her some medicine for the pain," the anesthesiologist said to Ned, as if I wasn't there.

"I'm not in pain," I said happily.

"You're legally stoned. Enjoy," said Ned.

Josh was burrowed into my chest, his mouth already rooting around for my breast.

"I'll get Kate," said Ned. "She's probably in the waiting room."

I nodded. Josh's head fit into the palm of my hand, and his fingers were curled into tight fists. I stared at his pointy little chin, his floppy neck, his smooshed-up nose. The morphine made me fuzzy, and I lost track of time. I had no idea how long Ned had been gone before he finally came back and sank down on the edge of my bed. He was breathless.

"She's gone," he said.

"What do you mean?" I asked through the haze.

"I don't know where the hell she is. I've looked everywhere." He stood up again and paced the room. "Think, Rachel. Where could she be?"

"I'm sure she didn't leave the hospital," I said. "She wouldn't know where to go."

Ned shook his head.

"One of the nurses told me she saw her running out the door. She said Kate looked like she had seen a ghost."

I SPENT THE FIRST SEVERAL HOURS OF JOSH'S LIFE ALONE with him. First in the recovery room, he slept burrowed under my arm as I was monitored, and then in the private room Ned had somehow managed to wangle. I was relieved about Josh and worried about Kate all at once, but truthfully I had been given a lot of morphine—it was physically impossible for me to panic. Ned had gone looking for her, and he would find her. Josh's mouth had fastened around my nipple and he was squirming, pulling hard. He's a survivor, I thought to myself. My children are survivors.

Once in my room, I kept fighting sleep. I was roused by a knock on the door. An orderly came in, carrying in a huge arrangement of yellow roses that I knew instantly my mother had sent. Yellow roses were her trademark. Phyllis had loved them ever since a suitor sent her two dozen back when she was dating, before she married my father. Perhaps because she was a bus driver's daughter from Brooklyn, Phyllis found all forms of material excess to be the height of sophistication. Rolls-Royces, yachts, big diamond solitaires, Chanel jackets—all of these impressed her. My father, who had certainly done well financially, was never quite in the league of all the boyfriends Phyllis had before him, when she was a career girl in New York City.

The orderly placed the roses on the windowsill, blocking

the view. They were long-stemmed, leafy, just starting to open. There were at least two dozen, maybe three. He handed me a small white card. *My dear grandson; Welcome to the world! Love from your Grandma Phyllis.* Grandma Phyllis. To distinguish herself from Grandma Jane—it was already starting. Phyllis had been competitive with Jane all of Kate's life, and now she had a new victim. What was she going to send Josh, to top whatever his Hawthorne grandparents gave him? When Kate was two, Phyllis bought her a motorized car. I remembered Kate, her tiny feet barely touching the pedals, screaming in frustration because we had taken out the batteries. Who would let a two-year-old drive a motorized car? Was that why Phyllis did it? To make us seem like mean parents and to cast herself in the role of beneficent grandmother?

I looked at the clock on the wall and realized that it had been hours since Ned had left to look for Kate.

I pushed a button next to my bed, and a voice blasted over the intercom in my room. "Yes, can I help you?"

"I was wondering if you knew where my husband went," I said.

"Sorry, I don't."

"Is there any way you could page him?" I asked. "Ned Jensen?"

"Sure, hon."

Another knock on the door.

"Hey, there." I heard my mother-in-law's unmistakable accent. *Thee-uh.* "Are you decent?"

"Come on in," I said.

Jane and Arthur walked gingerly into the room. Arthur was holding an enormous teddy bear. It was a Friday morning, and they were both in their Jensen Realty attire: New England tweedy casual blazers, with their brass name tags pinned to the lapels.

"There he is," Arthur said jovially. He leaned over me and looked at Josh, who was sound asleep in the crook of my arm.

"I hear you had a hard time in there," said Jane. She stood next to Arthur in her flesh-colored stockings and one-inch heels. Her face was bright pink, as it almost always was these days. If you looked closely you could see a map of veins running across her nose and cheeks, her nightly pint of gin finally catching up with her.

"He's okay—that's the important thing," I said. I knew what Jane thought: that I was a fragile little Jewish girl, a complainer, not cut out for the rigors of childbirth. Jane herself had popped out her two boys, Ned and his younger brother Steven, in less than two hours start to finish.

"Look at that little face," said Jane. "That's the Jensen chin, you know."

"Where's Ned?" piped Arthur. He was already moving away from the bed, from my sweaty corpulence. And why not? My breasts were practically hanging out of my hospital gown, and Arthur was squeamish to begin with. Ned had told me that in all his years growing up he had never once seen his father naked.

"He went to look for Kate hours ago," I said. I could hear my words slurring. I was in a dangerous state, not clearheaded at all.

"What do you mean, look for Kate? Isn't she here?" asked Jane. "We haven't seen her since—"

"There he is! There's the new father!" Arthur suddenly boomed. I swiveled my head to the door, and there was Ned, standing with Kate, who skulked like a collared dog. His mouth was one thin line of fury.

"What happened?" I asked from the bed.

"We'll talk about it later." He gave Kate a little shove into the room.

"Katie, look at your baby brother!" said Jane.

Instead, Kate walked into the room, past me, and over to the window where she stood with her back to all of us.

"Kate!" said Arthur. "Don't you want to—"

She shook her head hard.

"Now, now, young lady—"

"Drop it, Dad," said Ned. "Leave her alone."

Jane and Arthur raised their eyebrows at each other. This would no doubt be discussed over drinks later that evening. *It's all because of the way Rachel raised her,* I imagined Jane saying. I was so stoned that their faces started going in and out of focus, and the room was revolving slowly, not altogether unpleasantly. *So much permissiveness. Like some sort of hippie, if you ask me.*

"Who's a hippie?" Jane asked.

My hand shot over my mouth. Had I spoken out loud?

"Hippy. I'm going to be so hippy," I responded weakly.

Ned looked at me as if I had lost my mind. He had pulled a chair up to the clear plastic bassinet where Josh now slept soundly on his side, his head covered with a tiny pink-and-blue knit cap.

"Have you called your mother, Rachel?" asked Jane.

"I left her a message," said Ned.

"Those flowers are from her." I pointed to the yellow roses.

"Of course," said Jane. "Lovely."

Jane and Arthur had tried to befriend Phyllis when Ned and I were first married. They invited her to family occasions—even family occasions at which the mother of their new daughter-in-law need not be included. They felt sorry for her; that was part of it. She was widowed, all alone in New York, and her only child had moved far away from her. For all of our differences, I knew Jane and Arthur were decent people. They tried to do the right thing, not simply out of an Emily Post protocol but because the right thing was what came naturally to them. And so, when Phyllis started misbehaving, it was deeply surprising to them. *What would cause her to act that way?* Jane used to ask me, in the years before she gave up entirely on my mother. *Why would she be so nasty to us?* I tried to tell Jane that it wasn't personal; Phyllis was an equal-opportunity spreader of bile. The butcher, the greengrocer, her daughter, her in-laws—she couldn't contain the bucket of rage that was inside of her, bubbling to a boil, constantly in danger of spilling over. Now, in her late seventies, she had no friends left.

"Is she going to visit?" asked Jane brightly.

"Yeah, let us know so we can take a trip to the Bahamas," said Arthur.

Jane swatted at him, laughing.

"I don't know. I haven't decided what to do yet," I said. "The last time she was here, it was awful."

"Kate? I brought some chocolate—do you want a piece?" asked Jane.

Kate's long hair swung back and forth as she shook her head.

"Where was she?" I whispered to Ned.

"Home," he said. "She had thumbed it back to Hawthorne."

"Hitchhiked?"

He nodded. We had expressly forbidden Kate ever to hitchhike. We knew some of her friends did it, but she swore to us that she never would.

"How did you figure it out?"

"I—there were only so many places I could think of that she could go. I mean, where the hell was she going to go in Boston? She doesn't know anybody in town."

"What are you whispering about?" Kate turned away from the window. I knew it would get to her—ever since she was a kid she couldn't stand it if she thought we were keeping a secret from her.

"What do you think?" I asked.

She blinked. Her eyes were red-rimmed, and her nose was running. She had obviously been crying for hours.

"Katie, I'm so sorry. You must have been scared out of your wits," I said.

She wouldn't look at me.

"Please, honey. Come over here so I can hug you," I said.

"We're heading out," said Arthur. He and Jane had stood and were hovering by the door at the mere mention of a hug. "House to show. We'll see you guys later."

Ned nodded, and I waved from my bed. Kate came over and sat next to me, carefully moving the tube from my IV out of the way. Her eyes were glued to the bassinet where her new baby brother was snoozing away peacefully.

"Wow," she said. "He's so tiny."

I could see a hundred thoughts flickering across her face, and I realized we weren't going to punish her—not for running off, not for hitchhiking.

"It's okay, Kate," I said. "I understand."

"Maybe your mother does, but I have to say—" Ned started, but I shot him a pleading look.

"This was terrible judgment on our part," I said. "You never should have been exposed—"

"I thought you were going to die," she said, looking at Josh. Her expression was unreadable.

"I know, baby. It must have been scary. But everything's okay now."

I fought through my haze, trying to reach her.

"I thought something terrible was happening to you in there," she went on. Her voice was curiously flat, but I saw that her lips were trembling.

"Oh, Katie," I said, and reached out a hand to her. She ignored me and leaned over so she could see Josh's face through the side of the clear plastic bassinet.

"His nose is smooshed," she said.

"So what do you think?" I asked. "Should we keep him?"

Kate straightened up and looked at me impassively, as if I hadn't been joking.

"I'll let you know," she said.

THE FIRST COUPLE OF DAYS AFTER WE BROUGHT JOSH HOME are a time I cherish, hours filled with so much joy that, if I could have harvested that joy, it would have lasted me for the rest of my life. The house was overflowing with flowers. So many bouquets! Because of Jane and Arthur's business, it seemed that every real estate broker in the state of Massachusetts had sent an arrangement. Glass vases filled with bright summer flowers teetered on tables and windowsills and mantels. Ned had brought home a bunch of lullaby CDs and set up a boom box in the bedroom, so there was a soundtrack to those early weeks—songs I can remember still.

A constant buzz of activity surrounded me, but all I had to do was lie there in the center of it like a queen bee, with my new baby snuggled against my chest. I was recovering from surgery, so I spent most of my time in bed, wearing a pair of men's pajamas that Ned had bought for me at Brooks Brothers. Josh seemed always to be hungry, and breast-feeding was easy—so much easier than the first time around. With Kate, the truth is I didn't enjoy breast-feeding. I felt like a cow, completely unsexy, as if my body wasn't my own. Perhaps it was a function of age, but now I loved the intimacy, the ability to give Josh everything he needed, the miracle of what my own body produced. I kept him close all day long. He slept and ate, and Ned brought me yogurt, toast, and endless cups of herbal tea. Kate was through with school, and we weren't going to send her to camp—it seemed to us that camp was where all her troubles had started the year before—so she was home with us, restless and bored. She spent a lot of time sitting in the wing chair in the corner of the bedroom near my vanity, just watching wordlessly as I nursed Josh.

"Do you want to hold him?" I asked her each day—and each day she shook her head no. It is only in retrospect that I see she was slipping away; the fissure inside her had begun to grow. Later, I would wonder why I didn't worry more that Kate physically kept her distance from Josh for a whole week: the four days I was in the hospital, and three days after that. But at the time I was in a cocoon of new motherhood; the world felt safe to me, all of us protected. I was like a mountain climber who, having scaled a difficult peak, rested there without noticing that the way back down was full of jagged, difficult terrain.

"Katie, why don't you get outside?" I asked.

"There's nothing to do. Everybody's away."

It was true that most of her friends were gone. Most of the kids from the academy were already at their summer houses.

"Hey," said Ned from the door. "Look who's here!"

Liza and Tommy poked their heads around the corner.

"Oh my God! I thought you guys were in Paris!"

"We got home last night," said Liza.

She bent over me in a cloud of sweet French perfume and kissed me on both cheeks.

"You look amazing," she said. "Not like a woman who just had a C-section."

Tommy crossed the room and gave me a hug.

"So this is the little guy!" he said. Tommy had shaved his head when he started to lose his hair and was a very arresting-looking figure with his dark blue blazer, faded Levi's, and that shiny bald head.

He stroked Josh's cheek.

"Wash your hands, Tommy!" called Liza.

"What?"

"The baby. Germs. Wash your hands."

Liza looked more serene than usual, and when she wrinkled her forehead the space between her eyebrows didn't move. I wondered if she'd had the kind of procedure I had read about in *Vogue* or *Harper's Bazaar:* collagen injections, or botox, or some other rite-of-passage for the pushing-forty set. I always read the fashion magazines, buying them each month and devouring them in one sitting. They were my guilty pleasure, even though they had nothing to do with my life. Reading them was like browsing through a guidebook to a country I knew I'd never visit.

"Look at this little creature!" she exclaimed, picking Josh up out of my arms.

As Liza cooed over the baby, I watched Kate. Her shoulders sagged, and she seemed to wilt after Liza came in without even saying hello. Kate had always hungered for Liza's approval. She was so glamorous, so urbane, such a force of nature. I tried to signal Liza with my eyes, to let her know that she should pay attention to Kate, but she was oblivious.

"He's your spitting image," she said.

"Anybody want a beer?" asked Ned. Countless times in our

marriage, in tense moments, this is what Ned has come up with: a beer. As if the rituals of suburban life—beer, barbecued chicken, picnic tables, *hey, how ya doin'?*—could make up for the roiling tension underneath.

"Good thinking, buddy," said Tommy. "I'll come down with you."

Liza perched on the edge of my bed, cradling Josh.

"He's just beautiful, Rach."

"Thanks."

Kate jumped up out of the wing chair. She stood at the foot of the bed for a moment, her eyes huge and glassy. Her fists were clenched.

"He's just beautiful," she spat out, in an awful, mimicking voice. Then she stormed out, slamming the bedroom door so hard the walls shook.

"Katie!" I called, but she didn't answer. I tried to sit up, but every time I moved it felt like my stitches would pop. I fell back down onto the pillows.

"Holy shit," Liza said. "What was that about?"

"She's having a hard time."

"But I thought things were getting better."

"Me too."

"Do you think—the new baby?"

"Yeah, and—"

"Oh, God. I just blew right past her, didn't I?" Liza looked horrified, though her forehead was still unwrinkled. "I'm such an idiot."

I could see a shadow under the closed door. Kate had been hovering there, listening. How much had she heard?

"I'm sure it would mean a lot to her if you'd—" I whispered.

Just then, Kate walked back into the room, her cheeks pink.

"Katie!" Liza stretched out her arms. "Let me look at you, gorgeous."

She pushed Kate's hair out of her eyes, held her face between her palms.

"Do you know you could be a model?" Liza asked.

Kate's cheeks turned even redder.

"I'm serious. One of my clients runs an agency in New York. I bet they'd snap you up in a minute."

"Really?" Kate stood up taller. "You would do that?"

"Sure, honey."

"Um, Liza?" I said, trying to give her the "drop it" message.

They both turned and looked at me expectantly.

"We don't really want Kate to—"

"Mom!"

"No, really, Kate. That isn't something—"

"What's your problem?" Kate snapped, her eyes flashing.

"Well, for one thing, you're fourteen," I said.

"Yeah, so what?"

"I didn't mean to stir anything up," murmured Liza.

I shot Liza a look. She just didn't think. She was one of those people who said whatever came into her head, screw the consequences.

"What do you care what I do?" Kate asked.

Josh was nursing again, clamped down on my raw, sore nipple.

"What's that supposed to mean?"

"You're . . . busy."

"Listen, Kate, never mind. I should have cleared this with your mother," Liza said.

"We can see, maybe next year—" I started to say.

"Shut up!" Kate screamed. She started pulling at her own hair, so violently I expected to see clumps of it in her fists. "Shut-up-shut-up-shut-up!"

I covered the baby's ears.

"You ruin everything!" Kate screamed at me. Her face was twisted into a rageful mask, her mouth an open cavern. "Why do you ruin everything, you stupid fucking bitch?"

She ran out of the room again, and I heard her pounding down the stairs, taking them two at a time. The front door slammed as she left the house.

Liza sat down in the wing chair. She sighed deeply, looking suddenly very serious. She leaned forward, elbows on knees. "I'm so sorry, Rach."

I blinked away the tears that I felt welling up.

"It's gotten so much worse," I whispered. "I thought it was getting better, but now—"

"She needs help."

"I know," I whispered.

"Listen. Tommy knows a very good man in Boston. A psychiatrist who specializes in adolescents."

"Of course." It was suddenly hard to breathe.

"Maybe she just needs some medication. It could be something simple."

I nodded.

"Our friends Lorna and Jim sent their kid to this guy," Liza went on. "His name is Zelman. I'll make a call."

"What do you think it is, Liza?" I asked. Josh nestled deeper into the folds of my pajama top. I steeled myself against words she might use. *Typical teenage stuff* wasn't on the list anymore.

"I don't know. But something's wrong," she said slowly.

"Yes, yes," I said. "But what?"

"I don't know. Maybe it's chemical. Or maybe Josh being born."

"She had a really hard time during my delivery," I said quietly. "It was pretty scary for her."

"It'll be good for her to talk to someone," said Liza. "Get it all out."

"I hope so," I said. I pictured whatever it was inside of Kate like a poison, seeping, finding its way into crevices where it would remain for years.

I heard Ned and Tommy climbing the stairs, the sound of their easy male laughter. I began to cry, my shoulders shaking in silent sobs. Liza crossed the room and held me. I rocked Josh, and she rocked me.

6

"WHAT CAN I GET YOU?" THE BARTENDER AT BACK STREET asks, sliding two napkins across the polished mahogany bar. Thankfully, he's no one we know. Often Hawthorne restaurants and stores are staffed by local kids; kids we used to watch jumping through sprinklers or skateboarding down the street now serve us drinks or find us paint thinner in the hardware store.

"Bombay martini," says Ned. "And my—"

He falters. He almost said *my wife.* As in: My wife will have a glass of white wine. My wife will have a scotch on the rocks. My wife is my wife. I long to hear the word come out of his mouth, to feel that sense of belonging, of being half of a couple again.

"Diet Coke," I say.

Ned looks at me.

"Not drinking?"

"I have to pick up Josh from your mother," I say.

"Come on, Rach. I need a drink and I don't want to drink alone."

The bartender places Ned's martini on the napkin in front of him. It's brimming, and he leans forward to take a sip like a kid hunched over a slurpee at a soda fountain. I can't remember ever seeing Ned have a drink while it was still light out.

He sits back and closes his eyes for a moment.

"What a day," he says. "What a complete and total nightmare."

"Preschizophrenic." I form my mouth around the word.

"They didn't say she's preschizophrenic. They just said they can't rule it out."

Ned leans back and closes his eyes. Those long lashes—Kate has them too—casting shadows across his face. His mouth, slack and moist from the sip of martini. A lock of sandy hair falling across his forehead, more creased even just in the last six months. He opens his eyes, leans forward, and takes another sip. Is he afraid his hands will tremble if he tries to raise the glass to his lips? We're both tense, our nerves shot. We look around the room, out the windows of the restaurant—anywhere but at each other.

"At least the snow stopped," I say.

I finish my Diet Coke and suddenly want a real drink, but I can't. There are very few controls in my life anymore, but one of them is this: I never have a drink when I have to drive with Joshua. Never, never.

"Could I have another Diet Coke please?" I call to the bartender, and then turn to Ned. "How are we going to afford this?" I ask one of the questions I've been silently asking myself the whole drive home.

"Maybe they give athletic scholarships."

"Very funny."

"I'll go to my parents again."

Ned looks away from me and around the dark room. In the fading afternoon light reflected off the snow outside the tall windows, the room has an eerie, almost fluorescent glow. The bar is horseshoe shaped, and there's one other customer, a man in a watch cap sitting on the other side. I've never seen him before, and I wonder what he's doing here. Who would be sitting at the Back Street bar at four on a winter afternoon?

"Oh, Ned. I don't want you to have to do that."

"What choice do I have?" he snaps.

"We could go to Tommy and Liza," I say slowly, realizing that I've been thinking about this all along. The whole drive back from New Hampshire the thought has been forming in my head, as if in a dream. Tommy and Liza and their endless cash—Tommy and Liza who *embody* cash, who are walking money, impossible to look at anymore without thinking of it. Especially for us.

"No," says Ned. "Absolutely not."

"Why?"

"I just don't want to. That's all."

"You'd rather go to your parents. With everything they'll—"

"Yes."

"What is it . . . pride?" I see the look on Ned's face and realize I should just shut up. Of course it's pride, and Ned is entitled to it. The last thing he wants is for Tommy to write us a check. I know Ned finds that unacceptable. Ned has been shrinking and shrinking for the last couple of years—or, if I'm honest with myself, probably longer than that. He'd rather bow and scrape in front of his parents once more, who at least are family, than make himself smaller than he already feels in front of Tommy Mendel.

I put a hand on his arm, feeling the muscles taut beneath his skin.

"It's okay, Ned," I say. "I understand."

He takes a big gulp of his martini.

"No, you don't, Rachel. But that's all right."

He pushes himself off his bar stool and heads for the bathroom. While he's gone, one of the waiters takes a quarter from a cup and sticks it in the jukebox. An old James Taylor song comes on, and it reminds me of high school, of boys with faded corduroys hanging from their skinny hips, the bleached outlines of cigarette packs in their back pockets. The waiter can't be older than a high school boy himself, and he's mouthing the lyrics as he sets paper place mats on the tables, lines up the forks and knives.

"Rock-a-bye sweet baby James," croons Ned, as he slides back onto his stool next to me. He puts his arm around me and signals the bartender.

"Another one for me, and she'll have a Dewars on the rocks," he says.

"Ned, I can't."

"I called my mother," he says. "She'll keep Josh overnight. She said it's no problem."

"Still, I—"

"She'll make him eat his peas. Don't you want him to eat his peas?"

Ned still has his arm around me.

"What are you doing?" I ask. We are reflected in the mirror behind the bar: Ned and I, our two heads bobbing above the dozens of bottles. The image of us—seeing us together—is eerie, surprising to me, like catching a glimpse of two strangers who remind me of people who are dead and gone.

"Can't I order a drink for my wife?"

"Ned, what are you doing?" I repeat quietly. What I mean, what I really feel like saying, is, *Don't play with me. Don't play with my heart.*

Ned leans forward, takes my chin between his thumb and forefinger, and holds my face very still as he kisses me. I close my eyes and give in, feeling everything and nothing all at once, my mind spinning, as if this were a first kiss. The roughness of his cheeks, the gin on his lips, the soft warmth of his tongue, and most of all those fingers holding me just so, exactly the way he wants me. A sound escapes me, a sigh.

He pulls away and looks at me, inches away from my face. I haven't seen Ned this close since he moved out of the house. He looks like a little boy, his eyes gentle, frightened, questioning. I stroke the back of his neck, his scraggly hair.

"If this is just because—"

"No, Rach. Stop thinking."

"I can't," I say. Tears are suddenly spilling from my eyes. "I can't stop thinking, not even for a second, Ned."

He wipes my cheek with the back of his hand.

"I know," he says softly. "Me neither."

"I keep thinking about what if. What if we hadn't—"

Ned puts a finger to my lips.

"You can play the what if game all the way back to the beginning," he says. "Back to the day we met. What if I hadn't stopped and talked to you? What if you had gone to the diner instead of Veselka? What if I had been shy that day, or if I had been with some other girl, or—"

"That's not what I mean."

"Yeah, but that's the truth, Rachel. You can't pick and choose your moments. They're like dominoes. You set the first one in motion, but the rest isn't up to you."

"That's not what you said earlier."

"When?"

"In the car. You said it was all my fault."

"I was angry."

"But you meant it."

The waiter deposits our two drinks in front of us. Ned pulls away from me and takes a sip of his second martini. Something in me snaps, just breaks in two, and I reach for my scotch and down it in a couple of gulps. I can still hear Kate's wails echoing in my head, and if I don't drown out the sound of that horrible shrieking I think I'll lose my mind. The scotch burns going down.

I wave to the bartender and ask for another one. For a minute, I'm just going to stop being terrified, even if later there's a price to pay. I need to stop thinking about our children, or about how we're going to get home if we're drunk, or even about what anybody in Hawthorne will think about Ned and Rachel Jensen boozing it up at Back Street late on a Thursday afternoon. It has been so long since I have felt no worry, no sickening thud in the pit of my stomach. I pick up my glass. *Just an hour,* I think to myself. *Just a day. Just a night.*

FAMILY HISTORY

THE KNOB ON OUR FRONT DOOR IS MY FOCAL POINT, and I'm jabbing at it like a blindfolded kid trying to pin the tail on the donkey. *Our* front door, *our* because I am with my husband, tall still-handsome Ned Jensen who is weaving by my side, three martinis later, of no help whatsoever when it comes to fitting the key into the lock.

"Help," I say, handing him my key ring.

"Why'd you lock the door?" he asks.

"I was going to be gone all day," I say. "The Wilsons were robbed last week—someone came in and took Chrissie's bike right out of the garage while Marcia was upstairs."

"Really."

"Yeah, and—"

"Rach?"

"What?"

"I don't care about that right now."

"Oh."

"I just want to get inside."

"Oh."

The way he says *inside* makes my knees go weak.

He leans into me, presses me up against the front door, and I feel his hardness through his pants, through the thick wool of my skirt. A car passes slowly by, and I wonder who's seeing us. Within hours, everyone in town will know: Ned and Rachel are back together. Or, at least, Ned and Rachel were making out under the light of their front porch, and why can't decent people do that sort of thing in private?

He reaches behind me and turns the key in the lock.

"Lightweight," he says, nudging me inside.

I take Ned's hand and climb the stairs. Night after night I have walked upstairs alone and climbed into bed, the only sound in the house the creaking of my footsteps and Josh stirring in his crib. There have been nights when every page I've turned in a book sounded as loud to me as a crack of thunder. This house was never meant for solitude. Its old walls and crumbling plaster call out for a family to fill it with noise.

"Wait," Ned says from behind me, as we walk into the bedroom. The bed is unmade, the sheets creased and covered with magazines I wish I could just brush away. I don't want Ned seeing my recent reading material: *People, In Style, Us Weekly.* I have lost the ability to concentrate on anything more substantive than the latest Hollywood divorce.

"What?"

"Let me look at you," he says, his hands on my shoulders, turning me around. His eyes are bloodshot from too much booze, but his hands are steady as he unbuttons each tiny mother-of-pearl button of my cardigan and pulls it off.

"Too many clothes," he mutters.

"It's twenty degrees out."

"Take off your shirt."

He stands back and watches me, the way he used to when we were first together. Ned watching me—this was part of the seduction. With his painter's eyes he seemed to look into me, through my skin to the bone. I had never felt so appreciated or desired. But then again, I was twenty-two, and even though I could have recited a list of what was wrong with me, looking back I realize I was close to perfect. Ned hasn't seen me naked in a long time—long enough to see me anew. As I pull my T-shirt over my head, I'm aware of every little thing: the roll of flesh around my stomach that I've had since Josh was born. My plain cotton bra, stained under my arms. I wasn't expecting anyone to see me take my clothes off today.

I reach behind my waist and undo my skirt, then sit on the edge of the bed and unzip my boots. He's still standing there, watching me.

"Stop," I say. "Come here."

"I want to look at you."

"Don't, Ned."

I feel heat rising across my chest, the twin flames of desire and shame.

"You're beautiful," he says. His voice is thick, swallowed in his throat.

He walks over to the bed, pulls his sweater over his head, and drops it on the floor. I grab his belt buckle and undo it with one hand, unzipping his fly with the other. The bedroom door is wide open—there's nobody home, nobody coming home. No children, no baby-sitters or in-laws, or students, or the guy who trims the hedges. None of that. Just Ned's warm hands on my breasts, his fingers brushing my nipples, and then a moan as his mouth reaches down for me, his rough cheek against my breast.

"God, Rach."

He reaches down and grabs my hip, his hands traveling all over me, appropriating me, taking me and making me his. Something unfurls inside of me, twists and pulls in a way I haven't felt in years. All desire has been gone, bled out of me since before Josh was born, and now it's back and I barely know what to do with it. It feels almost scary, the way it felt the very first time, when I was Kate's age. Uncontainable. Impossible to control.

I pull Ned on top of me. His hipbones push into mine. He's lost so much weight, I hardly recognize the feel of him.

"Hold on a minute," I say, shocking myself. The last thing I want him to do is stop, but still I blurt it out. "Ned, wait."

He looks down at me, his hair falling into his eyes, his mouth swollen.

"What?"

"Have you been with anybody else?" I ask him. I believe I'll know if he's telling me the truth; I just will.

He blinks, then rolls off me and props himself up on an elbow. "Why are you asking me this now?"

"Lots of reasons," I say. Though I already know the answer. If it were no, he would have just said it—indignant, emphatic. *Of course not.* I feel the truth in the pit of my stomach. Ned squints at me, the way he does when he has something to tell me that he knows will hurt.

"Who?" I ask softly. "Just tell me."

"Oh, God, Rach. Come on."

"Goddammit, you tell me who!"

"Nobody. No one you know."

I fall back on the pillows. It's impossible, only it isn't. Everything I've rooted my life in has been slowly sucked away. Healthy children. A faithful marriage. Who the hell did I think I was, all these years, to have the right to such privilege? Health, happiness, faith—these are not to be simply expected. I'm an idiot for thinking that Ned had been living a parallel life to mine all these months, alone in Pine Dunes, lying in bed watching television and just trying to get through the night.

I roll away from him. Suddenly all I want in the world is to be alone, in my big bed with nothing but the television to keep me company. I can't believe Ned could have slept with someone else.

"Come on, Rach," he says. He traces a circle on my back.

"Leave me alone," I say. My voice is small, and I am even smaller. If I could I would crumble into pieces, I would disintegrate, vanish.

"It's not like we were together," he says. "I mean . . . we were separated. What was I supposed to do?"

A million answers run through my mind. *Wait,* I want to scream. *You should have waited for me.*

He puts a hand on my hip and rolls me over.

"It was one night," he says. "That's all."

"Oh, like that's supposed to make it better?"

"It was just sex."

"What the hell does that mean, just sex?"

I'm aware that my voice is getting louder, shriller.

"It meant nothing. She was just someone I met in a bar."

"Where?"

"Boston."

"How old was she?"

"I don't know."

"About how old, do you think?"

"Thirty or so."

I push this out of my mind fast, hoping never to think about it again. The only thing worse than your estranged husband sleeping with somebody else is when that somebody is ten years younger than you are.

"Where'd you do it?"

"Rachel, stop."

"I want to know."

"Her apartment," he says faintly. And then, "I used a condom."

"Oh, that makes everything all right, then."

Ned sits up and pulls the sheet and blanket around him.

"Are you going to quit this anytime soon?" he asks.

I examine Ned for a good long minute, the bedroom so quiet that I can hear the ticking of the wall clock downstairs in the foyer. I wonder if I'll ever be able to look at him again without thinking about it: a dark bar, a frosty mug of beer, and a girl—did he approach her? Did she sidle up to him? Did he undress her, or did he ask her to undress herself while he watched? I shake my head hard, as if I can rattle the thought away.

"What?" he asks.

"Nothing."

"What are you thinking?"

I grab his left hand and look at his fingers. Even though it's the middle of winter there's a faint, faint tan line where his wedding ring used to be.

"Listen," I say. "I just can't stand the idea that—"

"I know," he says. He pulls me toward him until I'm up on his lap and he rocks me back and forth slowly. This is what I need, this gentle rocking, to be held like something precious, something that just possibly could break.

"I love you," he whispers.

"Me too," I say. He kisses my nose, my cheek, the top of my head. He showers me with kisses the way we used to kiss Kate every single morning. A hundred kisses, we used to say, as she squirmed and laughed. There was no such thing as too much love. I close my eyes against the image of Katie as a delighted little girl, her head thrown back, her mouth wide open, dimples flashing. The contrast between my memory of her and the wasted apparition we saw this afternoon is something I feel deep in my body—a knife in my belly, in the place where I will be her mother forever.

"What are we going to do?" I ask.

"Ssshhh, not now."

"But—"

"Later."

Ned lays me down on our bed, the bed upon which we conceived two children, the bed which moved with us from the cramped studio in New York to this old house, the bed of fevers, tears, fights, and ten thousand nights of entangled sleep. He's still cradling me as he enters me slowly, with ease, and I wrap my arms around his neck. At first my mind is racing: Is Josh okay at Jane's house? Does she have pajamas for him? Did Kate calm down, did they have to sedate her? The woman Ned slept with—was she beautiful? Was she good in bed? But then slowly, it all begins to fade, and thought is replaced with sensation. The minutes pass between us, in a blur of hands and fingers and mouths and whispers and moans that make no sense, until finally the world stops spinning. The world disappears.

IT'S STILL DARK OUT WHEN I WAKE UP FROM A TERRIBLE dream. In my dream, Joshua is an infant and he is falling, outlined against a pale blue sky, his chubby legs pedaling as he laughs. He doesn't know he's in danger—he doesn't know anything about danger—since nothing bad has ever happened to him. He thinks he's flying. He flaps his hands up and down like a bird and laughs his beautiful laugh, a pure sound of joy. And I am tied to a chair, my arms and legs bound with twine. Who has tied me up? I am helpless to stop him from falling.

My own scream, scratching raw against my throat, wakes me up. My heart is pounding, and I look around the room, trying to steady myself. I'm in my safe bed in my safe room, and Josh is in his nursery down the hall. No. That's not right—Josh is sleeping over at Jane's house. Why is he at Jane's? It all takes me a minute to sort out. My heart is pounding so fast, and my head feels like it's going to split open.

Ned. I reach over to his side of the bed—it's still his side of the bed—and feel nothing but cool empty sheets. And then the sound of a car engine, turning over on the street, just outside the bedroom window. I look out front and see Ned climbing out of the driver's side with a scraper; his car, parked outside since we left for Stone Mountain, is buried in snow. He moves slowly, like a sleepwalker; he has no idea I'm watching him. The exhaust from his car's engine billows into the starry night, rising above him in plumes of smoke. *I love you. Me too.* And, unsaid: *Don't hurt me again. I won't.* He scrapes the windshield methodically, by rote, the way all good New England boys raised in blizzard country do. Back and forth, back and forth. His hands were on me only a few hours ago, steady, sure of themselves, moving across my breasts, pinching my nipples with just the right amount of pressure, tracing my belly with the certainty that comes from a thousand nights of love.

What the hell is he doing? I scramble around the bedroom for some warm clothes. My flannel pajamas are on the floor near the vanity, and I pull them on and stick my feet into my Bean boots, not bothering with socks. I run downstairs, grab my down jacket off the rack in the front hall, and open the front door. Ned looks up when he sees the front door open, a pale stream of yellow light cast across the snow.

"What's going on?" I keep my voice down. The houses are close together, and it's the dead of night, when voices carry.

"Just cleaning off my car," he says.

"That's evident."

We both stand there, arms dangling.

"Were you leaving?" I ask.

He nods. "I have to be up at the crack of dawn. An appointment in the Salem office."

"You were just going to go? Like that?"

I hug my arms around myself, wrapping my down jacket around me like a quilt.

"Rach."

He starts to walk toward me, and I back up a step.

"Don't," I say. "I can't believe you were doing this. Did you think about me? Did you think that maybe I'd wake up in the morning and you'd be gone, and I'd wonder what the hell had happened?"

"I couldn't stay," he almost whispers. "I was freaking out."

"Why?"

"I don't know."

Clouds of vapor drift from our mouths, fading into nothing. It's all hopeless, is what I'm thinking as I look at my husband, the man I trusted with my whole life. We're never going to be okay again. We can't possibly be.

"Come inside." I reach out a hand to him. He's standing knee-deep in snow, still holding the scraper. "It'll take you hours to dig out."

He looks at the car, then back at me. He knows I'm right. He's not getting out of here. The temperature has dropped during the night, and the snow covering his windshield has frozen into a solid sheet of ice.

He follows me inside. I walk through the house and into the kitchen, where I put up a kettle to boil. Ned comes in behind me and sits down at the kitchen table. He bends over his boots, undoing the laces. They drip puddles on the floor. I used to care about that sort of thing: dripping boots, orange juice containers left on countertops, coffee stains in the sink. It used to bug me, the way Ned and Kate would both just leave their messes for me to clean up after them.

"Decaf Earl Gray, Lipton, or chamomile?" I ask. My voice shakes.

"Rach."

"Don't Rach me."

"Rachel."

I wheel around and look at him.

"Are you trying to destroy me?" I ask. "Is that what you want?"

"No!" He looks pained at the thought.

"Why did you go to bed with me, then, if you were just going to sneak off in the middle of the night?"

"I didn't know."

"Didn't know what?"

He swallows hard and looks away from me. I wonder what he's thinking, looking around this kitchen where we've spent so much of our lives—talking over our morning coffees, quietly reading the paper together, or sitting with Kate when she was a kid, watching Saturday morning cartoons. I haven't touched this room, haven't changed a thing since Ned left. A grocery list in his handwriting is still pinned on the fridge, next to a photo of Josh and Ned sleeping curled up together. And his collection of dried wishbones in a glass jar—it's all exactly as he left it. I guess I've had the superstitious feeling that if I kept things just as they had been, in a state of suspended animation, perhaps there would be room for Ned to just walk back into our lives as if nothing had happened. *Honey, I'm home!* And our lives would resume, not exactly as if nothing had happened but with the proud forbearance of grief overcome. Tragedy averted. A near miss.

"I'm such an idiot," I say.

"Don't say that."

"But I am."

The kettle begins to screech. It's one of those sleek modern kettles that makes a loud, tinny, off-key sound when water begins to boil. A gift from Jane and Arthur that I've never been able to get rid of. I grab the handle, forgetting how hot the metal gets.

"Ouch!" I bang it back down.

"Are you all right?"

I wave my hand in the air. "Shit!"

Ned gets up and takes a couple of mugs from the cupboard.

"Sit down," he says. "Let me make the tea."

I lower myself into the kitchen chair Ned just vacated and watch him as he putters around the kitchen. He brings me a dish towel soaked in cool water and wraps it around my hand. He doesn't look up at my face, just presses the cool cloth into my palm.

"There," he says. "That should take the sting out."

I close my eyes and try to stop the words bubbling up inside of me. *Please stay,* I want to say. *Don't go. We'll work it out.* But I know I can't say anything. I can't beg him. It will only make both of us feel worse.

"Let's talk about Kate," I say. All business. This, I know how to do. If someone put a gun to my head and asked me to describe myself in a split second, the first word that would come to mind would be *mother.* That's who I am, who I have always been since Kate was born. All these years I have been Ned's wife, Phyllis's daughter, Liza's best friend, an art restorer, a transplanted New Yorker—there have been a dozen ways I could describe myself but only one that I truly felt to the core of my being.

"I told you, I'll bring it up with my parents," says Ned. "I'm seeing them tomorrow." He glances up at the wall clock. "Or, rather, later today."

He puts a steaming mug of tea in front of me.

"That's not what I mean."

"What, then?"

He pulls up a chair next to me. I look at his hands—those hands that were all over me just a few hours ago. Why do I feel like I can't reach out and touch him now?

"Are we doing the right thing?" I ask. "Leaving her there?"

"We don't have a choice."

"There's always a choice."

"Rachel. You have to recognize how sick she is."

"I refuse to just take their word for it," I say. "They don't know her."

"We've been through this already."

"But I could—"

"It would kill you."

I bury my nose into my mug, inhale the sweet-smelling tea. I don't say the true thing: it's killing me already. I should be able to heal my own daughter.

"She's so unhappy," I say.

"Unhappy isn't the word."

"Sick."

"She wouldn't be safe here, Rachel. You know that, right?"

I nod. I do know it. I remember, when Kate was a toddler, hovering over her as she tried to get into trouble. The oven, the toilet, the knife drawer—she gravitated, like any toddler, to whatever was going to cause her the most damage. But I never really worried, because I was there to protect her. They don't tell you, when you become a parent, that the hardest part is way, way down the road: when your children are old enough to cause damage to themselves and there's nothing—absolutely nothing—you can do about it.

"I want to ask Tommy for the money, then," I say.

"No."

"It's nothing to him. He probably spends more than that on docking fees for his goddamned boat."

"That's not the point."

"I know. But I hate the idea of going to Jane and Arthur again."

"Look," Ned says. "I've got three houses closing in the next week. I'm not doing badly, financially speaking. I may even be able to swing it myself."

"Ned, you can't afford it. Come on, don't let pride be the reason—"

"Fuck you," he says.

I sit back in my chair, physically recoiling from the force of

Ned's anger. He has never cursed at me, never once in our marriage, not even when he's lost his temper so badly he's crashed dishes and wine goblets.

"I don't have any pride left, Rachel. I'm just trying to do right by my family."

Ned scrapes his chair back, bends over, and puts his boots on. I see the rage coiled in his body; over the years I have learned the signals, and I know not to say a word. He carries his mug across the kitchen and puts it in the dishwasher, as if to erase any trace of his having been here.

"We'll talk later," he says stiffly. "I'm sorry, but I have to go."

I don't stop him this time. I wait until I hear the front door close with a soft click, and then I take my tea and walk upstairs. When I get to the bedroom I push back the curtains and watch him. Just as I thought. He's left his car buried beneath the layers of snow and ice, and in the thin gray light of dawn he is trudging uphill, toward Pine Dunes, his head down, hands deep in the pockets of his parka.

IN THE MORNING, I DRIVE TO MY IN-LAWS. JANE AND Arthur live in a prosperous leafy section of Hawthorne near the country club. It's been a while since I've visited them, and on the way there I'm momentarily disoriented when I realize that I'm driving through the newest Jensen Realty project. On the land around the country club are several dozen McMansions: neo-Tudor gives way to neo-Federal, which is next to, God help us all, a neo-Southern plantation whose veranda overlooks a mountain of dirt and several cranes digging up the foundation for a house next to it. A small green sign with gold lettering announces the name of this new neighborhood: REGAL RIDGE. Some of the houses have swimming pools, but they're all set close to one another on no more than half an acre. Ned has told me that the draw of this development is the country club itself, with membership thrown into the deal. Walk to the golf course! Have dinner at the club!

Back in the old days, Ned and I used to sit around sometimes with Jane and Arthur, brainstorming names for their developments the way parents try out names for their future children. Even though Jensen Realty paid good money to market researchers, Ned and I often ended up creating the names that stuck.

"If you were a Boston banker with three kids, what would you want your street to be called?" Ned would muse.

"How do you know this particular banker has three kids?" I asked.

"Who else would buy a house this size?" Ned said, thumping his fist on a glossy brochure of six- and seven-bedroom houses.

"Okay," I said with a sigh. "Abercrombie Court."

"Not bad." Ned scribbled it down on a yellow legal pad. "How about White Oak Bluff?"

"Bluff's no good."

"You're right. White Oak Terrace."

"Hickory Manor."

"I've got it!" Ned jumped up with a certain amount of pretend enthusiasm. He paused dramatically: "Snowcrest."

"Snowcrest what?"

"Just Snowcrest. Sort of like: just Madonna."

It was a strangely powerful feeling, to name streets. To realize that no matter what happened to any of us, we were creating addresses—fragments of nonsense, really, but nonetheless streets and boulevards and avenues where people would live long after we were gone.

The country-club houses give way to elegant turn-of-the-century mansions. Despite their propensity for all things faux, Jane and Arthur live in the real thing: a beautiful turn-of-the-century brick house with white columns that has retained all its original charm, even though the kitchens and bathrooms have been modernized with only the best: Poggen-Pohl bathroom fixtures, a Sub-Zero, even a state-of-the-art laundry room that Jane managed to let slip cost $15,000. I pull into the driveway, relieved to see Jane's

Range Rover parked there, next to Arthur's little sports coupe. I had been afraid she might have left early to take Josh to preschool.

I park alongside Jane's car. They're plowed out already; they have a guy who comes with the heavyweight machinery as soon as the snow stops. Even their front walk is so clean you can see the old brickwork. As I make my way to the front door, I'm suddenly conscious of how I must look. Hung over, no sleep, a baggy cardigan thrown over the T-shirt I slept in, and a pair of jeans I picked up off my bedroom floor. I just wanted to get here in time, but now that I'm here, I'm aware of how my mother-in-law is going to see me. I rake my fingers through my hair and ring the doorbell.

"Good morning!" Jane opens the door. She's wearing her usual blazer, the brass JENSEN REALTY name tag already pinned to her lapel. Her hair, done once a week at a salon downtown, is a lacquered perfect gray bob.

"Mommy!" Joshie comes careening down the long front corridor and bangs into my knees. "Mommy, Mommy, Mommy!" he cries.

I bend down and scoop him up. I have never, in his short life, been away from him overnight. He flings his arms around my neck, and I hold his squirmy body close.

"Hi, baby," I murmur into his ear. "Mommy missed you."

I know you're not supposed to say that. The kiddie psychology books all say that telling your children you miss them makes them feel guilty—after all, what if they didn't miss you? But I can't help it. I'm in a perpetual state of yearning for my children.

"How'd he do?" I ask Jane.

"Just fine," she says. "Joshua, tell your mother what you ate for breakfast."

Josh looks at her blankly.

"You had . . ." she prompts.

"Cheerios!" he yells.

"And . . ."

"Mommy, come!" he commands, sliding down my body and

grabbing my hand, leading me into Jane and Arthur's den. Arthur is sitting in the black leather recliner, his nose buried in the *Wall Street Journal.* Hanging on the wall behind him are a half-dozen framed photos of the Jensen family, taken when Ned and his brother were in high school. Two shaggy-haired boys—they look like slightly less beautiful versions of Kate.

"Hi, Arthur," I say.

He mumbles a hello, rustling his paper. Arthur doesn't know what to do with me ever since Ned moved out. The whole thing is an embarrassment to him—separation, Pine Dunes, a granddaughter in reform school, as he puts it—and unlike Jane he doesn't have the ability to pretend. I used to think, when Ned and I were first together, that Arthur might be some sort of father figure to me. I missed my own father terribly, and Arthur looked the part: he had a shock of white hair, twinkly blue eyes, and the same set of deep dimples that were passed down to Kate. He smoked a pipe and was a lunatic baseball fan just like my father was—though he rooted for the Red Sox, not the Yankees. But the similarities stopped there. Arthur made it abundantly clear, early on, that he wasn't about to fill those shoes. He was always nice enough, but in a remote way that made me feel even more bereft.

"Tower!" Josh points to a set of Winnie the Pooh blocks piled taller than he is.

I know what's coming next, but I don't stop him.

"Wreck!" Josh shouts, with a swipe of his hand, and sends the whole thing flying—wooden blocks in every direction, including a small Eeyore block right smack into Arthur's newspaper.

Arthur slowly puts down the paper and blinks at Josh.

"Papa." Josh beams. He's too young to know his grandparents have had just about enough of him. "Again, again!"

"No, not again. Papa has to get to work," says Arthur.

"Work," repeats Josh.

"That's right. Nana and Papa have to go sell houses."

"So how's everything, Arthur?" I ask, trying for a light, cheerful tone but winding up sounding reedy and anxious.

"Just fine," he says. And then nothing. Just a long stretch of silence as Josh turns his attention to the buttons on the television set. Arthur has still not looked me in the eye. I wonder what they know. What did Ned tell them yesterday when he called them from Back Street?

"Joshie, stop," I say. I pry his fingers off the volume button.

"No-o-o!" he screeches.

"Here, let's look at—"

I grab an *Architectural Digest* from the coffee table and start flipping through the pages.

"Ooh! What a pretty house!" I say. Josh looks at me as if he knows exactly how lame I'm being.

I hear the neat click of Jane's heels on the wooden floor.

"So how was yesterday's meeting at the school?" Jane asks. She's standing in the door, her coat already buttoned.

"Fine," I say. "But I don't think we should—"

I gesture to Josh. I don't want him to hear a word about Kate. Jane's mouth tightens, but she doesn't say anything. She doesn't need to. Over the years I've learned to read her as well as I read my own mother. She disapproves of this whole situation—and who can blame her? I disapprove of it too.

"Artie, would you watch the baby? I need to talk to Rachel," she says.

Arthur doesn't look too happy about it, but he gets down on the floor next to Josh. When I follow Jane out of the den, Josh cries after me.

"Mommy, no!"

"Just a minute, Joshie," I call. "Mama needs to talk to Nana."

Jane and I walk back into the kitchen. She goes over to the sink, pulls on a pair of rubber gloves, and starts scrubbing out the coffeepot, still bundled in her heavy wool coat.

"Tell me what happened," she says.

"Ned didn't fill you in?"

She doesn't even respond to this, and I'm not sure how to answer. If it were Phyllis doing the asking, I know exactly what I would do: I would lie through my teeth, say whatever I had to say to keep her at a distance. But this is different. Jane and Arthur may not be my type of people, but they're not bad people—not at all. Their lives have been fairly smooth sailing until now. They've built a business, raised two healthy boys, stayed together in their hometown. All this puzzles them, and it pains them. They don't understand that you can do everything right, and still it can go terribly wrong.

"Kate got into some trouble up there," I finally answer.

"How do you get into trouble at a school for troubled kids?" Jane cuts through it all in her usual blunt manner.

"It's a difficult situation."

"Don't spare me, Rachel. I have a right to know what's going on."

I wonder if her right to know has to do with her love for Kate, or the money they're paying to the school. Both, probably.

"She hurt herself, Jane."

Jane stops scrubbing, turns off the faucet, and turns around.

"She bashed her head into a radiator, and she burned her hands," I say.

"Oh, sweet Jesus." Her eyes are teary. "What can we do?"

I shake my head. "Nothing." I pause. "You could say a prayer, I guess."

"I want to see her."

"They don't allow visitors up there. The only reason Ned and I went up was that we were summoned."

"And why were you summoned?"

"They wanted—" I falter.

"It's about money, isn't it."

"No, that's not what—"

"They want more money."

I hear the den door creak open and the sound of Josh's feet pounding down the hall. He dashes into the kitchen and pulls at my sweater.

"Mama, go!" he says.

Arthur follows Josh into the kitchen and shrugs apologetically at Jane.

"He wouldn't stay with me," he says. "He wanted his mother."

"Well, of course he did," Jane snaps. "You were supposed to distract him."

Arthur looks at her, surprised.

"What's the matter?" he asks.

"The school wants more money," says Jane. "And Kate—"

"Please!" I say sharply. "I don't want to talk about this in front of Josh."

"Mommy, go!"

"We're going, Joshie," I say, gathering his sippy cup and Ziploc bags of Cheerios and crackers and stuffing them into his diaper bag.

"He doesn't understand," says Jane.

"I can't take that chance," I say.

Arthur clears his throat.

"Rachel."

I look at my in-laws. They're standing next to each other in the middle of their perfect homey kitchen, and suddenly they look small—small and old. Arthur is stooped over, and his eyes look yellow, rheumy.

"You know we'll do whatever we can to help."

"I know, Arthur."

I pick up Josh, along with his diaper bag, and head out the back door.

"Say 'Bye, Papa! 'Bye, Nana!" I whisper.

" 'Bye, Papa, Nana!"

"Please let us know what's going on," calls Jane. "Ned doesn't always."

"I will."

"And Rachel? Are you sure it wouldn't be better to—"

I close the door behind me, but not soon enough.

"—bring her home?"

7

WHEN JOSH WAS ONLY A FEW WEEKS OLD, OUR DOORBELL rang, and when I answered it Kate was standing there next to Skip Jeffries. Skip was an old high school friend of Ned's who had stayed in Hawthorne all his life and was now one of the senior members of the police department. He was in uniform, with his cap on—and he looked uncomfortable.

"Hey, Rachel," he said. Then he glanced down at Josh, who was attached to my hip in a sling. "There's the little one!" He smiled awkwardly.

"Skip?"

"Um—we had a little problem down on Main Street," said Skip. "Kate, do you want to tell your mom about it?"

Kate shook her head.

"Come inside."

I stepped away from the front door. I admit I was worried about what the neighbors would think.

"Seems Kate slipped a few things into her knapsack down at the CVS," said Skip.

"What do you mean?"

He shifted and looked over my head, as if addressing a taller person.

"She took some fountain pens, a couple of refrigerator magnets—"

"Took—you mean stole?"

"It seems to be shoplifting, yes," said Skip.

"Kate? Is that true?" I turned to her.

She pushed past me and ran through the front hall and up the stairs, slamming her bedroom door behind her.

"They're not going to press charges," Skip said. "They told me to tell you."

"I can't believe it," I said. But the problem was, I could. A police officer showing up at my door was not surprising to me. Things had taken a turn for the worse with Kate, just in the few weeks since Josh's birth. She was barely speaking to us at all; any attempt to engage her in conversation was met with an icy, hateful stare. Ned and I had an appointment scheduled for the following day, in fact, with the Boston psychiatrist Liza had recommended.

Skip tipped his cap to me.

"Try not to get too upset, Rachel," he said. "These things happen."

"Do they?" I asked.

"Sure they do." He started to leave. "I do this kind of thing all the time—you'd be surprised."

NED AND I DROVE SILENTLY FOR THE FIRST TWENTY MINutes of our drive into Boston until the traffic slowed to a crawl on Storrow Drive. Josh was strapped into his infant seat in back, and I was sitting next to him. We weren't giving him any bottles yet, so I couldn't leave him with Jane, even for two hours.

Ned broke the silence.

"I was just thinking about how when I was a kid I used to cut out of school and Bruce Wertz and I would take the bus to Kenmore Square and we'd buy one-dollar bleacher tickets at Fenway."

"Why were you thinking about that?"

"Oh, I don't know. I guess just that I used to do crazy stuff as a kid."

"This is more than that."

We lapsed back into silence.

"I guess you're right."

"She's lucky," I said. "She's lucky that you and Skip are old friends."

Josh let out a squeak as we lurched through traffic.

"The kid's not even a month old and he's going to a shrink," said Ned.

"It's not for him!" I said.

Ned turned around and shot me a look. "It was a joke, Rach. A joke. Get it?"

We circled for a good fifteen minutes until we finally found a parking space near the address we'd been given in the Back Bay. There was a nice breeze in the air as we walked past the well-maintained facades of townhouses with manicured boxwood hedges in front gardens. Wisteria was in bloom; bursts of sweet-smelling purple flowers climbed up the sides of buildings. Josh was snuggled against my chest in the Baby Bjorn; Ned and I loosely held hands. An older woman carrying shopping bags smiled as she passed us; I knew we looked for all the world like a happy young family out for a stroll. I squeezed Ned's fingers and glanced up at him. He was squinting at the addresses. I wanted to say something to him—something reassuring—but all the words felt hollow.

"There it is." He pointed to a small brass plaque engraved MARVIN W. ZELMAN, M.D., just inside a heavy iron gate. Ned rang the bell, and I wondered what the *W* stood for as we were buzzed inside. We didn't even have a chance to sit down before Dr. Zelman poked his head out from behind a dark wood door.

"Mr. and Mrs. Jensen?" he said. "Please—come in."

Ned and I followed Zelman into his office and were confronted with a variety of seating options: sofa, several comfortable chairs, a leather recliner. I undid the Bjorn and pulled Josh out; he was half asleep.

"Sit wherever you feel comfortable," he said. Was this a test? Ned and I perched side by side on the sofa, and I cradled Josh against me. Zelman sat in the chair opposite us and crossed his legs. He pulled out a yellow legal-sized pad. He was a short slightly built man with dark curly hair and thick expensive-looking glasses.

"So if I understand correctly, you're considering treatment for your daughter."

We nodded.

"Why don't you tell me a bit about what's been going on."

"We just found out she's stealing—" I blurted out.

"Only once," interjected Ned. "But that isn't why—I mean, we had already made an appointment to come see you."

"The police brought her home yesterday," I continued. "I mean, she stole refrigerator magnets."

"I think she's just having a rough time as a teenager," said Ned. "We thought maybe if she talked to someone."

"Now, Mrs. Jensen told me on the phone"—he glanced at his pad—"Kate is fourteen?"

"Yes."

"And this infant is your only other child?"

We nodded.

Zelman made some notes. I wondered what he was writing.

"I've been worried—she hasn't seemed herself for a long time," I said. I knew Ned would be mad at me; he wanted to downplay the whole thing. But I saw no point in that. We needed to let this doctor know what was going on, otherwise there was no reason to be here.

"What's a long time?" Zelman asked.

I thought for a minute.

"Almost a year. We both thought it was just rocky adolescent stuff—"

More scribbled notes.

"But lately it seems to have escalated."

I looked around Zelman's office. It was spare, impersonal, beige. A small bookcase contained psychiatry textbooks; the lower shelf had some toys piled neatly into baskets. I wondered how young some of his patients were.

"Is she involved with drugs at all?" he asked.

Ned and I responded simultaneously, tripping over each other.

"Maybe," I said.

"I doubt it," said Ned.

We looked at each other, dismayed.

"So you're not certain," said Zelman, looking back and forth at both of us.

"Well, of course we've talked about it with Kate," I said. I was suddenly, irrationally furious with Ned. He just wanted to whitewash this whole thing. I knew he was as frightened as I was; I didn't understand why he couldn't admit it. "But she lies," I went on. "So it's impossible to know."

"Tell me about other behavior," said Zelman.

"Sullen. Prone to outbursts. She pushes us away," I said. I felt the sting of tears against the backs of my eyes. I wasn't going to cry, goddammit.

"She isn't really eating very much," said Ned. "She just plays with her food."

Zelman nodded and kept on writing.

"And before this last year?" he asked.

"She was perfect," I said.

Zelman lifted his head from writing and looked at me through his tortoise-shelled glasses. "Perfect?" he repeated.

I felt myself flush. It was the wrong word, of course.

"Not *perfect,*" I said. "Obviously. But she was a delightful, loving, sweet girl."

"How was her performance in school?"

"Excellent," said Ned. "Straight As. And she's a gifted athlete—she goes to Hawthorne, where she's captain of the junior varsity field-hockey team."

"Currently?" Zelman raised an eyebrow.

Ned nodded.

Zelman pushed his chair back slightly and flipped a page on the legal pad.

"I need to take a family history from each of you," he said. "Let's start with you, Mrs. Jensen. Are your parents living?"

"My father died twenty-three years ago," I said. "And my mother is alive, well, and living in New York."

Zelman didn't crack a smile.

"How did your father die?"

"Lung cancer," I said.

"Any significant medical history on either side, other than your father's cancer?"

"No."

"And what about psychiatric history?"

"Depression on my father's side," I said. "Both my father and my grandfather."

"Were either of them treated?"

"No."

"What about your mother?"

Ned let out a short nervous laugh, and Zelman looked over at him.

"Sorry," said Ned. "It's just—Rachel's mother is in a class by herself."

I glared at Ned. It was fine for us to joke about my mother, but not in front of a perfect stranger.

"Let's just say Rachel's mother is difficult," said Ned.

Zelman turned back to me.

"You're going to let him talk that way about your mother?" he asked, with his first small smile.

"Well, it's true," I said. I was covering for Ned, even though I was very angry. "She is difficult. She's been classified as a borderline—I think *narcissistic personality disorder* is the term."

"So she's been in treatment?" Zelman asked.

"Oh, no. This was by a friend of mine who is a therapist."

"I see."

He kept writing.

"And what about you, Mr. Jensen? Your family?"

"Parents both living," Ned said. "They drink too much, but that's about it."

"No psychiatric problems?"

"Not that I know of."

As Ned and Zelman continued to discuss the flawless Jensen family history, I held Josh, sound asleep, in my lap and felt the room begin to disintegrate around me. The subtle shades of beige, the wood-slatted window blinds, the children's toys and thick leather spines of books started to bobble and weave, breaking into kaleidoscopic bits. I was sweating. My head throbbed. It was as if an invisible hand had seized me by the throat and forced me to swallow the ugliest possible truth. It didn't matter what I did. It couldn't possibly have mattered less how hard I tried. I came from a sick and faulty genetic line and had passed it all down to my daughter.

"Rach?" Ned was patting me on the shoulder. "Are you okay?"

I nodded. I was afraid that if I opened my mouth it would all come pouring out. The poison inside of me—a lifetime of fighting the sad, pathetic, lonesome darkness of Phyllis. I blinked back tears and tried to bring the room back into focus.

"Well, I'd like to see Kate," Zelman was saying. "We'll start with one session and see how we connect."

He stood up and walked over to his desk, then flipped the pages of a calendar. "How's next Tuesday at four-fifteen?"

"Fine," I said. I fastened Josh back into the Bjorn. I felt Ned's hand on the small of my back, steadying me.

"And you understand that whatever Kate tells me is confidential," Zelman said, as he ushered us to the door. "I won't be able to speak to you without her permission."

"What if she's doing something dangerous?" I asked. "Would you call us?"

"In a situation where she is putting herself or someone else at risk—yes, I would contact you."

Zelman shook Ned's hand and then mine. It was a quick professional handshake, but his eyes were warm. I wondered if Kate would take to him.

"I hope you can help her," I said quietly.

He gave a slight nod and then closed the door behind us.

"I'm sorry," said Ned, as we headed back to the car. "I never should have said that about your mother."

"It's okay," I said, grateful that he had apologized.

I leaned into him as we walked. All our adult lives, Ned and I relied on each other in ways that were unspoken between us. We were—it is true—almost unfailingly kind to each other.

"Do you want to get a cup of coffee?" he asked.

I patted the top of Josh's head.

"No, we'd better just go home."

We proceeded slowly, like an old couple, unsure of the ground beneath our feet.

JOSH WAS SEVEN MONTHS OLD WHEN WE DECIDED IT was time for a trip down to the city. By *the city* we didn't mean Boston. We meant New York, the place we had left, the place that still held, for Ned and me, the shimmering promise of our youthful dreams. It was also, of course, where Phyllis still lived, in the same rent-controlled apartment on Central Park West I had grown up in—a huge sprawling duplex that some glitch in the system allowed her to rent for a pittance all these years. We had seen Phyllis only once since her disastrous visit to Hawthorne. She had come briefly the previous summer, when Josh was about six weeks old.

It was December, my favorite time in New York. I thought it

would be a treat for Kate to see the tree lit up in Rockefeller Center, the holiday window displays at Lord & Taylor and Barney's. She had never felt the thrumming, swirling energy of New York during the holidays, and I wanted that for her. She had been seeing Zelman for a while, and though I wouldn't exactly have said she was *better,* she was calmer. Her outbursts were less frequent, and there had been no more incidents like the one with Skip Jeffries. Whether this change in her was due to the talk therapy or to the antidepressants Zelman had prescribed, I wasn't sure. I was hoping that maybe a family vacation would do us all some good.

As for seeing my mother, I suppose enough time had elapsed to allow me to forget once again what it was like—what it was always like—to be with her. No matter how much I understood in my head, in my heart I was still the pathetic little girl who wanted—no, *needed*—her approval. Surely, she would enjoy seeing Ned, Kate, and particularly the new baby. She would understand that I had built a life for myself, a life that was good even though it was different from hers. I had managed to forget the pangs of disappointment that always hit me from almost the very first second I saw her. Or the way I found it impossible to speak to her in a normal, natural way—the way I spoke with everyone else in my life. With Phyllis, I was conscious of my mouth physically forming words; I was paralyzed with self-consciousness. And I was disgusted with myself for not being able to push past all the uncomfortable feelings and find something—anything—to enjoy about being with her.

"Ta-dah!" said Phyllis, opening the door of her apartment. "Come in, dear children, come in!"

Ned raised an eyebrow at me, as if to ask who Phyllis was impersonating. She was wearing some sort of silk caftan, the kind of thing advertised in expensive catalogs as an "at-home entertaining" outfit. It billowed around her thin frame. And she'd had her hair streaked bright red. I had noticed, over recent years, that my mother had begun to surround herself with ever brighter colors, as if her own fading looks could be held in place by an orange seat cushion or a vivid green sweater.

"Let me look at my gorgeous grandson!" Phyllis cooed. Ned had Josh strapped into a Baby Bjorn. Josh had been restless the whole five-hour drive down from Hawthorne, and he was still wired, kicking his feet out and gurgling.

"What a resemblance," breathed Phyllis. She ran a bejeweled hand over the top of Josh's curls. "I just can't get over it."

"Resemblance to who, Grandma?" chimed in Kate. She shrugged off her huge knapsack, and it clattered to the marble floor of the foyer.

"To *whom,*" corrected Phyllis.

Kate blinked. "Whom."

"To my whole side of the family, of course," said Phyllis.

"Do I smell coffee?" asked Ned.

"Would I deprive my son-in-law of the world's best coffee?"

I felt my face start to arrange itself into the familiar mask I always wore around my mother. Kate came up behind me and pinched my side in commiseration. The one advantage of being around Phyllis was that it always seemed to bring Kate and me closer together.

"Are you going to say hello to your other grandchild?" I asked. I couldn't help myself.

"I said hello!" Phyllis snapped.

"No, you didn't."

"Yes, I did. Kate?"

Phyllis turned to Kate, who was hovering in back of me now. In trying to protect her, I had inadvertently put her in the last place she wanted to be: the center of attention.

"Grandma," Kate said faintly.

"Hello, *bubeleh.*" Phyllis swept around me, caftan flying. My mother reverted to Yiddish when she wanted to give the appearance of maternal warmth, summoning up the language of her big-bosomed, peasant ancestors. She grasped both of Kate's hands and gave her *the look.* Intense, penetrating, searching—and yet at the same time turned inward. Seeing nothing.

"Hi."

"What a *shaineh punim*!" said Phyllis. "Tell me, have you gotten rid of that disgusting thing in your belly button?"

A long pause, broken only by Josh's thin wail.

"He's hungry," I said, moving to unsnap him from the Bjorn.

"Do you need some milk? I've got some two percent in the fridge," said Phyllis.

"No, I've got my own," I said, gesturing down at my blouse.

"Oh, Rachel. Don't tell me you're still—"

"He's seven months old, Mom. Everybody breast-feeds nowadays until the baby's at least six months."

"That can't be healthy."

"Actually, it's very healthy."

Phyllis wrinkled her nose in distaste, turned, and headed into the kitchen.

"Oh, God," I said, under my breath.

"We don't have to stay here," said Ned.

I sat down on the sofa, undid the top three buttons of my blouse, and unhooked my nursing bra.

"Where would we go?" I asked.

"We can stay in a hotel," Kate said. She sounded hopeful.

"We can't afford it, sweetie," I said.

"Just a couple of nights," said Ned.

"There's no way. We'd need two rooms—do you know how much hotel rooms cost here?"

"Aren't Liza and Tommy in New York?" asked Kate. "Where are they staying?"

"The Pierre," I said.

"Are we going to see them, by the way?" asked Ned.

"I don't know."

Josh burrowed into my soft belly and started feeding. I tried to relax—my milk always flowed better if I was relaxed. A few days with Phyllis, and I might end up dry as the Sahara.

"What's that about a hotel?" Phyllis asked, as she walked back into the living room, two mugs of coffee in hand. But before any of us could think of what to say, she noticed me sitting with Josh on her sofa.

"Not on the Ultrasuede!" she shrieked. "Please, Rachel!"

"Where would you like me to sit, then?" I asked, trying to keep my voice neutral.

"Over there." She pointed to a leather-and-chrome chair I had never seen before. It looked more suitable to some sadomasochistic act than to nursing a baby, but still I got up, cradling Josh, and moved over to it.

"Thank you," said Phyllis.

She averted her eyes from my exposed breast and looked, instead, out the window at the bare branches of the treetops along the edge of Central Park. I had always loved this view. The apartment was on the sixth and seventh floors of a prewar building, high up enough to keep street noise to a minimum but low enough to feel like a part of the city. As a kid, I used to sit on the window seat in my father's study (which had been transformed into "the pink room" after his death) and watch people hanging out in the park. My parents didn't let me go into the park, not even with my friends. It was like having a backyard where it wasn't safe to play—but I didn't mind, and I certainly didn't feel sorry for myself. I didn't know life could be any different. I was used to being alone, to living life within the confines of my own head; I assumed everyone lived in similar isolation. I used to make up stories about those people in the park, imagining that they all went home by themselves to rooms in which they sat alone.

"I've put you and Ned in the blue room upstairs. And Kate in the pink room. I thought the baby could stay in the den."

"The baby still sleeps with us, Mom."

"Oh."

"What?"

Ned shot me a look that said don't go there.

Phyllis perched on the edge of the pristine white sofa. "Nothing."

"No, really, what?"

"Aren't you spoiling him?"

A dozen answers darted through my head, all of them mean, all of them hurtful. *You're the last person I'd go to for mothering advice* is what I wanted to say.

"Yes," I said instead. "Absolutely, we're spoiling him."

Phyllis turned her attention to Kate. "So what's new, pussycat?" she asked.

Kate looked at me, puzzled.

"It's an expression, sweetheart."

"People don't say that anymore?" Phyllis asked.

"No," said Kate.

"What do they say instead?"

"I don't know."

Kate looked itchy, uncomfortable. She had squeezed herself into a corner of the sofa, as if she were trying to disappear.

"Try, Kate. I want to be modern."

"I don't know. Stuff like, 'Yo, wassup?' "

"That's not even English," said Phyllis.

"Whatever." Kate shrugged.

"*Whatever.* Now you see? That's a perfect example."

"Lay off her, Mom."

"Can I go for a walk?" Kate asked, jumping up. She looked like she was about to explode. But I couldn't let her go out by herself. Phyllis's apartment was at the end of a grand stretch of beautiful buildings—if it were a co-op it would have cost millions—but just a few blocks north there were tenements and drug dealers on the streets. If there was trouble to be gotten into, Kate would find it. Besides, she was only fourteen.

"I'll take her," Ned said, putting down his coffee mug. Of course he wanted to take her. It was perfect for him. They'd both leave and be gone for hours, and I'd be left, trapped with Phyllis and the baby.

"No, I could use some air," I said. Josh had just finished nursing, and I handed him off to Ned, who was looking like he was about to kill me. The only thing worse than me being alone with Phyllis was him being alone with Phyllis. I was sacrificing him for my own sanity.

"Are you sure?" he asked. What he was really saying was *You're going to owe me big.* He had a slightly crazed, hysterical expression on his face, but he put Josh over his shoulder and started to burp him.

"I'm sure," I said. "Come on, sweetie."

"Can we go to The Gap?"

"I don't see why not."

KATE AND I WALKED THREE LONG BLOCKS WEST TO BROADway. It was a cold afternoon. Passersby were hunched against the wind, heads down, barreling forward. I had forgotten that about New York: the sense of purpose with which people walked. Everybody had somewhere to go, and fast. A tall woman held her fur coat closed with one gloved hand as she rushed from beneath an awning, crossing in front of us to grab a taxi stopped at a red light.

"Are you warm enough?" I asked Kate.

"Yeah."

"Are you happy we're here?"

She shrugged. Her long blond hair whipped across her face, and she pulled it into a knot and tucked it into the collar of her down jacket.

"I guess."

It had been a long time since Kate and I had done anything alone together. I stopped myself from reaching for her hand or putting my arm around her. Instead, I shoved my hands in my pockets. I strained to find a way to be with her, a way to be lighthearted and easygoing, so I wouldn't have to watch her face grow stony or worse. Walking on ice: that's all we did, these days, with the help of carefully doled-out tiny yellow pills.

Kate's mood seemed to lift when we reached the corner of 86th and Broadway and she saw a Banana Republic on one side of the avenue, a Gap on the other, and a Club Monaco a few doors down. These stores were like homes away from home; she and her friends hung out at the North Shore Mall whenever they could. I was constantly in fear that she'd shoplift again, and this time she wouldn't be brought home by a friend of her father's. But it hadn't happened—at least not yet.

"Can we go in?" She pointed to Banana Republic.

"I thought you wanted to go to The Gap."

"Can't we do both?"

I bit my tongue.

"I'll wait in the front of the store," I said. Kate looked relieved to be rid of me and made a beeline for a rack of army pants near the cash register. She riffled through them with an almost professional grace, like a blackjack dealer shuffling a deck of cards. I watched from a distance as she blended in with the other shoppers, her fair hair streaming over her black down parka, her cheeks pink and healthy. To look at her, there was no hint of the girl who had shoplifted and lied, who had screamed at us so hard I thought she might explode from within. We were, none of us, transparent.

"They have my size!" she came running up to me with her first genuine smile of the day. "They were out of these at North Shore."

"Do you need to try them on?" I asked.

"No, they'll fit," she said. She held them close to her chest, as if I might rip them away from her.

"Okay," I said, handing her a hundred-dollar bill. As she took it, I wondered if she had any idea that money was finite—that Ned and I didn't have endless supplies of hundred-dollar bills. Our financial situation had grown tighter since Josh's birth, and her therapy was expensive. Even though we had always made it clear to Kate that we didn't have a lot of money, I knew she thought we were rich, because of the way Jane and Arthur lived, with their fancy cars and round-the-world trips. Their names were on plaques all over Hawthorne: Jensen Park, the Jensen Soccer Field, the Jensen Concert Series. I think she suspected that Jane and Arthur's money and ours were one and the same and that we were secretly holding out on her.

She handed me back fifteen dollars in change.

"Don't you think we should get back? Dad is probably going nuts," Kate said. Her mission had been accomplished. I realized with a painful jolt that she didn't want to spend a minute more than necessary alone with me.

"Oh, Daddy can handle himself."

"Dr. Zelman thinks—"

I whipped my head around and looked at Kate, surprised. She never talked about Zelman.

"What were you going to say?" I tried to sound casual.

"Nothing."

We walked out onto Broadway.

"Only"—she struggled to zip up her parka—"that we don't have good enough communication."

"We don't have—" I repeated slowly.

I looked away from Kate so she couldn't see the expression on my face. It was the late-afternoon rush hour, and people were getting out of cabs and scurrying into their doorman buildings, carrying briefcases and shopping bags. There were thousands of lives behind the old stone walls of those buildings, and in that moment I imagined that they were all happier and more orderly than mine.

"Do you think Dr. Zelman is helping you?" I dared to ask.

"I don't know." She paused, biting a hangnail. "Maybe."

Horns blasted all around us as a double-decker tour bus tried to make a turn onto Columbus. We were walking down 86th, directly across from the temple my father used to attend when I was growing up. It was still there, and miraculously it was still a temple. It hadn't been converted into condominiums with stained-glass windows yet. An older man, a janitor, was sweeping the steps. A glass-encased announcement board spelled out the week's activities: SATURDAY, 9 A.M.: DAVID PERLMUTTER'S BAR MITZVAH. SERMON: WHERE IS GOD WHEN YOU NEED HIM?

When we first moved to the Upper West Side, I was six years old and I used to go with my father to that temple, where I sat on his lap and listened to him sing songs in a language I didn't understand. When I was ten or eleven, thanks to Phyllis's campaign for assimilation, I no longer thought it was cool to go to synagogue, and on Saturday mornings I hung out with my friends instead. I was never bat mitzvahed, and I didn't go to Hebrew school. By the time I went to college, my father had given up on his spiritual side altogether. He played racquetball on Saturday mornings instead, his middle-aged face twisted into a paroxysm of rage as he smashed the ball against the sides of the court again and again.

"Katie." I sighed. "I just want you to be happy."

Kate was looking at a group of teenagers slightly older than she was. They had just gotten off the crosstown bus and were standing in a huddle, lighting their cigarettes. The boys' pants were so baggy they were almost falling off, and the girls looked older, more sophisticated than Kate's friends back home. Their lipstick was dark, their hair sleek and shiny, pulled tightly back ballerina style.

"I hate my life," she said.

"I'm sorry, baby."

I risked a quick glance at my daughter. A tear rolled down her cheek, and she swiped at it angrily. She was so miserable. I wanted to reach my hands inside of her and rearrange things, find the tiny pearl-sized seed of discontent that had grown so unmanageable.

"What is it?" I asked. "If you could just talk it out, maybe—"

"I can't."

"Why? You have everything in the world going for you," I said, then abruptly stopped, wishing I could stuff the words back into my mouth. That was the last thing she wanted to hear. I remembered hearing the same thing at her age. Brains, beauty, privilege, family—it all meant nothing if she was troubled inside.

She walked faster, her head bowed.

"I'm sorry, Katie. I shouldn't have said that. I know it doesn't matter."

An old couple, gray-haired and stooped over, walked out of a deli and hobbled slowly across the crowded street. No one stopped to help them; no one even noticed them. I thought, simultaneously, of Jane and Arthur—how lucky they were to live in the relative bucolia of Hawthorne—and of my own parents, and how sad it was that they didn't have the chance to grow old in each other's company.

Kate bundled her jacket around her. Her teeth were chattering.

"Are you and Dad okay?" she asked. The question felt like it was completely out of the blue. Of course Ned and I were okay! I couldn't imagine why Kate would ask such a question.

"What in the world do you mean?"

She shrugged and looked down at her feet.

"Your father and I love each other, Katie," I said. "Always have, always will. That's not something you ever need to worry about."

She didn't say anything. Her hair hung in a curtain over her face.

"Did you hear me?" It suddenly felt essential that I make her understand at least this one thing. "Kate?"

"Uh-huh," she mumbled. She finally made eye contact, and the expression on her face was so dead, so devoid of anything I could connect to, that I felt instantly exhausted.

"Let's just go home," I said.

BACK AT MY MOTHER'S APARTMENT, I FUMBLED THROUGH my bag for my key and then realized I didn't have one. I rang the bell and heard heavy footsteps on the other side. Ned opened the door. He looked oddly happy, given that he had been with Phyllis for the past hour and a half.

"Guess who's here?" he said.

"Who?"

Kate and I followed Ned through the foyer and into the living room, where I heard voices. No one ever visited Phyllis—literally no one, ever. The only "visitors" she ever had were people who did work for her: the drapery man, the carpet cleaner, the woman she hired to teach her bridge. As we grew nearer, the voices became more distinct, and I heard a familiar tinkling laugh.

"You called them?" I asked.

"Yeah, and it turned out they were free tonight. So they came right over."

Liza unfolded herself from the Ultrasuede sofa, where she was cradling Josh in a blanket against her perfectly cut black suit. She had gotten her hair cut into shaggy bangs and highlighted pale blond. Every time I saw Liza, she looked younger. Pretty soon she was going to be carded in bars. Meanwhile, I was marching toward dowdy middle age.

"Hi, honey." She kissed me on both cheeks.

Tommy engulfed Kate in a bear hug.

"How's my girl?" he asked.

Phyllis was sitting across from Liza, *kvelling,* as she might say in Yiddish. She loved Liza and wished I were more like her: a fashion plate married to a gazillionaire.

"I can't believe you guys are here," I said, forcing a smile. I was feeling so down after my outing with Kate.

"If it's a bad time—" Liza said quickly.

"No, no."

"Well, good," said Tommy, "because I just booked us a table at Danube."

"Booked a table," breathed Phyllis. "What a wonderful au courant expression."

"We can't go," I said.

"I told them that," said Ned. "Tommy won't take no for an answer."

"We don't have a baby-sitter," I said.

"We'll call a service," said Liza.

"I'm not leaving Josh with some stranger."

"Maybe your mother can—" Ned started, but I shot him a look that stopped him.

"Actually, Phyllis, why don't you join us?" asked Liza.

"Oh, I can't possibly, dear," said Phyllis, "but how nice of you to ask." She smiled pointedly at Ned.

"Maybe we could all just order in Chinese," I said.

"Chinese!" Liza laughed, as if I had just said the quaintest thing.

"You don't need a baby-sitter. I'll watch Josh," Kate suddenly piped up.

"Oh, Kate, I don't think—"

"And I'll be here," said Phyllis. "I have been a mother for nearly forty years, after all."

Ned and I glanced at each other, surprised. The room grew so quiet I could hear the ticking of Phyllis's wall clock. Kate had put Josh to bed a few times—once, Ned and I even ducked out to the movies—but never in a strange house, in a strange city.

"What a sweet offer." My mind was racing. It might be good to give Kate the responsibility, to show her that we trusted her. All she'd have to do would be to put him in his port-a-crib and then just hang out downstairs, watching television. She could handle that—and it might make her feel good about herself. And though the thought of my mother being around didn't exactly comfort me, she *was* an adult presence in the house.

"I don't know—"

"Really, I want to."

"Maybe just a quick bite," I said reluctantly. "Where's this restaurant?"

"Tribeca," said Tommy. "Come on. My driver's outside."

"Ned?" I turned to him. Why wasn't he saying anything? He was bowing out, the way he often did when the stress level got too high. "Do you have any thoughts about this?"

"I think it's okay," he said.

"Oh, go on," said Phyllis. "Really, it's hardly a trip to the moon."

Our bags were still packed and sitting at the foot of the staircase. "Ned, would you help me take these upstairs?"

Ned followed me up the stairs, carrying our luggage. The curved wall along the staircase was lined with photos from my mother's travels since my father's death. In every city around the world, she stopped someone and asked to have her picture taken in front of a major monument. There was Phyllis in front of the Taj Mahal, Phyllis standing next to a guard at Buckingham Palace, Phyllis with her hair tied back in a kerchief, one hand touching the Western Wall. At the top of the stairs hung the one remaining photo of my father: smiling, his eyes crinkled at the corners, holding his pipe. I touched the frame as I reached the top step.

Ned and I went into the blue room and closed the door.

"Do you really think we should do this?" I asked.

"I don't see why not," he said. "It'll be good for her."

He checked his watch.

"It's six o'clock. He'll probably go down at seven and sleep through until we're back. And if not, she can always give him a bottle of formula."

"I hate giving him formula."

"Come on, Rach. A bottle now and then isn't the end of the world."

I sat down on the bed.

"I'm just so tired," I said. I was on the verge of tears. Nights out with Tommy and Liza required a lot of energy, and after the five-hour drive down from Hawthorne with Josh fussing in his baby seat and Kate insisting on hip-hop music, I was ready for bed.

"Please?" Ned asked.

I looked at him. Ned needed these Tommy-and-Liza extravaganzas more than I did. Over the years we had gone to every great restaurant up and down the East Coast, and whether we were at an inn in Kennebunkport or a four-star restaurant on the Upper East Side, it was always the same: the maître d' would fall all over himself the minute Tommy walked in. The finest bottle on the wine list would appear at our table. The chef would sprint out from the kitchen with special treats for us and would often join us at the end of the evening. We would sit late into the night drinking grappa, or very old port, or some ridiculously expensive cognac while Tommy and the chef argued about which distributor had procured the best morels that season. Not that it wasn't fun. It was fun while it lasted, like getting a nice buzz from a drug even though you knew there'd be hell to pay the next morning.

I pulled my makeup kit from the side compartment of my suitcase and searched through it for some blush. Everything I had brought with me seemed old and drab. The kit itself was ancient, filled with the dust of years' worth of compacts, eye shadows, sticky bits of spilled foundation. I saw it clearly, just as I saw that the sweaters I had brought all had pulls or small moth holes. In Hawthorne, I didn't care. But being in New York—especially being in New York with Liza—made me aware, suddenly, of the fifteen extra pounds I was still carrying from my pregnancy, and the bags under my eyes from all the sleepless nights. My hair fell around my face like a dull dirty mop. I needed an overhaul. Maybe I could get Liza to take me to some fancy day spa where I'd get buffed and steamed and waxed.

"Don't do that."

Ned was frowning at me.

"Do what?"

"You're pulling at your face."

"Sorry," I said, my voice muffled by a couple of bobby pins in my mouth. I swiped at my cheeks with blush and patted some concealer under my eyes. I stuck a barrette in my hair and put on some dangling earrings.

"Why are we doing this?" I asked.

"Because it'll be fun," said Ned. "Because we haven't been out to dinner in seven months."

He leaned over me and looked in the mirror, squeezed some hair gel into his palms, and raked his fingers through his hair. It had been a while since I had looked at him as anything other than the father of my children. He was right. It would be good for us to have a night out on the town.

"My handsome husband," I said, reaching for him.

"My beautiful wife."

OFTEN I THINK BACK TO THAT NIGHT, TO THE SERIES OF moments stacked precariously, one on top of the next like a house of cards, and try to see if I can remove any one of the cards without upsetting the balance. It's a sick game I play with myself, not unlike the sick games Kate now plays with herself. I draw the razor of memory across my skin, tracing each image as lightly as possible, still drawing blood.

What if Kate and I had stayed out later? What if Tommy and Liza had gotten tired of waiting for us and had left for dinner by themselves? What if Kate hadn't offered to baby-sit? Sometimes I take it back farther: What if I had never met Liza when I was in graduate school? What if we hadn't become friends? And still farther: What if my father had taken a different route, the day he first saw the lovely dark-haired girl my mother once was? What if a honking horn had distracted him, or if he had glanced down at his watch at just the moment she passed? Turn one corner, and everything lines up differently. Everything we do matters. Every single blessed thing.

"There's my guy," said Tommy, as we walked out of Phyllis's building. He pointed to a Lincoln Navigator idling by the curb, its driver obscured by tinted windows.

"That's not a car, it's a pimpmobile," said Ned.

"I think it's very handsome," said Phyllis. She had come downstairs to see us off.

"Everybody, this is our driver, François," said Tommy.

We all chorused hello except for Phyllis, who offered François a limp hand and actually said *enchanté.*

We piled in, waved goodbye, pulled onto Central Park West, and started downtown. François wove in and out of traffic to 79th Street, turned south on the West Side Highway, and suddenly everything stopped. Before us there were endless red brake lights, and in the distance something was flashing.

"Great," said Tommy.

"Sorry, sir."

"Not your fault, bud."

We sat for a while in silence until Tommy started fiddling with the CD player up front. A female voice filled the air with a heavy acoustic beat.

"Who the hell is that?" asked Ned.

"J. Lo," said Tommy.

Ned looked at him blankly.

"Jennifer Lopez," said Liza.

"Man, I knew it." Ned slapped his knee.

"What?"

"Tommy Mendel's secret wish."

"Yeah? What's that?"

"You want to be a music mogul," said Ned.

"Give me a break."

"Oh, come on. The Navigator. The shades at night—"

"—I happen to have an eye infection."

"Uh-huh."

The guy behind us leaned on his horn, and Tommy rolled down the window and jabbed his middle finger into the air.

"Tommy!" Liza exclaimed, half laughing, even though I knew that the crude side of Tommy bothered her.

"Fucking asshole," said Tommy. "People like that should be shot."

The horn blared again, and this time all of us turned around to look at him. A skinny guy in a Volkswagen gave us the finger back.

"Oh, that's mature," muttered Tommy. "Short man's complex." Then he turned to François.

"Is there anything you can do to get us out of here?" he asked.

"Got to wait it out, sir."

It was then that my cell phone rang. At first, I didn't even know where the ringing was coming from. All of us reached for our cell phones—even François.

"It's yours, I think," said Ned.

I was fumbling through my bag, the only bag I had—an enormous satchel. My phone was buried under my wallet, keys, loose tissues, baby wipes. I grabbed it and flipped it open.

"Hello?" On the other end, static crackled. For a second I thought it was a wrong number. That happened sometimes. "Hello?" I repeated.

Then I heard Kate's voice, and she was screaming.

"Kate?" I said. "What happened?"

She just kept screaming. She was trying to talk, trying to say something to me, but she couldn't catch her breath. I could make out a sound underneath Kate's screams, another kind of shriek, high-pitched and unstoppable: Josh. All I could think was that we had only been gone fifteen minutes. Nothing could have gone wrong in fifteen minutes.

"Katie?" My voice was shaking. The car got very quiet. Everyone was staring at me.

"He fell," Kate managed to gulp out.

"Where did he fall? What do you mean, he fell?"

"I'm sorry!"

"Kate?" I figured if I kept repeating her name, she'd come to, like a coma victim. She'd stop screaming, stop hyperventilating, and I'd be able to get a clear picture of what was going on.

In the front seat, I saw Tommy lean over to François, who jammed his hand on the horn, drove up onto the divider, and made a sharp turn off the West Side Highway and onto a midtown street. Horns blared all around us, but we were in a bubble, the soft purplish interior of Tommy's car. Everything got very slow—slow and freezing cold. I had left my trembling body; I was floating, adrift in a nightmare. Ned grabbed my arm and was shaking me.

"What happened?" he asked. He was white, his eyes huge.

I held up a finger, stopping him.

"Is he hurt, Kate? Can you tell if he—"

"He hit his head," she wailed.

I heard static again, and then the sound of my mother's voice.

"Rachel? Can you hear me?"

"Get off the phone now, Mom, and call 911. Can you do that?" I asked.

I heard muffled sobs, and then something I couldn't understand.

"What?"

"I already did." She wept into my ear.

"Don't move him. Just wait for them to get there. Do you understand?"

On the other end there was silence.

"Hello?" I screamed into the phone. "Hello?"

I flipped my phone closed.

"I lost them," I said.

Everybody started talking all at once. Words ricocheted around the car, words like *accident* and *hospital* and *emergency.* It seemed impossible to me that I could have been sitting in the back of Tommy's car, looking out at the Hudson River, while my baby hurt himself just a mile or two away. How could I not have known? I should have felt a searing pain in my own head, a premonition that something had gone wrong back home.

"He hit his head," I said.

"Is he conscious?" asked Liza. "Was he crying? That's the most important thing. You don't want them to lose consciousness. I remember Sophie once hit her head on the side of the kitchen table—do you remember that, Tommy?—and I was so sure she had a concussion. But she was absolutely fine."

"He was crying, I heard him," I said.

Liza leaned across Ned and stroked my arm.

"That's good," said Liza. "It's probably nothing, then. I'm sure Kate's just . . ."

Liza's voice faded, as Ned and I locked hands. I felt a current of energy running between us. Then Ned's cell phone rang.

"Yeah?"

He paused for a minute and rubbed his eyes.

"Phyllis, could you put him on the phone?"

Another pause. I could hear noise and, still, that high-pitched wailing.

"Phyllis? Put the policeman on the phone."

Policeman? I saw Tommy and Liza exchange a quick, frightened glance. Terror surged through my body, a physical sensation. I wanted to slam my fist through the window, bust out of the car, and go tearing off in the direction of my baby.

"Yes." Ned reached over and grabbed my hand again. "Yes. Fine, that's fine."

"What's going on?" I asked. I couldn't stand it. "Ned?"

"Which hospital?" he asked.

"Oh my God!" I cried.

Liza was looking at me, her eyes steady and direct as if she might be able to keep me calm. She had known me the longest of anyone in the car. She had been with me when my father died and nursed me through my grief. She had been there the very same day I met Ned. How crazy was it, that we were together now, she and I—we almost never saw each other anymore and now she was here with me, during this . . . emergency. I didn't want to call it an emergency, even though as the minutes marched on it was becoming clear to me that life was never going to be the same again. Somehow, I knew it. Whatever had happened, it was all going to be different now. Even if everything turned out to be fine, something had been shattered. We weren't safe—nothing was safe.

"They're taking him to Mount Sinai," said Ned.

"Why not Lenox Hill?" asked Tommy. "Lenox Hill is the best."

"That's where they're taking him, Tommy," snapped Ned.

"Sinai's good," said Liza. "They have an excellent pediatric unit."

I wondered how she knew that, or even if it was true.

"What did the cop say?" asked Tommy.

"Why is there a cop?" I blurted out. "What's a cop doing—"

"They always come for something like this," said Liza.

"He said if it were his kid, he'd want him in the hospital," said Ned.

FIVE MINUTES MIGHT HAVE GONE BY, OR TEN, OR TWENTY by the time we pulled up to the emergency room. I had closed my eyes and was trying to pray. But I didn't have much practice, and all I felt, with my eyes closed and my lips moving, was that there was a black void, an emptiness into which I was hurling my prayers. No one was there. No one was listening. I tried to take comfort in the fact that whatever had happened had already happened. There was nothing I could do. The worst thing was not knowing, and in a few minutes we'd be rushing through the hospital and I would see my baby. Knowledge was better than no knowledge. Without knowing, my imagination ran wild.

Tommy jumped out of the car ahead of us and barreled forward through the hospital doors. He was just being Tommy, just trying to take care of things as if this were a restaurant or a first-class hotel where who he was might make a difference.

"Patient's name is Jensen," he barked to an older black woman in a white coat who was seated behind a glass partition. "Joshua Jensen."

She stared at him for a moment, as if deciding what to do about the level of entitlement with which Tommy had approached her. She didn't want to be helpful. On the other hand, this was an emergency room, not the department of motor vehicles.

"Say the name again?" she asked.

"Jensen. He's an infant," said Ned. He had come up behind Tommy and had angled his way in. "My son."

The woman looked from Tommy to Ned and then sighed, glancing down at the patient list in front of her.

"I'll buzz you through," she said.

All four of us rushed to the side door.

"Just the parents." Her voice was amplified by the intercom.

"I love you," I said to Ned as we pushed the door open. It was an odd thing to say, perhaps, incongruous—but I needed to say it, and I thought he might need to hear it.

Through a partially opened curtain I saw Josh lying in a hospital crib. A nurse bent over him, checking his blood pressure with a tiny cuff. I pushed past the curtain and rushed to the side of the crib, afraid to touch him, terrified that moving him would make things worse. He had a bump on his forehead, a bluish-green swelling there, and his eyes were closed, his lashes matted with tears.

"Is he conscious?" Ned asked the nurse. His voice was shaking and he could barely get the words out.

"He's floating in and out," she said.

I reached into the crib and stroked Josh's hand. Josh responded to my touch, taking a deep shuddering breath. His hand curled into a fist.

"The doctor will be here in a minute," the nurse said.

"Has he been seen yet?"

"No, he just got here," said the nurse.

It was then that I noticed Kate. She was sitting just outside the curtained-off area on a metal folding chair. Her head was down, and she was rocking back and forth, weeping.

"Kate?" I walked over to her. She was my baby too, and though part of me wanted to throw her against the wall, the rest of me wanted to pick her up and hold her.

She looked up at me, her whole face crumpled. I sat down next to her.

"You need to tell me what happened," I said.

"I . . . fell . . ."

She was breathing hard, and she was so pale I could see the thin blue veins beneath her skin. Her pupils filled her eyes. I reached into my purse, where I remembered I had a Ziploc full of formula packets. I emptied the packets into my purse and handed Kate the Ziploc.

"Breathe into the bag," I said. "Hold it over your mouth and breathe."

A young Indian man in a white coat slid aside a curtain three partitions down. I caught a glimpse of a child on a bed, surrounded by equipment. The doctor quickly moved to Josh's side. He lifted first one eyelid, then the other, peering into each eye with a small flashlight. He ran his fingers lightly over the bump.

"How old is he?" he asked.

"Seven months," said Ned.

"And what was the nature of the accident?" The doctor put two fingers inside Josh's wrist, checking his pulse. Ned, Kate, and I were hovering at the foot of the crib.

Ned and I looked at Kate, waiting. But she stood there, frozen. She was staring at Josh, and I couldn't read her expression.

"Kate," Ned said.

"I was carrying him downstairs," she said. "I had just changed him into his pajamas." At this, she broke down weeping again.

"It happened so fast," I suddenly hear my mother's high-pitched voice behind me. "Lord forgive me, it's my fault, I never should have taken my eyes off—"

"That's not what we need right now, Phyllis," said Ned.

"How far did he fall?" asked the doctor.

"I don't know . . . maybe six or seven steps," Kate said.

"There's no carpet on those stairs," said Ned.

"I always meant to put a runner," my mother murmured.

"We're going to need to do a CT scan," said the doctor. "Is he allergic to any medications?"

"Not that we know of," I said.

"Why?" Ned asked. "What do you need to—"

"He has to be sedated," said the doctor.

"But he's—"

"In case he wakes up. He needs to be absolutely still for the X-ray."

"Do you think he's all right?" I asked. "I mean—"

"We'll know more after the CT scan," said the doctor.

He and an orderly released the brakes on the crib bed and began to wheel Josh down the corridor. Josh looked so small against the white sheets, the metal rails, his dark curls framing his face, his perfect rosebud of a mouth. I watched his chest rise and fall, his eyelids flicker. I thought of my father, as I always did when I was in a hospital. My father hadn't been an old man when he died, but he was certainly of an age when sickness and death were not a complete and total abomination. This—Josh being wheeled into radiology, unconscious, a swelling on his head—this was unacceptable.

I could hear my mother moaning behind me.

"Kate, would you please take Grandma to the waiting room outside?" I asked. My voice was eerily calm. I knew Phyllis was hurting, but she was the last person on earth I could bear to have near me.

"But—" my mother protested.

"Tommy and Liza are out there," I said. "They'll take care of you."

"You'll have to wait out here," said the orderly, as he swung the doors open. The gleaming white machinery was visible inside, a futuristic-looking thing with a tunnel running through its center.

"We're coming in," I said.

"It isn't safe, ma'am. There's a lot of radiation."

"I want to be with my son," said Ned.

The orderly stopped and looked at Ned for a second, sizing him up. Then he shrugged.

"All right," he said. "One of you can come."

I paced the waiting area outside radiology. My legs felt heavy, like I was walking through sand. I was beset by images of Josh being slid into that monster of a machine. The minutes ticked by. What were they seeing inside his little head?

"Mom?" Kate appeared by my side. Her eyes were puffy, but she looked a little calmer. "How long did they say it would take?" she asked.

"They didn't."

"Where's Dad?"

"Inside, with Josh."

"Did they say—"

"They don't know anything, Kate."

"But they don't think—"

She wanted so badly for me to tell her it was going to be okay. After all, I had spent her whole life fixing things: anything broken or bruised could be repaired. Kiss it better, she used to say, offering me a banged elbow, a bumped knee. But I couldn't kiss this better. I couldn't even try to comfort her. Babies suffered and died. It happened all the time. Why should we be spared? I had to keep moving. I walked over to an empty nurses' station and noticed a phone there. I picked it up, listened to the dial tone, then replaced the receiver. Who was I going to call? There was nobody. Everyone who mattered to me in the world was within these hospital walls.

Kate sat down on the ice-cold floor and wrapped her arms around herself. I plopped myself down next to her. I knew I should try to focus on her, but I couldn't. In retrospect I realize that I was furious with her, angry beyond comprehension—that the truest test of unconditional maternal love was being exacted upon me. One of my children had put the other one in grave danger. How could I forgive that?

All I could see was Josh: Josh's face, superimposed like a transparency over everything else I was seeing. He had smiled at me when we left for dinner. He had reached his fat little arms up toward me when I bent down to kiss him goodbye. *Goodbye, Joshie! See you soon!* I was always breathing him in. Inhaling that delicious infant smell as if I could still hold him inside me. *He looks just like you, you know. Not a drop of Jensen in him.* People in Hawthorne were constantly stopping me on the street, exclaiming over his dimples, his black ringlets, his deep-set dark eyes so much like my own.

Kate was talking, but I hadn't been listening. She was looking at me, waiting for an answer.

"Sorry. What did you say?"

"It was an accident," she said.

"Of course it was."

"It was an accident," she repeated more urgently.

"I know that."

"You don't believe me," she almost shouted. Her eyes were wild. Two nurses walking down the hall turned and glanced at us.

"Ssshhh," I said.

She was picking at the skin around her fingernails. She had always been a nail biter, but this was worse. The skin was raw, almost bloody. On a few fingers, she had shredded the skin down to her knuckles.

"Stop it." I grabbed one of her hands.

"I can't."

She wrenched her hand away from me and kept picking at the pink skin. She swatted angrily at the corners of her eyes, which threatened tears. Her lower lip was trembling. She looked like a little girl.

Two men in suits approached us. At first I thought they were hospital administrators, or maybe salesmen of radiology equipment. But then one of them cleared his throat.

"Excuse me, are you Mrs. Jensen?"

"Yes," I said.

One of the men flipped open a leather case and flashed a badge at me.

"Sergeant Roter, ma'am, from the Sixty-sixth Precinct. We'd like to ask your daughter a couple of questions."

"Me?" asked Kate. Two bright pink circles appeared in her cheeks.

"Why in the world would you want to question her?" I asked, putting my arm around Kate.

"It's standard procedure. In any case involving a baby."

"It's fine, Mom. Go ahead," said Kate. Her chin was jutted out, and every muscle in her body looked tightly coiled, ready to spring.

"Can you tell us what happened?"

"I fell down the stairs at my grandmother's house. I was carrying my baby brother."

"Was anyone else at home?"

"My grandmother was in the kitchen."

"Where is your grandmother now?"

"In the waiting room," I interjected. "Is this really necessary?"

"We'll want to have a few words with her as well," one of them said, then turned back to Kate. "Please, go on."

"I lost my balance. I was wearing socks, and it was slippery."

The other cop was scribbling into his notebook. Was Kate in trouble?

"There's no rug on the stairs," I blurted out. "I've been telling my mother for years—"

"That's all right, ma'am," the sergeant interrupted. He turned back to Kate. "Go on."

"I dropped him," she said, her voice lowered. "He flew out of my arms. I don't know how it happened. He just started rolling away from me, down—I don't know—four, five, six steps before I caught him."

"Did you hurt yourself at all?"

She pulled up her sweater and, for the first time, I saw a nasty scrape on her elbow.

"Kate! We should get that looked at!" I said. There was caked blood around the scrape.

"I'm fine," she said quietly.

"Okay—thank you very much," said the sergeant. The other one flipped his notebook closed. "That's all we need for now."

I watched them leave. Kate was shaking next to me. I hugged her close and found myself rocking back and forth, murmuring Hebrew prayers from my childhood, melodies and words I didn't even know I remembered.

"What does that mean?" she asked.

"I don't know," I said. I kept my eyes shut tight, trying to find a place of strength inside of myself. Like a rock climber, I was looking for a place to grasp, to dig in my hand and keep us all from falling.

"Rachel?"

I blinked open. Ned was standing in front of me.

"They're finished," he said.

"What did they say?"

"They didn't tell me. The doctor has to read the results."

The orderly wheeled Josh out of radiology, and we followed him down the hall, in the direction of the emergency room. He was completely unconscious, his head rolled to the side. A white cotton blanket was pulled halfway over him, and his foot, clad in a dark blue sock with white treads, poked out from the bottom.

I was focused on Josh's foot—how tiny and perfect it was—when suddenly I heard my mother's voice. Why hadn't Liza kept her away?

"You tell me where they are this instant! I will not take no for an answer!"

Her presence here was wrong, all wrong.

"There's my grandson!"

She rushed over to Josh's crib, blocking the orderly's path. She leaned over the crib rail until she was inches from Josh's face. I was afraid she'd fall over.

"Please, Mom."

I pulled her away. I looked at her. I don't think I had ever seen her quite so agitated, not even when my father was dying.

"What are they saying, Rachel? Please, tell me what they're saying."

"We're waiting to talk to the doctor now," I said.

"You can't just wait! You have to make yourself known to these people. Otherwise—"

"Please, Phyllis. Everything's under control."

Ned was squeezing my hand tightly.

"You think it's under control. But I've lived longer than you and in my experience—"

"You're not allowed in here, Mom," I interrupted.

"Not allowed?" Her eyebrows shot up.

"You need to go back into the waiting room. With Tommy and Liza."

I felt sorry for my mother in that moment, I really did. She looked old and frail and terribly frightened. But she was making things worse for all of us.

"Jensen?" The doctor approached us, holding an X-ray.

"Yes," Ned said quickly.

"Your son has suffered a contusion on his brain," said the doctor.

"What does that mean?"

"A bruise," said the doctor.

For a moment I was flooded with relief. A bruise—well, bruises weren't so bad. But then I looked at the doctor: His serious eyes. The crease between his brows. His hands held out to us, pointing to a few metal chairs.

"Please—sit down," he said.

I knew that being told to sit down wasn't good. That wasn't good at all. When a doctor told you to sit down, you knew you were in trouble.

"This was a very serious fall," said the doctor. "We're going to have to wait and see what happens."

"What do you mean, wait and see?" Ned asked. "Wait and see what?"

"We're going to keep him here—I'm moving him over to the pediatric ICU. There's the possibility of a bleed, of his going into shock."

"He's going to be okay, right?" Kate asked. She was gripping the bars of Josh's crib.

"We don't know that yet," said the doctor.

"Oh my God," moaned Phyllis. "My grandson, my precious little—"

"Get her out of here," Ned said to me, under his breath.

"Mom, I'm going to take you to the waiting room now," I said, standing up.

"He has to be okay," said Kate. Her voice was shrill. "He has to be!" She grabbed the sleeve of the doctor's white coat and started tugging at it. "He has to be, you have to make him—" She was almost yelling.

I should have seen it coming. It happened so precisely, so slowly, as if it had been choreographed.

"Kate, stop it," said Ned.

She started to scream, just as she had on the phone. She was shattered, my daughter, she couldn't stop; she just couldn't hold herself together. Everyone was staring at us. The doctor moved away from her. The nurses looked up from their station, pens poised in midair. A woman in a trench coat, who was waiting for her own news, shook her head, then covered her ears. And Ned took two giant steps toward Kate, grabbed her by her narrow shoulders, and shook her. She pulled away from him and then she slipped and fell, banging the side of her head hard against the metal railing of Josh's stretcher.

She stopped screaming. She touched her cheek and looked up at all of us in shock.

Ned's lips trembled. "I'm sorry, baby," he said, "I was just trying to stop you from—"

A drop of blood dribbled from Kate's nose, across her mouth, down her chin.

"Oh, God." A sob escaped him.

"You hate me," Kate said softly.

"Katie, no!"

"Of course you hate me," she repeated.

"No, no, no!" He moved to hug her, but something in her eyes stopped him. I saw it too. Whatever remained of the little girl she once was—whatever ghost selves that still clung to her and kept her healthy and safe—those ghosts fled right there under the fluorescent lights of the emergency room.

8

THE PARKING LOT OF THE LITTLE ACORN IS JAMMED WITH SUVs and minivans. The moms of Hawthorne are performing their morning ritual, buckling and unbuckling car seats, pulling strollers and diaper bags from trunks, checking lunch boxes, blowing kisses. They're a good-looking bunch, the Hawthorne moms: in shape from their twice-weekly soccer games, their hair cut into no-nonsense bobs, their fingers and toes polished regularly at a salon downtown. Several of them wave as I pull up in my Volvo with Josh. I flick on the hazards, then let Josh out of his car seat.

"Hey, Rachel!" Maggie Conover jogs up to me. Her daughter Zoë is in Josh's preschool class. "We were just talking about putting together something special for graduation. Do you want to come to Starbucks after and talk about it?"

"Um—" I brush my hair out of my eyes. "Sure, okay."

I'm dumbfounded that she's asking me.

"Great. See you soon." Maggie dashes back to her Ford Explorer and pulls out of the parking lot. I scoop up Josh along with the lunch I've packed him, and carry him inside, past the paper cutouts of acorns that adorn the halls of the school, no matter what the season. As I bounce him on my hip, I steal glances at the chubby folds of his neck, the soft curve of his cheek, his moist little mouth so perfect that it's all I can do, sometimes, to stop myself from kissing him square on the lips.

"You're delicious," I murmur to him, a singsong. "You're delightful, delectable."

He giggles, liking the sound of the words.

"You're yummy," I whisper in his ear.

"Yummy, yummy," he repeats, smacking his lips.

I deposit him at the door of his classroom, and he dashes inside.

" 'Bye, Joshie!" I call.

He ignores me and runs toward the train set. He never says, "bye-bye" like other kids his age. I keep telling myself it's just his personality—that he doesn't like hello or goodbye—but it never fails to frighten me. *Please-be-okay, please-be-okay, please-be-okay.* I turn quickly so he doesn't see the tears stinging my eyes. Each time I leave him, I feel wrenched. As I drive away, I have to push past a sick empty feeling inside of me—an invisible secret wall. How is he doing in the classroom without me? He's not as far along as the other toddlers, he's just not. The teachers say not to worry, but when I'm with him, I do nothing but worry. His eyes look too cloudy, too dreamy to me. And he repeats things—echoing phrases instead of speaking in sentences like the other kids. I have to get away from him, just so I can forget for hours at a time that I'm a mother, until suddenly I'll glance at my watch or hear a child shouting and remember. But I know it's what keeps me sane, the forgetting. If I lived inside of my love for Josh and Kate all the time, I would be trapped. I would burn up from the intensity of my own feelings, and nothing would be left of me but a little pile of ash.

I head downtown. Graduation, Maggie said. My God. Planning a graduation from preschool! I have the urge to call Ned and tell him about it—Ned's companionship being one of the prime reasons why I never felt lonely in Hawthorne. After all, this is exactly the kind of thing we used to laugh about. *Can you believe it? What, are they going to have caps and gowns? Special diapers?* But I don't know if I should call. Since the night we spent together, I have been careful not to push too hard. Ned retreated after that night, and I can't say I blame him. He's afraid to hope, terrified of disappointment. I want to reach out a hand to him and say, *Me too, but let's try anyway.* I want to tell him there's a freedom in the worst thing having already happened. But instead I have kept my distance. One week, now two.

Oh, screw it. Stopped at a red light, I pull my phone out of my bag. It's nine o'clock. I dial his cell phone, my fingers moving nimbly across the numbers.

"Hey, it's Ned. Leave a message."

"Hey, you." I turn left onto a side street near Starbucks where there's metered parking. "Listen, can we talk? I need to talk to you. That night—"

And then I falter to a stop. What do I want to say about that night? That it was wonderful? Terrible? That I want him to sleep beside me every night, to feel his hands grope for me? That I want to hear him call my name in his dreams? That I never want to see him again? That I want to start my whole life over and skip the part where he and I met—I want to see how my life would unfurl from that moment, at age twenty-four, when I decided that I had met my future and its name was Ned?

"Call me," I say, then flip the phone shut. I'm parked right in front of the chocolate shop, the place where Ned has bought me chocolates for birthdays, anniversaries, Valentine's Days, and even sometimes for no reason at all. Dee Dretzin, the nice lady who owns the place, is trudging down the block toward the store, moving slowly, as if the air is too thick for her. Her husband recently passed away from a brain tumor. How hard it must be, to have a companion for fifty years and then suddenly to be alone. I watch from my car as she unlocks the glass door to her shop and lets herself inside.

I rest my head against the steering wheel. The world feels impossibly sad to me. Still, I know this: given the choice—and given everything that's happened—I would still choose to have met

Ned that day more than fifteen years ago in the East Village. I would still choose it all, even at this moment when I don't know how any of it is going to turn out. How could I have missed being Kate's mother? Or Josh's? How could I turn my back on all those years of bounty? Because that's what it was—every minute of every day: overflowing bounty.

My phone rings, and my heart jumps. Every time it rings, I panic. I know it's understandable, but still I wonder if I'll ever feel normal again.

"Hello," I answer quickly.

"Yeah," says Ned's voice on the other end. "You called."

"I did."

"Where are you?"

"On Pine Street. Outside Dee's shop."

"What are you doing there?"

"Trying to summon up the strength to walk into Starbucks and have a tall half-caf skim caramel macchiato with Maggie Conover and company."

"Why?"

I hear the amusement in his voice, so I press on.

"Graduation," I say. "Graduation from preschool."

"You're kidding."

"They want me to help."

Silence.

"To be a part of things."

"That's a new twist."

"Yeah. It's kind of weird, actually."

"Oh, they're probably just trying to be nice to you because—"

Ned stops. The unsaid words hang between us. Because of what happened between us? Because of Kate? Or Josh?

"Anyway," says Ned, "I think I just sold this house. So that's a good thing."

"Great!" I say. I'm not sure how excited I should sound.

"Eight hundred grand. And they haven't even broken ground yet."

"This is one of Jane and Arthur's?"

"Uh-huh. It's a development they've asked me to oversee, actually."

Now I really don't know what to say. I've hoped Ned would get back to the things he cares about. His art may be too big a step for him to take, but at least teaching is something he still can do. That he cares about. Not this. If he keeps selling houses he's going to wake up one morning, look in the mirror, and see his father's pink, sagging face staring back at him.

"Oh, Ned."

"It's a lot of money," he says. There's an edge to his voice, but I press on.

"Money's not the only issue."

"Right now it is."

"We can find another way to deal with it. I know we can. If you start managing a whole development project, it's going to mean—"

"An extra thousand bucks a week," says Ned. "That's what it'll mean."

"Listen, I've been thinking about that."

He doesn't say anything. I wonder where he is right now. That's the thing about calling people on their cell phones; you can't picture them.

"I've been thinking," I say, "that we shouldn't do it."

"Do what?"

"You know. The school."

"Oh, come on, Rach. What choice do we have?"

I hear music in the background, the sound of a door slamming.

"Where are you?"

"A coffee shop in Haverhill."

I feel like backing out of this parking spot and speeding toward Haverhill. It's fifteen minutes away. By the time I get there, he'll be gone.

"We have choices, Ned. I think part of the problem is that we've forgotten that."

"I've got to go," he says.

"Wait. We need to discuss this."

"Not now."

"Well, when?"

"Later."

"Later, when?"

I hate this. I hate trying to pin him down, acting like some nagging, lovelorn idiot. A flash of rage tears through me, white-hot, leaving my fingertips tingling. I can make my own decisions—about Kate, about Josh, about the rest of my life.

"Tonight," he says. "I'll come over after work."

The fury leaves as quickly and silently as it arrived.

"Okay," I say. "I'll see you then."

I hang up, then open the car door. Dee sees me for the first time and waves from behind the counter. I'm sure she knows about Ned and me. Everybody knows. It's one of the things I miss about living in a big city; you can walk down the street there and be surrounded by strangers. There's comfort in that—no one knows your business.

I walk to the Starbucks on the corner. Five years ago, there wasn't even a place to get a decent cup of coffee in this town, and to do any shopping you'd have to drive to the mall. Now, besides Starbucks, there are three different Gaps: Baby Gap, Gap Kids, even something called Gap Body. And I heard that Banana Republic is moving into Mr. Bagley's hardware store. Pretty soon all you're going to need is a roof to call this town a mall.

Maggie Conover is sitting with two other moms at a table by the window. They see me and smile, motioning me inside. Now there's no going back. I go to the counter first and order a double espresso. I don't know the other two women, even though our kids are in the same preschool class. I make my way to their table, feeling the way I did in the cafeteria on the first day of junior high school. Here's what they almost certainly know about me: teenage daughter in reform school; son took a nasty fall a couple of years ago. Son's still a little slow. Developmentally delayed? No one's talking. Oh, and separated from her husband. He's a Jensen of *those* Jensens. And the husband—well, that's a whole other story.

I smile and sit down. My face feels like it's going to crack.

"Rachel, have you met Patty Baker and Sarah Jane Phillips?"

Hi's all the way around. The three women have sheets of paper spread across the small table, with notes—notes!—that they've obviously been taking about graduation. Sarah Jane is a tall rangy woman whose husband is the local ophthalmologist. And Patty looks like she was once young and pretty, but all those kids—how many, three? four?—have wrung the life right out of her. She's wearing overalls with appliqúed sheep on her bib. I can't help it—I take an instant dislike to them, and I'm sure it's mutual. How could they like me? I've kept to myself since Josh started at the Little Acorn, too afraid to join the world of normal mothers talking about their normal children. I hear them sometimes: *Evan asks me to read* Goodnight Moon *ten times every night! Molly knows all the letters of the alphabet!* I understand these conversations; they aren't about bragging so much as a proud exchange. But I can't take part in it, and the forced smile I feel on my face when I talk to these mothers is enough to keep me away. After all, they don't want to hear my sad, scary story. *Josh looks so far away sometimes. Like he's not really there—you know? Does Evan ever look that way? Or Molly?*

"So we were thinking"—Maggie leans forward—"about a duckling theme."

"Duckling," I repeat.

"Baby ducklings, teacher ducklings, mama ducklings," says Patty. "In actual costume."

"Fuzzy yellow outfits," says Sarah Jane. "It would be the cutest."

I nod. What else can I do? I try to imagine cajoling Josh into a fuzzy yellow duckling outfit.

"You do something with art, don't you?" asks Maggie.

"I'm a conservator."

"Can you paint?"

"Not very well."

"We thought a background of a field—something green—maybe with some flowers?"

"You want me to do this?" I ask.

They nod.

"We don't need it until June—but I thought we should start planning now," says Maggie.

"Okay," I say slowly.

"Excellent!"

This, a conversation that could have taken two minutes in the parking lot of the Little Acorn, has required a meeting plus notes. I sink down in my chair and half listen as they talk about the rest of the day. Mommy-baby yoga, play group, music class. I want to scream *Do you know how lucky you all are?* I was not thankful enough. I know that now. *My child hit his head—and it was not a little playground mishap. Do you understand?*

I down my espresso in two gulps and reach to the floor for my purse.

"Oh, Rachel, don't go yet," Maggie says. Her hands are clasped under her chin and she's looking at me expectantly, as if watching the opening credits of a movie.

I hold my bag in my lap. I'm perched, ready to flee.

"Do you want to bring Josh to play group this afternoon?" Patty asks. "We'd love to have you."

"Sorry, I have to work," I say. "But thanks for asking."

I pull my coat from the pile on the extra chair, say a quick good-bye, and make my way outside. I count the number of steps it takes to get to the door. Once outside and past their line of vision, I sprint down the street to my car. I feel desperate to get out of here, out of this town, away from anyone who thinks they know anything about me or my life. I saw it on the faces of those other mothers: pity. Ned was right, they feel sorry for me. That's why they asked me to join them. *Let's try to involve her,* I can almost hear them saying. *Maybe ask her to paint something for graduation.*

I fumble with my car lock.

"Rachel?"

I whirl around. Dee Dretzin is standing in the doorway of her shop. She doesn't have a jacket on in the chilly spring air, and she's holding out a small paper bag.

"Hi, Dee."

I feel like I'm going to scream.

"I made these up for you," she says. "Your favorites."

Tears spring to my eyes.

"Oh, Dee. You didn't need to do that."

I walk up to her and take the bag, which I know has milk chocolate caramels, white chocolate pralines, and almond bark inside.

I can't speak. If I open my mouth, a wail will escape me. I wipe my eyes and shake my head hard, as if I can loosen all the sadness and anger inside me.

"Oh, honey," she says. A soft hand on my cheek—a maternal touch, unlike anything I know. "Do you want to come in for a minute?"

I slip in the door, into Dee's shop, and lean my back against the glass door. The smell—a sugary homespun sweet scent—makes me double over, and before I know what's happened I am sobbing.

"It's okay." This woman I barely know soothes me. "Whatever it is, you'll get through it." She pats me everywhere she can reach: my bare head, my face, my back through my thick wool coat.

"I'm sorry," I manage to blurt out through my tears.

"Don't be silly," she says.

"But you have your own—"

"We all have our own problems," says Dee. "And you know what, hon? We're stronger than we think."

I NEED A FRIEND. THAT'S ALL I CAN THINK AS I FINALLY dry my eyes, eat five caramels, and start to drive home. I've let myself become so isolated over the years. I guess it happens to most of us who work and raise families. The rest of life gets gobbled up by car pools, lists, chores, taxes. When I was in college, before I met Ned, I must have had a dozen girlfriends. We'd talk on the phone for no reason at all, or meet for coffee or drinks and find that hours had passed without our even knowing it. Of those women I knew, there are maybe three with whom I still exchange holiday cards. And then, of course, there's Liza.

I hit the speed dial.

"Liza Mendel's office," her secretary says.

I hate this. I hate calling Liza because she always has a new secretary who never knows who I am.

"Is she there?"

"Who's calling?"

"Rachel Jensen."

A pause.

"Will she know what this is in reference to?"

"It's personal. I'm a friend," I say, too shortly. It isn't the secretary's fault. The very fact of Liza, ensconced in her corner office high above State Street, bugs me no end, though I am loath to admit it.

"Please hold a moment."

I drive slowly, one hand on the wheel, the other holding my cell phone to my ear. I'm listening to a Muzak version of Mozart's Sonata in A Major and passing the Stop & Shop, wondering if we're running low on soy milk, when Liza breaks onto the line.

"Sweetie!"

"Hey, Li."

"What's doing?"

I glance at the car's digital clock. It's 10:15.

"You aren't by any chance free for lunch, are you?" I ask.

Liza and I never have lunch. I don't ask, and she doesn't offer. Time is money for her. What are her billable hours now, four hundred? Five? Besides, I avoid going into Boston during the day, unless I have a business meeting myself. Too much traffic.

"You know . . . I think I could be," says Liza. "I was going to do Pilates, but—"

"I don't want to stop you from anything."

"No, no, I'd love to see you."

"Are you sure?"

I pull up in front of my house and park at the curb. The mailman's already been here; a thick wad of envelopes and magazines is poking out of the slot in the front door.

"Why don't we meet at noon. I'll make us a reservation at Olive's."

"That's kind of fancy, Li."

"We deserve it, don't you think? Besides, it's on the firm."

"Well, in that case, okay."

I rush inside. I have hardly any time to dress in something decent and slap on some makeup. Black skirt, black sweater, black opaque tights, black boots. That'll work. I'll look like a New Yorker—I've never really stopped looking out of place here—but it's better than a sweater smeared with Josh's strawberry yogurt. Everything about me screams *mommy:* the Volvo with sticky juice spilled all over the baby seat in back, the hastily applied lipstick, the Cheerios that seem to cling to me no matter what I'm wearing. When I get undressed at night, little bits of cereal drop to the floor. I rummage through my dresser for a lipstick, spritz on some cologne, and head out the door.

LIZA DOESN'T SEE ME AT FIRST, WHEN I WALK INTO THE restaurant. She's shaking hands with some guy in a suit. He's leaning toward her as if she's magnetic—literally magnetic. She draws people in, speaking softly, making them move closer if they want to hear a word she says.

The maître d' leads me to the table.

"There she is!" Liza reaches her arms toward me. I bend down for a kiss, feeling curiously childlike. She's a year younger than I am, but she's always made me feel like I'm the young one. She presses her cheeks to mine—first one side, then the other.

I take my seat across the table.

"Hey," I say. "It's good to see you."

"You too, babe."

"You look gorgeous," I say.

"Thanks."

She examines me, looking at me closely as if I were a painting in a museum or a piece of furniture she's considering. This doesn't put me off. From the time we were in college, Liza has always studied me, and I've never minded because I've been interested in what she sees.

"You look like shit," she says.

I nod, smiling. "That's just great. Thanks. Don't mince any words."

She takes a sip of water, sits back in her chair, and folds her arms: her lawyer stance.

"Well, you do."

"I've had a rough morning."

"You've had a rough couple of years, honey."

I bite off the end of a breadstick.

"So. What happened this morning?"

"I spent some time with the Hawthorne mommies."

"Sounds scary."

"You may laugh—but it really was."

"What the hell are you doing, still living in that town?"

I inhale sharply. Here we go. Liza Mendel is going to fix my life in five easy steps.

"Where should I go, Liza?"

"Boston. Or back to New York. You're not a small-town person. You moved there because of Ned. Never in a million years would you have lived in a place like Hawthorne, and you know it."

"Well, I'm sort of stuck there now. I can't just move."

"Of course you can. What's stopping you?"

It would never occur to Liza that there might be financial reasons why Ned and I have stayed in Hawthorne all these years. That the proximity to Arthur and Jane, the tuition breaks we got at the academy, made living there affordable—and living anywhere else seem like pure folly.

"We can't afford it."

"That's self-defeating. You know, when Tommy and I started out we lived above our heads—we lived *as if* we were successful and then we *became* successful. You have to take chances sometimes. *Act as if,* as they say in the twelve-step programs."

She says all this in one breath, and then she opens her menu as if the subject is closed.

"The tuna tartare is very good here."

"Liza?"

She looks over the top of her menu at me.

"Fuck you," I say.

Her perfect eyebrows shoot up.

"What did I do?"

"You don't get it. You just don't get it," I say. My face is growing hot. My cheeks are burning. "My life is—"

"Ssshh. Lower your voice," says Liza.

I try to get a grip on myself. I am not a woman who raises her voice in restaurants. Or cries in public. And here I am, doing both at once.

"My life," I begin again more quietly, "is not some elastic, flexible thing. I'm not twenty-five. I have two sick children. I don't know what's going to happen with either of them, and—"

"Wait a minute. What's wrong with Joshie?"

I haven't said it before. I've thought it, I've worried endlessly, but I haven't said it out loud.

"He's barely talking. He's two years old, and he hardly says a word."

"Oh, honey. Einstein didn't—"

"I know, I know. Einstein didn't speak until he was three. But Einstein didn't fall down a flight of stairs and have a contusion on his brain either."

"What do the doctors say?"

"Oh, you know. Not to worry."

"Well, then, don't you think you should listen to them?"

"He's my *child,* Liza. How would you feel if Sophie—"

She reaches a hand across the table, almost knocking over the small vase of flowers.

"I'm sorry. I'm an insensitive asshole."

"Yes, you are."

We both laugh.

"I slept with Ned," I say.

"What?" she practically shrieks.

"Ssshh," I mock her.

"What do you mean?"

"Well, we took our clothes off, and then—"

"Oh, shut up. How did it?—so do you think this means—?"

"I don't know what it means. It happened two weeks ago, and we haven't seen each other since."

"Do you think you will?"

"I hope so. I want to." I shrug. "I guess it's up to him right now."

"Rachel! That's so exciting!"

"Yeah. I slept with my husband. Pretty racy stuff."

"You have a lot going on."

"You're telling me."

A waiter materializes, and Liza orders the tuna tartare for both of us.

"Do you want a glass of wine? I think I need one," she says.

"No, thanks. I'm driving."

"So." Liza leans back and crosses her arms once more. "What's going on with Kate?"

"She's a wreck. I think she's even worse than when she got to Stone Mountain. I keep on thinking maybe we should bring her home."

I realize that this was why I wanted to see Liza, why I needed to talk to a friend today. There are things in my life I can't control, but this—what to do about Kate—is something I can.

"What do they say at the school?"

"They want to put her into the highest level of security and therapy. It's a lot more money, and—"

"If money's the issue—"

"No. That's not it. I just don't know if we're doing the right thing."

The waiter serves Liza her wine. She inhales from the bowl of the glass, then takes a sip.

"What does Ned want to do?"

I sigh.

"I don't think Ned knows what Ned wants to do. He's as confused about all this as I am. He's saying—"

The waiter appears again, this time with two pinkish gray glistening mounds of raw tuna.

"He's saying he wants to keep her there. That there's no way we can keep her safe at home."

"Well, if that's true then there's no question," says Liza. She squeezes a lemon slice over her fish. I've completely lost my appetite.

She puts down her fork and looks at me.

"I don't know," she says. "I'm so sorry, Rachel. I feel like if we hadn't—"

"Please don't."

"I can't help it. We sent her to Zelman. Some of this might never have happened if we—"

"You can't second-guess," I say. I don't know how to respond, because it's true. If Liza hadn't referred Kate to Dr. Zelman, it's possible that some of this nightmare might have been avoided. Zelman was the whistle-blower, after all. But we'll never know. Maybe all this had to happen. Maybe it was karma, or fate.

"And we dragged you out to dinner that night. I know you didn't want to go. You didn't feel comfortable leaving her with—"

Liza takes a big gulp of wine.

"How can you even look at me?"

In all the years I've known Liza, she has never had a moment of self-doubt, much less self-flagellation. But here she is, crying in a restaurant, in full view of her partners at nearby tables.

"It's not your fault," I say, patting her hand.

"You know what I think?" She dabs at her eyes. "I think that whether or not you bring her home right now, what Kate needs to know, more than anything, is that you love her."

"She knows we love her," I say quietly.

"But does she know that you forgive her?"

I say nothing.

"*Do* you forgive her?" Liza asks me.

The noise in my head is deafening. I am stock-still, trapped by my oldest and best and only friend into an admission I have not made until now, even to myself.

"I don't know," I say. "Liza, I just don't know."

9

THE STREETS OF NEW YORK WERE DUSTED WITH A LIGHT coat of snow that Christmas we spent at Mount Sinai Hospital. We were there for four days, while the doctors monitored the bleeding in Josh's brain. Ned and I paced the corridors of the pediatric intensive care unit, each of us making our private bargains with whatever God we were able to conjure. The fragile, bruised tissue inside Josh's skull was all I saw when I closed my eyes.

The unit was decorated for the holidays with paper cutouts of Christmas trees and Hanukkah dreidels, and small white lights twinkled along the edges of the nurses' station. I crawled into Josh's hospital crib with him, careful not to disturb the tiny IV in his arm, the needle covered with a small fistful of bandages and tape to keep him from scratching at it. I curled up with my baby—I fit if I stayed in the fetal position—and held on to him each night as nurses came in every hour to open his eyes and check his pupils to make sure they were dilating. While I stayed with Josh, Ned spent half his time on his cell phone outside the hospital, standing on Fifth Avenue amid the holiday shoppers hurrying home with their packages. He was calling everyone we knew to find the best pediatric neurologist in the country.

"I think we're in good hands here," I whispered to him. We were, after all, at one of the best teaching hospitals in New York City.

"I want to be sure," he said. His hair was disheveled, and he had a three-day growth of beard. He looked like a wild man.

"But I really think—"

"Look, Rach. This is what I have to do, okay?"

I understood. Ned was trying to control what he could. As for me, I was trying to bargain and control the uncontrollable. Sometimes, in the eerie half-light of three or four in the morning, I would open my eyes and stare at Josh sleeping. I'd be inches away from him, and I would will myself to keep staring, not to blink, not to fall back asleep. I had the completely irrational thought that if only I kept watching him I could keep him safe. That the dam inside his head would hold, that the tissue would begin to heal instead of giving way.

The morning after the accident, I finally left the ICU and went down to the cafeteria for something to eat. Liza was there, standing in front of a coffee machine, a Styrofoam cup in her hand.

She grabbed my arm.

"What's going on?" she asked.

"We don't know," I said.

"But he's going to be okay, right?"

"We don't know," I repeated. I broke down sobbing. I so wanted to be able to give her another answer, a different ending to the story. *It was a close call,* I wanted to say, *but he's fine.* She grabbed me and held me close. I could feel her heart beating. They had been there all night too, Tommy and Liza, in the emergency room waiting area. At about three in the morning Tommy had sent Phyllis home in his car.

Liza took my arm and pulled me out of the cafeteria.

"Let's get some air and some decent coffee," she said. I knew it was all she could do. Take care of the little things. She pulled a pair of black sunglasses from her purse and covered her own reddening eyes. In the early morning sun, she looked exhausted. Her black suit, which had looked so stunning the night before, looked funereal. I wanted to rip the jacket off of her. *What are we doing here?* I wanted to scream.

"Listen," she said, as she steered me down the street to a small French bakery on Madison, "I think Tommy and I should take Kate home. She shouldn't be here."

"I don't know, Liza. I don't want her that far from me."

"But she's a kid. This is too much for her. She shouldn't be exposed to all this. She's terrified, she's upset—"

I wondered how much Liza knew. Kate had fled the emergency room after Ned had shaken her. She had run past Tommy and Liza, weeping—but what did she tell them?

"Tommy and I could drive her back to Hawthorne, stay in the house with her."

"What about Sophie? What about your work?"

"Sophie's with her girlfriend in Newton. And the office doesn't expect me back until Monday."

We walked back down 98th, holding our paper coffee cups. Everyone on the block seemed to be headed toward the hospital. There were green-coated doctors, white-coated nurses. A very pregnant woman being helped along by a skinny man. An old woman in a wheelchair pushed along by a caregiver.

"You're a good friend, Liza," I said. "Let me talk to Ned about it."

Liza looked at me quickly at the mention of Ned. In her glance I saw it all: Kate had told her about falling in the emergency room.

"And that way she could see Zelman right away," she said. "I think it's important for her to see him. Especially right now."

"You're probably right," I said.

"She blames herself for what happened to Josh," said Liza.

I was so tired my bones ached. I was having a hard time focusing on Kate. All my heart, all my worry was taken up with Josh and what was going to happen to him.

THE QUESTIONS ABOUT THE LONG-TERM EFFECTS OF Josh's fall hung in the air, clouding everything around us as we finally bundled him up and left Mount Sinai Hospital the day after Christmas. The immediate danger had passed us over, thank God (and I was thanking God, suddenly and temporarily having developed a sense of faith), but none of the doctors would tell us what was going to happen down the road. We wanted to hear that this was over, that Josh was going to be absolutely fine, but no one was saying that. We don't know. They shrugged, palms up, as if entreating us to be happy with where we were, grateful for what they had done to save our baby. And we were grateful, but we were also terrified. How were we supposed to live with not knowing? *You have no idea how lucky you are,* the chief resident said. I felt like slugging him. He had the soft chin and shining eyes of a pampered, coddled child. What had he ever been through in his life?

Lucky, lucky. I pulled on Josh's onesie, snapping it over his diaper, then buttoned him into the fleece snowsuit Ned had picked up from our suitcase at Phyllis's house. I pulled one tiny sock over each foot, keeping my focus on the task at hand. But I kept looking up at the enormous bump, rising like a deformity, a blue-green tumor, from Josh's perfect forehead. I carefully pulled a knit cap over the gauze padding. He grinned at me, two pearly teeth flashing.

"Mama loves you," I cooed. "Mama loves Joshie."

"Do we have everything?" Ned asked. He looked around the room. We had barely left the pediatric ICU in four days. We'd had food brought in, and changes of underwear and socks. My mother had brought me an old tennis sweat suit of hers—I hadn't even known she owned a sweat suit—and I had worn it night and day. I gave a quick look around the room, as if it were a hotel room we were vacating.

I lifted Josh from his hospital crib and held him to my chest as we walked down the hall, into the elevator, and through the hospital lobby. With each step away from the pediatric ICU, we seemed to be moving closer and closer to the normal world. The lobby doors slid open with a frigid blast of air, and, as planned, Phyllis was waiting for us just outside the hospital's awning in our Volvo. She'd had her doorman load up the trunk with our suitcases, and she'd convinced us that she could manage to drive it across town. She had been good in the crisis; I had to admit it. After the first night's hysteria, she had settled down and seemed to grasp that this situation didn't revolve around her.

"I bought you some sandwiches," she said. "For the road."

"Thanks, Mom," I said. I opened the door and put Josh in his car seat.

"Pastrami on rye, from Barney Greengrass," she said.

"My favorite," said Ned.

"Call when you get home," said Phyllis. "I'll worry."

Ned and I both hugged her goodbye, then watched as she bent inside the back door and kissed Josh right next to the bump on his head.

"Sweet *kepelah,*" she murmured. When she straightened up again, she had tears in her eyes.

As we pulled away, I turned to see Phyllis standing on the corner of 98th and Fifth, waving goodbye.

"My God, she actually seemed human," said Ned.

"I know. She really did."

Ned turned on 96th and headed for the FDR Drive. He was driving more cautiously than usual. We were heading home with our already-dozing infant in the backseat. I reached for Ned's hand.

"Are we going to be okay?" I asked.

"Are you kidding?" He squeezed my fingers. "You and me? We're fine."

"And Katie?"

Ned let go of my hand and downshifted as we approached the FDR Drive.

"This is all going to seem like a bad dream someday," he said.

I swallowed what I wanted to say—*How do you know? How do you know it, Ned? What are the odds here?* There was no point in sharing all my doubts and fears; it would only make him feel worse. In our marriage, he was the optimist and I was the pessimist. We had always balanced each other well—but then again, we'd never been here before. All my life I had guarded against disaster, and I now realized it was just magical thinking: somehow I had believed that if I worried enough, the worry would protect us. But those years of worry had done no good. I looked at Joshua, sleeping peacefully, his head flopped to the side. He had to be all right. He had to be.

I turned my thoughts to home. We'd be back in five hours, if there wasn't too much traffic. The timing had worked out well. In the early afternoon, Liza was driving Kate into Boston for an emergency appointment with Zelman. We'd have time to settle in with the baby before they got back. I wanted to unpack our bags, clean out the fridge, maybe even put some soup on for supper. If I could just fill our house with the smell of good food and get a couple of loads of laundry into the wash, maybe things would feel safe and normal—or at least normal enough.

I kept checking on Josh. He had slept through Stamford, New Haven, Hartford. I watched his chest rise and fall. I had a growing urge to wake him.

"Do you think it's safe for him to take such a long nap?" I asked Ned.

"I don't think they would have let him out of the hospital if it wasn't," said Ned.

"You have more faith in them than I do."

"What else are we going to do, Rach?"

We fell into silence. Trusting people had never been one of my great strengths. I was suspicious, cynical, always wondering about hidden motives, secret agendas—except when it came to Ned and to the world we had created within our home. There, I believed.

"I made an appointment for us to see this guy Kaufman at Boston Children's," said Ned. "He's the best guy in town."

"When?"

"Next Monday."

"Why so long?"

"Because you don't just call the best pediatric neurologist in Boston and get in the next day, that's why."

"Okay. I was just asking."

"And also, there's nothing he can actually do right now. It's a waiting game. He said it himself on the phone."

"You talked to him?"

"Yeah, a couple of times."

"Why didn't you tell me?"

"I didn't want to get into it while we were at Sinai. Those guys don't like it when you start fishing around for second opinions."

He was right. As usual, Ned was right about how to handle people, what to say and what not to say. He was better at that sort of thing. He just had a natural ease about him. I was more prickly. Even when I tried to ingratiate myself, I often sounded harsher than I wanted to.

I rubbed the back of his neck.

"I'm sorry."

"For what?"

"I know I'm being sort of snappish."

"We're both being snappish. It's a stressful time."

"You're the best husband in the world."

He smiled. It was the first real smile I had seen on his face in four days.

"Try to relax a bit. Take advantage of the fact that the baby's sleeping," he said. He turned the radio to a classical station, and a Chopin prelude drifted through the car, a simple slow piece in a minor key. I found myself actually starting to relax, and I must have drifted off to sleep. I napped for about an hour, and when I woke up we were still on the highway but nothing was moving. Traffic was at a complete standstill.

I blinked my eyes open. I was disoriented.

"Where are we?"

"Not far from the Mass Pike toll booths," said Ned. "There must have been an accident."

"Oh, great. That's all we need."

Josh stirred in the backseat, then let out a thin wail.

Ned looked at me sideways. "Well, he's up." I turned around.

"Hi, Joshie," I said softly. "Hi, babycakes."

Josh's face scrunched up, then turned bright red.

"Uh-oh," I said.

"What?"

"He's pooping."

"When we get to the other side of the toll, I'll get off at the rest stop so we can change his diaper."

I couldn't even see the toll booths ahead of us. We were probably a half hour away from being on the other side. Josh started wailing, as he always did as soon as he had a dirty diaper. I felt a low-level maternal panic that I knew Ned didn't feel. I couldn't stand it when Josh cried. The sound pierced me, and I would do anything to make him stop. The need to comfort him was almost physical.

"What are you doing?"

"What does it look like I'm doing?"

I climbed over the console and into the backseat.

"You can't change him here."

"Why not? We're not moving."

"Rachel, you can't take him out of the car seat until we're parked somewhere."

Josh shrieked louder.

"Fine. He'll just scream until he throws up, then."

"Don't be mad at me."

"I'm not mad."

Traffic finally started breaking up, moving slowly. Off in the distance, I saw the flashing lights of a tow truck.

"That could have been worse."

Josh had not stopped screaming for one second. He was looking at me as if to say, *Why aren't you changing my diaper?* I couldn't explain it to him. No wonder kids grow up to hate their parents. Ned finally pulled into a rest stop at the first Mass Pike exit. I dove over Josh, unbuckling him, lifting him onto my lap to change his diaper. I didn't care if I got poop all over me. All I wanted was to make the crying stop. His legs pedaled in the air, and his mouth was open in a shriek.

"Sshhh," I whispered. "Almost done."

He whipped his head back, almost catching the side of the door.

"Joshie, stop!" I said sharply, which of course made him cry even louder.

I fastened the Velcro of the diaper and buckled him back in. My eyes burned. I was about to burst into tears myself. When had everything gotten so hard?

BY THE TIME WE PULLED UP TO OUR HOUSE, WE HAD been in the car for seven hours, and it was the middle of the afternoon. I saw Tommy's car parked across the street. Goddammit. Liza was already back from Boston with Kate. I tried to take some deep breaths, to fill my head with something other than a loud, anxious stream of thoughts.

"You take the baby inside, I'll get everything else," said Ned.

I walked up the front steps with Josh in my arms. Coming home felt bizarre. Everything had changed, and yet here was our house with its creaky front door, the week's mail arranged in a neat pile—I recognized Liza's handiwork—on the hall table.

"Hello?" I called. "Anybody home?"

I shifted Josh to my hip and riffled through the pile of mail. Bills, mostly. Some second notices. And catalogs, endless catalogs. Baby clothes, clothes for teenagers, household gadgets, faux-Provençal dishware, and—my personal favorite—Martha Stewart's catalog. I had never ordered anything from there, but I liked to imagine that some day I would: ribbon sorters, cake decorations, cookie molds in the shapes of birds and trees. Some happy woman out there had to be buying that stuff and making use of it. I wanted to be elbow-deep in flour and sugar with nothing more on my mind than making the perfect bird cookie.

"Hello?" I called again. "Katie? Liza?"

I had left the front door open for Ned, and I could see him, bundled up in his green down parka and ski hat, slowly unloading our stuff. He was in no rush to get inside.

"Well, let's get you upstairs," I said to Josh.

Each stair creaked as I headed up with Josh. We had to rebuild the staircase; it had been on our to-do list for ten years, each year assuming a lower and lower priority as the rest of our expenses grew. The house smelled different. I tried to figure out what it was, and then I realized that it was actually the absence of smell. No one had been cooking. They had probably gone out for every single meal, including breakfast.

I walked down the hall to Josh's room. It was good to be home. Maybe Liza and Kate had gone out for a walk or something. I put Josh down on his play mat and undid his fleece snowsuit. He had probably been too hot in the car; maybe that was why he had slept so long. He whimpered when I pulled off his hat, and I wondered if his head hurt. This was the hardest part: he couldn't tell me if he was in pain. I lifted up the bandage and looked at the bump.

"My poor, poor baby," I whispered, and bent down to kiss it.

A shadow fell over the play mat, and I spun around. Liza was standing in the doorway.

"Hey!" I said. "I thought you guys were out somewhere."

She walked a few steps into the room and crouched down next to me, looking at Josh. She was dressed in my clothes—an old pink turtleneck and a pair of faded jeans that were baggy on her and only came to her ankles. Her face was bare and swollen, and her hair looked like it hadn't been washed in days. I had never, in all the years I had known her, seen Liza like this. Through illnesses and fights with Tommy and deaths in the family, she always managed to look like she had just walked out of the pages of a magazine.

"My God, Liza. What's wrong?" I asked. She didn't say a word. She rocked back and forth on her ankles.

"What's going on?" I asked again.

She reached down and touched the top of Josh's head. A tear rolled down her cheek.

"Liza, what the hell is—"

She turned and looked at me.

"Oh my God, is it Kate? Has something happened to Kate?"

She shook her head. "No, nothing like that. But you'd better go talk to her," she said quietly. "She's in her room."

"Li, you can't just—I've been on the road for seven hours, and I'm scared half out of my wits about the baby. Please, just tell me."

She sat down on the floor next to me. I could hear Ned downstairs, bringing in the last of our bags, then slamming the front door.

"It's terrible," Liza whispered. "Just terrible. I am so, so sorry, Rachel."

"What? Liza, *please*."

"Listen, I know it's not true," she said. "But still, it's going to cause all sorts of huge problems, and I just don't know how—"

I jumped up. "I don't know what the hell you're talking about, but you're scaring me," I said.

I walked down the hall to Kate's room. My knees were weak, my legs wobbly. Usually there was music pounding from behind her closed door, but today it was dead silent, and her door was open a crack.

"Kate?" I nudged the door open. I didn't want to just walk in on her. "Katie?"

Through the crack I saw her, lying on her unmade bed. She was facing the wall, where a framed Babar poster had hung since her early childhood. Snapshots were tucked into the sides of Babar's frame: Ned and Kate at Great Adventure, Kate and Sophie Mendel in tiny bikinis on the beach at Wellfleet. Her hair spilled over the side of the pillow. She was barefoot, her knees scrunched up around her chest.

I walked into the room and stood at the foot of her bed. Her eyes were closed, and she was shaking with silent sobs.

"Oh, honey," I said, sitting down next to her. "Honey, honey, honey."

She started to cry even harder. I swung myself onto the bed so that I was holding her, cradling her from behind. I wrapped my arms around her and held on tight.

"No-o-o," she wailed.

"The doctors say Joshie's going to be fine," I said.

I figured that fudging the truth was, in these circumstances, not only understandable but necessary. Kate must be feeling so guilty about what happened. I wanted her to know it wasn't her fault. It was an accident. It could have happened to anybody.

"We're all home now. It was a bad dream, but it's over," I whispered into her ear. "Please, Katie. Listen to me."

But she kept sobbing. I had never seen her cry so hard, not even in the hospital. I gathered her hair in my hands and started to comb my fingers through it, something I had done to soothe her since she was a little girl. But she shook me off.

"Kate, you need to tell your mother what's going on." I heard Liza's voice behind me. She had walked into Kate's room, holding Josh against her chest.

"Go away." Kate's voice was muffled.

"I'm not going away," Liza said. "Kate, you have to tell your mother what you told Dr. Zelman."

Kate rolled over on her stomach and buried her face in the pillow.

"Tell me what?" I asked.

"Go away," she cried.

I looked up at Liza. I was so confused. Usually I had some idea of what was going on; I girded myself for all kinds of disasters by imagining them in advance. Even Joshie's fall, on some level, was something I was prepared for. I knew that babies fell. Or choked. Or simply died in their cribs. I knew all that. But I didn't know what Kate could possibly tell me. And what did Liza mean about Dr. Zelman? What did Zelman have to do with any of this?

Downstairs, Ned was whistling. It was one of his habits, probably not even something he was aware of doing. I heard him moving through the living room into the kitchen, where he was unpacking all the baby stuff we had with us: bottles, breast pump, organic cereal.

"If you don't tell your mother, I will," said Liza. She had a lawyerly tone: formal, tightly wound.

"Fuck you," said Kate. "This is none of your fucking business."

Liza blinked.

"Okay, then," she said slowly. She took a deep breath, and what she said next came out in a rush. "During her session with Zelman yesterday, Kate told him that her father—" Liza stopped. "Oh, God, I can't even say it."

"What, Liza?"

"That Ned had sexually abused her," Liza said.

The words scrambled and jumbled in my head. Kate's father. Ned? I was lying next to Kate on the bed. Her body had gone still, like an animal trying to camouflage itself.

"Kate?"

She didn't move.

"Kate? That's the most ridiculous thing I've ever heard in my life," I whispered. There is a breaking point—we all have one. This was mine. "Look at me," I said.

When she still didn't move, I pulled at her shoulders.

"Don't touch me!"

"What, Kate. My God! What the hell . . . you read this in a magazine? Or you saw it on *Oprah*? What put this idea in your head?" I asked.

Kate's face was red, her eyes tiny slits from crying. She sat up on her bed and crossed her legs into the lotus position.

"It's true," she said calmly.

"It's not true," I said. "It's absolutely not true."

"Rachel." Liza gave me a warning look. Then she turned back to Kate. "Honey, you need to tell us when this happened. Everything about it—everything you remember."

"Liza!" I exploded. "How can you even—"

She shot me the same look again, and I realized she knew what she was doing. She had spent her whole adult life as a prosecutor, and now she was trying to get Kate talking so she'd trip herself up.

"He came into my room at night," Kate said. Her voice was mechanical.

"When?" I asked.

"All the time."

"All the time? What does that mean? Every night? Every other night?"

"You know. Sometimes."

"How long has this been going on?" Liza asked.

"Since I was twelve," she said. And then she paused. "No. Eleven."

"Well, which is it? Twelve or eleven?"

"Eleven," Kate said, more firmly.

"And honey—what do you mean by abuse? Can you be more specific?"

"He touched me," she said.

"Where did he touch you?" Liza asked.

I interrupted. "Liza—do you really have to—"

"Did he penetrate you?" Liza asked.

Kate stopped for a moment then, as if wondering how far she could go.

"No."

"Why now, Kate?" I asked. "Why did you suddenly decide to come out with this now?"

She didn't respond. I still had the idea that I could reach her, reason with her—that we could stop this madness before it left her room. She was a robot, systematically destroying herself and everyone around her. I looked at the bed I had found at a roadside antique show, the desk Ned had built her out of some cherry wood left over from a Jensen Realty development. Babar, that happy elephant, had slowly been overtaken by posters of rock stars I had never heard of—pale-faced boys with studs in their lower lips, flat bellies peeking from low-slung jeans, and empty, empty eyes. What had Kate dreamt of, lying here late at night?

"Sweetheart," I went on, "you were so upset about what happened to Joshie, you must have just felt like flailing at anything and anyone—"

"It's fucking true!" Kate screamed.

I stood up and started to back out of the room. My only thought was to go find Ned. I needed to see him and touch him and talk to him—to remind myself of who he was.

"Rachel, there's something else," said Liza, clearing her throat. She jiggled Josh in her arms.

"What?"

"Zelman has a mandate to report something like this," said Liza. "There's a state requirement."

I felt dizzy. I held on to the headboard of Kate's bed to steady myself.

"He has a mandate to report . . ." I repeated slowly, and then turned back to Kate. I tried to keep my thoughts clear. My daughter was the enemy. "Please. Stop this nonsense." I heard a pleading tone in my voice and instantly regretted it.

Downstairs, Ned had begun whistling again. I listened to the sound I had always loved. He was organizing the kitchen—the clattering of forks, of glasses being taken out of the dishwasher. I knew his down parka would be flung over a chair, and he'd be stripped down to his gray henley in the warmth of the house. Our home. A home that this could happen in—where even the words could be uttered—had to have something terribly wrong with it.

"Kate, I swear." I was trembling so hard I could barely speak. "If there's nothing to this, if you're just making this up—"

She stared at me, and I felt my insides grow cold. I had said it: *If.*

10

BACK HOME AFTER MY LUNCH IN BOSTON WITH LIZA, I unpack the groceries. I'm still in my sweater and coat; I've been keeping the heat in the house around sixty-five degrees during the day, until Josh comes home from preschool, and then I crank it up. I don't even know if it saves any money on heating bills, but at least I'm trying. Ned thinks I don't know how much debt we're in—three credit cards are maxed out, and our other two are close to the limit—but other than economizing in little ways, what can I do? Lawyers, doctors, psychiatric facilities—not to mention running two households instead of one—it's expensive to have your life fall apart.

I put the soy milk and pasta in the pantry and load up the freezer with boxes of frozen peas and corn, which are the only two vegetables Josh will even look at. Without thinking, I eat three of Dee Dretzin's chocolates—dark almond bark and two caramels—before putting the bag in a drawer. Then I put a kettle on to boil for chamomile tea. The city has left me on edge, its energy more than I can stand. After fourteen years in Hawthorne, what I crave is peace and quiet.

Half an hour. In half an hour I have to swing by the Little Acorn and pick up Josh, and that will be the end of any time to myself. I have a couple of little jobs waiting for me upstairs, but I don't have the energy to tackle them. The kettle starts to whistle, and I pour the steaming water into a mug, steeping the tea while I stare out the back window. It's a gray afternoon. The bird feeder swings empty on the low branch of the oak, and the field between the house and barn is covered with a foot of melting snow from the blizzard two weeks ago. I haven't even opened the back door since the beginning of winter. I spend all my time in two rooms: the kitchen and my bedroom. Even my studio is unfamiliar to me now. Sometimes I find myself wandering around the house, running my finger along a picture molding or over the top of a chair and wondering who I used to be. Did I ever sit quietly and read a book, with nothing more on my mind than what to make for dinner or how much to charge for a restoration job? Who was the woman who spent hours arranging the furniture in the front parlor until it was just right?

A lone bird pecks at the bird feeder, then flies away. There's nothing here—nothing for any living being. The field behind the house is a perfect New England postcard, unmarred by a single footprint, and the big red barn seems to float on the horizon, bobbing like a ship in a placid sea. Kate rises out of the whiteness, bundled up in a bright blue snowsuit. She's eight or nine years old, and she's building a snowman, using all the vegetables in the house for eyes, nose, ears, and coat buttons. Behind her, where the land slopes down toward the barn, Ned is gathering up snowballs and lobbing them at her in slow, graceful arcs, and she is ducking, laughing, calling something out to him that I can't hear. And I am watching them—my daughter and my husband—cozy in my warm kitchen. My work is waiting for me upstairs. We're all together, solid and safe in our house, in the midst of winter.

I push hard against the back door, and it opens easily. I lift the barn key from its hook and, with my tea in hand, make my way across the yard. I'm knee-deep in soft melting snow, freezing through my heavy socks and boots. I wonder if I'm leaving footprints. What will I tell Ned, when he comes over later? Maybe he won't notice. It will be dark, and I'll turn off the back porch lights.

I fit the key into the old lock and jiggle it. At first, it doesn't give way, but I keep moving it in the lock. Finally the key turns and the door swings open with a heavy, mournful creak. My eyes adjust to the dim light inside the barn. There are canvases piled against every available wall, and a canvas flat on a worktable in the center of the barn, partly covered by an old sheet. A few open jars of paint, a palette, some paintbrushes in a glass. The whole place looks like someone ran out to do an errand and never came back. I walk in slowly, avoiding the few gaping holes in the floorboards, and make my way over to the table. My breath is a cloud of vapor in the air. Other than the mice I can tell have been here from their droppings, no one has been in the barn since Ned left.

My heart is pounding as I lift a corner of the sheet. I'm afraid to look, as if there might be a dead body underneath, not a painting. The last time Ned showed me his work, I wasn't impressed by it and made the mistake of telling him. He had been working on large canvases, experimenting with a kind of abstraction that didn't suit his gifts at all. His genius—and I do believe it is a form of genius—has always been in the figurative realm, and for reasons having less to do with art than with fashion, he had left it behind.

"You can't pander to the marketplace," I said to him back then. We had only been living in the Hawthorne house for a few years, and though I couldn't have put it into words, I had been watching Ned shrivel, becoming nervous and unsure as an artist before my very eyes. The paintings he was showing me made me angry. They were broad, sweeping, derivative.

"Don't tell me what I can and can't do, Rachel," he snapped. "You have no idea what I'm going through."

"You're right," I said. "But I do know this: you have no choice but to follow what's inside you. That's all you've got as an artist."

"What if nothing's inside me?" His eyes burned. "What if whatever little bit I had is gone?"

199

I LIFT THE TARP, OPEN MY EYES, AND LET OUT A GASP that echoes against the empty walls of the barn. The painting Ned abandoned, the very last thing he worked on before he stopped completely, is a blurry, photorealistic portrait of me. I'm hugely pregnant, it must be with Josh, and I am asleep on my side in our bed. The covers have fallen around me so that my belly and one breast are exposed, and an arm is flung over my eyes as if blocking out the morning light streaming in from a window above me. The effect of the painting technique is of a camera that has been slightly jarred. Everything is just slightly off, ghostly, a shadow in living color. Whole pieces of the painting are unfinished. A corner. One of my feet. The window curtain.

I walk around the perimeter of the barn, lifting canvases away from the walls, brushing off cobwebs. All the recent work is in the same vein, and it's all of our family. I recognize the images from the video footage Ned was always taking. Night after night, when he sat at his computer, downloading video, I thought he was just playing around. But instead he was beginning to create these wonderful blurred portraits, all of them unfinished in similar ways. Why didn't he complete any of them? Here is Kate, sitting in the window seat in the parlor, her head buried in a book. Her hair is tucked behind her ears and she's frowning in concentration. Another, of Kate and me in our usual spots at the kitchen table, talking late at night, the moon the only light in the room. In each painting, some element is missing. Here's one of me, bent over in the garden in a pair of overalls and gardening clogs—but the garden I'm tending is torn away from the painting, so that it appears I am tending to nothing.

I feel light-headed and sit down on the one rickety chair in the corner. Slowly I realize that the paintings aren't unfinished at all. This is precisely what Ned intended with the entire series. Why didn't he tell me? I remember the burst of energy he had while I was pregnant with Josh. It was the first time in years he had spent time in the barn, and he had that faraway look that he used to get all the time when he was working well.

How could he have left these paintings behind, just sitting in an unheated barn where they could be damaged? Didn't he know what he had done? He had cracked the world wide open in these portraits. I got up and placed my tea mug on the chair; I didn't trust myself to walk around with it in my shaking hands. If there had been something wrong with Ned's work, some reason—aside from the fickle nature of the art world—that he had never made it big over the years, I would have said it had to do with an earnestness he had never quite been able to rid himself of. It bordered on the sentimental, this earnestness; the viewer of Ned's paintings could never quite *enter* the painting, because the work itself seemed to be emoting; it was too full of feeling to allow anyone inside it. But these—these are a whole different story. The combination of the blurred images and the aspects left undone force the viewer to enter the painting. I make my way around the barn, turning over the canvases so they're face out, and when I run out of wall space I lean them against the sides of the table and the barn doors.

For the first time in ages, I wish I had a cigarette. I stand in the middle of the barn and try to take it all in. The beauty and originality of the work is indisputable. I could call any of my gallery-owner friends in New York—the ones who always ask politely after Ned when calling me about restoration work—and Ned would have a show. It would hardly be the first time an artist was discovered in middle age. In fact, this work couldn't possibly have been done at an early point in Ned's life. The paintings are too mature, full of pathos and instability. I circle slowly around the studio. There I am, at the beginning of my pregnancy with Josh. I'm sitting in the wing chair upstairs in our bedroom, attempting a needlepoint pillow that remains unfinished. And there's Kate with a few of her girlfriends, working on an art project on the back porch, their small sleek heads bent together like colts. I don't even remember that moment. How did Ned take it in? For me, life was something constantly happening, impossible to keep up with. But Ned was somehow able to stop and really see our family's life as it was unfolding. To freeze images in his memory and then create them anew in his work.

It's never going to happen for me, Rachel. I hear Ned's voice as clearly as if he were standing next to me. *I'm just not good enough, so let's stop pretending I am.* It was one of the only areas of discontent in our marriage, the subject guaranteed to make us fight. It was because somewhere inside me I had always known he was capable of this—and something was blocking him. I always harbored the secret fear that it was because we had moved back to Hawthorne. If we had stayed in the city and made our lives there, he would have been around other artists; he would have gone to gallery openings and met the people he needed to meet. Instead, he had lived a life of barbecues and football fields, neighbors and friends who talked about investments, town zoning, Little League.

My eyes fall on a single sheet of yellow paper, folded and tucked under the canvas on the table. I lift the canvas guiltily and slide it out. It's bad enough that I'm here—each of our studios has always been a sacred, inviolable space—but to be here and reading Ned's notes that are clearly meant to be private? I unfold the paper. I can't help it; I want to know the unknowable. I want to turn my husband inside out. I want to find the missing pieces of Ned and hold them up to the light, like shards from a broken glass. I want to examine them so I'll know how to fix us—how to put us back together.

In Ned's familiar scrawl, there is a list of titles, twenty or thirty of them, for each of the paintings in the barn. At first I'm disappointed. I was hoping for something more elaborate: a journal entry, a letter, notes from a dream. But as I start to scan the titles, I realize I've found exactly what I was looking for. *Kate with Friends. Kitchen Table #1. Kitchen Table #2. Rachel Asleep. Rachel by the Window. Kate in the Snow.* The titles go on, all simple, declarative, unadorned—just like my husband. He had no secret life, no dark thoughts he kept to himself. The final one in the series is *Rachel in Bloom.* I choke back tears as I look down at the painting to which the title refers. I was beyond bloom, full of life, days away from giving birth to my baby boy. Ned must have studied me while I was sleeping. He made me more beautiful than I could possibly have been at the time, my belly a perfect orb, my nipples dark against the pale milky color of my breasts. I remember those final days, when we were still a family of three. The house was quiet, the nursery all set up and waiting.

"How can you do that?" my mother asked me at the time.

"Do what?"

"Have all the stuff in the house. The crib, the sheets, the clothes."

"I'm not superstitious, Mom."

"You people who think nothing bad can happen."

I held the phone away from my ear.

"No," I said. "I just refuse to live my life assuming something bad *will* happen."

I said this, even though in fact I did assume it. I fought against that assumption every single day.

"You'll see. When you get old enough, you'll see."

I was almost forty. How old did I have to be before I passed Phyllis's maturity test? I suppose she'd think I had passed it by now. I glance back down at *Rachel in Bloom,* to the right side of the canvas, and feel the urge to finish the part that's unfinished—the bedsheet and my foot are simply not there, and I find it suddenly unbearable. Before I do something I'll regret, I throw the sheet over the painting, pick up my empty mug, lock the door, and rush away from the barn.

The house is all lit up across the field, the roof covered in snow, icicles dripping, pointing downward like daggers. I stop still in the center of the field. The wind is blowing, my feet are ice-cold, but for a moment I can't move. I feel I've forgotten something back in the barn. I retrace my footsteps to the old weathered door, turn the key, and push it open once more. Quickly, I gather two large canvases and a smaller one—the most I can carry—and take them back to the house with me. All the while, I am trying to pinpoint the exact moment that Ned stopped painting. Did he ever go back to the barn after finishing *Rachel in Bloom*?

In the kitchen, I set *Kate with Friends* against a cupboard, far from the sink or refrigerator or anything else that could damage it. Then I lift an old Nantucket watercolor from the wall in the front foyer and replace it with the small canvas of *Kate in the Snow. Rachel in Bloom* I carry upstairs to the bedroom and place on the mantel above the fireplace. I switch on a light. It's almost dark out—it must be close to four. I run down the stairs. How could this have happened? I'm an hour late to pick Josh up at the Little Acorn.

THE CAR SKIDS AS I PULL AWAY FROM THE CURB, THE back wheels shimmying. Traffic is fairly heavy by Hawthorne standards, a brigade of moms making their final daily rounds of ballet class, piano lessons, gymnastics. The dads are on their way home too, heading back from Boston or from their tech jobs nearby. I see them behind the wheels of their cars, alone before the deluge of kids and *Honey would you fix the porch light* and *Daddy, Daddy, watch me do a back bend!* The man next to me at the traffic light pulls his tie loose around his neck, his face slack with exhaustion. He catches me looking at him and his face quickly composes itself. Did Ned ever look that tired on his way home to me? That spent and middle-aged?

The light has turned green, but the car in front of me hasn't budged. I'm about to tap my horn, but then I think better of it. No one ever honks in Hawthorne. No one seems to be in a rush to get anywhere. I tell myself that thirty seconds isn't going to make any difference. Joshie's okay. They wouldn't leave him alone, obviously.

Did one of the teachers stay late with him? Or one of the other mothers?

Finally, the road opens up and I speed down the hill and swing into the driveway of the Little Acorn. There are only two cars parked in the lot: a van that must belong to one of the teachers and Ned's Subaru. Of course. Of course they called Ned. I'm more than an hour late. I rush inside, down the dim hall to the Twos' classroom. Through the glass door I see Ned sitting on a tiny chair, holding Josh in his lap. A pad of paper is open on the table, and they're drawing together. Ned gives Josh a red crayon, then guides his hand across the page.

I open the door, but neither of them notice. Emily, the teacher, looks up from her desk and smiles at me. She doesn't look even remotely annoyed, for which I'm grateful.

"Look, Joshie, what's that you've made? Is it a house?" Ned asks.

Josh shakes his head.

"Is it a dog?"

He shakes his head again.

"Tell Daddy."

Josh grabs a green crayon and scribbles on top of the red.

"Come on, use your words," says Ned.

Josh throws the crayons onto the floor and starts to fuss.

"Hey," I say softly.

"Where were you?" Ned asks, without taking his eyes off Josh.

"I'm sorry, I got tied up," I say. I don't want to exchange harsh words with Ned in front of Emily.

"We waited. I was worried about you."

"Mama!" Josh jumps up and grabs me around my knees. I hoist him into my arms and nibble on his ear.

"Ready to go, Joshie?"

Ned gathers together his jacket and Josh's jacket, hat, and mittens.

"I'm sorry we kept you," I call to Emily.

"No problem, Mrs. Jensen," she says, even though I have asked her a dozen times to call me Rachel.

We start walking down the corridor to the parking lot. Ned's walking fast, his long legs covering ground.

"I lost track of time. I'm really sorry."

"They called me on my mobile. I was just heading out to show a house in North Hawthorne."

"Look, I said I'm sorry."

"I stood up my clients, Rach. They had already left, and I couldn't get ahold of them."

"Shit."

"Shit, shit, shit," Joshie chirps.

"Great—that's just great. The kid barely talks and then that's what he says."

"You're in a foul mood."

"I can't afford to blow off appointments."

"What time were you supposed to be there?"

"Five."

I check my watch.

"If you leave now, you'll only be a few minutes late."

"My gas tank is almost empty. By the time I stop for gas—"

"We'll take the Volvo," I say.

"What do you mean, we?"

"Joshie and I will come with you."

I'm breathless from trying to keep up with him.

"Forget about it."

"Come on, it's no big deal. We'll drive you there and wait in the car while you show the house."

"I don't want to do this."

"Why not?"

"I just don't. That's all."

"Well, tough shit. We're doing it."

"Shit, shit, shit," Josh says again.

This time, we both start to laugh.

"Oh, all right," says Ned. He holds the door open for me and Josh. The sky is dark now, and the air smells of wood smoke. "Okey-dokey, smoky. Let's go."

THE HOUSE IN NORTH HAWTHORNE IS PART OF ONE OF the first Jensen Realty developments—fifty acres Jane and Arthur bought from a farmer in the early 1980s, when they foresaw that the new highway was going to make North Hawthorne a commutable distance from Boston. They held on to the land for about ten years and then built this neighborhood and named all the streets after us. Jane Street. Arthur Way. Edward Drive. Steven Circle. And, finally, Rachel Court. The houses are faux Colonial, with sloping lawns and three-car garages, backed up by swamps and woods. It's pitch dark by the time we pull onto Arthur Way. Lights are on in all the houses, windows glowing yellow.

"There they are," said Ned. "Turn into the driveway."

"Don't they want to see the house during the day?"

"The wife's already seen it. Now it's the husband's turn, and he can't get away from his job."

"Let me guess. He's a banker."

"Don't be such a snob, Rachel." Ned paused. "He's a lawyer."

I snort. I can't help it.

"Look, if you're going to be like this—"

"I'm just kidding."

Ned opens the door. "Why don't you guys come in and wait in the kitchen," he says. "It's too cold to stay in the car."

Ned waves to the couple in the idling car and motions to them that he'll be just a minute. He unlocks the front door of 12 Arthur Way and ushers Josh and me inside.

"Make yourselves at home," he says. "The family's away skiing."

The kitchen is perfect for Josh, who immediately plops himself down on the floor with a bucket of Legos. There are dozens of toys strewn in a path across the kitchen floor and into what is meant to be the dining room but instead is a massive playroom, with a full-sized toy kitchen, a tent, and a pool table on which an entire Brio train track is set up, complete with conductor, tiny wooden trees, and dozens of trains. I wander around the playroom as if wandering through a museum in a foreign country. Who are these people? The family photos framed on the walls show three small wiry boys and their blond parents who look so much alike they could be siblings themselves.

The back door slams, and I hear Ned entering the house with Mr. and Mrs. Lawyer.

"Your wife already knows this," Ned says, in a voice so wooden I find almost unrecognizable, "but the master bath had a twenty-thousand-dollar renovation last year, with granite floors and a glass-walled bath and Jacuzzi."

Josh looks up from the Legos. "Daddy?" he says.

Even though it's the middle of March, the refrigerator is covered with probably fifty holiday cards, stuck up with tape and magnets. Hawthorne and North Hawthorne families are on display. SEASON'S GREETINGS! MERRY CHRISTMAS! HAPPY HOLIDAYS! Three kids, or four, or five, gathered on beaches during last year's winter vacation or on ski slopes, grinning from beneath their goggles. I search the cards for pictures of families with only one child. There are none.

"And here," says Ned, in that same fake-robust voice, "is the kitchen."

I look up and catch Ned's eye. He shoots me a warning look.

"Hello," says the husband.

"This is my wife and son," says Ned.

"Hi," says the wife.

"Don't let us disturb you," I say.

"Oh, not at all," says the wife. She crouches down and smiles at Josh.

"Hi there. What's your name?"

Josh doesn't look up from his tower of Legos.

"Cat got your tongue?"

"He's shy," I say.

"How old is he?"

"Two."

Something, a shadow of something, crosses the woman's face. It's not the first time I've seen that look from a perfect stranger who thinks she knows something about my kid. What is she thinking, autism? Brain disorder? I feel like screaming at her to mind her own business, but it isn't her fault.

"Is he your first?" she asks.

"I have a sixteen-year-old daughter," I say.

She looks at me. "Impossible!" she says.

"That's very nice of you."

"Note the Viking Range," says Ned. In all my life, I could never have imagined such a sentence issuing forth from the lips of Ned Jensen. *Note the Viking Range.* Who is he modeling himself after, Bob Barker on *Let's Make a Deal*?

The couple follows Ned out of the kitchen, and they walk down the hall and then, soundlessly, up the carpeted center staircase. Jane and Arthur knew what they were doing when they built these houses. Every few years they've bought more land and created another new development, and the houses often sell before they're even finished. Their motto is JENSEN MEANS QUALITY. The most recent ones are faux Tudor and have cathedral ceilings, gas fireplaces, sunken Jacuzzis in the backyards, and direct satellite connections. But if you ask me, these slightly older houses are the nicest ones. They're simple and solid and don't pretend to be anything they're not.

"We're planning to have three." I hear the wife's voice on the top landing.

"Terrific," says Ned.

I hear the sound of a toilet flushing.

"Excellent water pressure," says the husband.

"Mommy, look!" Josh picks up something glinting on the floor. I bend over and take a discarded foil Nicorette packet from his open palm.

"Well, then." The husband's voice drifts downstairs, and I realize that the tour of the upstairs bedrooms is over. "It's certainly a very nice house."

"And at the right price too," says Ned. I feel like pulling him into the kitchen and telling him he doesn't have to strain so hard; he's overselling in his eagerness to make his 6 percent. He's going to blow this deal; I feel embarrassed for him. He's a terrible real estate broker. Just awful. The man who painted those brilliant blurred photorealistic images cannot sell a house to save his life. It's clear to me that the only reason he's done okay as a broker is because of Jane and Arthur. He's a Jensen and, in the end, JENSEN IS QUALITY.

"We'll be in touch," says the husband. The kiss of death. *We'll be in touch. I'll call you. Drop me a line.*

The door closes behind them, and Ned comes back into the kitchen.

"God, this place is a mess," he says. "They left it like a complete pigsty. How the hell am I supposed to sell it when it looks like this?"

He waves his arms around the kitchen, at the toys and animals and trains scattered everywhere, the half-finished bowl of cereal still on the kitchen counter.

"I think it looks homey," I say.

He sits down on a stool and rubs his eyes.

"They're not buying it."

"No, probably not."

"Goddammit."

"Dammit," Josh repeats.

"Does the kid have some kind of radar for bad words?" Ned asks.

He gets off the stool and crouches down on the floor next to Josh.

"Time to go, garbage-mouth."

"No-o-o-o!"

"These aren't our toys."

"No-o-o-o!"

Josh squirms in Ned's arms, his face scrunched and red. He

looks like a little old man. Ned bounces him up and down and turns to me.

"So what are we doing?" he asks. What is he asking? Does he mean are we having dinner together? Are we spending the night together? Are we going to be a family again? In the soft light of a stranger's kitchen, I want to reach out and cup him in my hands like water. I want to carry him home with me, careful not to spill him. He feels that fragile to me, that easily lost.

"Ned, I—"

"What?" he asks. Josh is hugging and kissing him, planting big sloppy kisses on his ear. He has gone from near-tantrum to giddy-toddler mode in two seconds flat. I wish I could change my mood so quickly.

"Nothing. Let's go. I'll make us dinner."

Ned carries Josh out through the garage and locks up the house. I wrap my jacket tightly around me. I'm shivering, too cold to be standing still. All around us, the houses on Arthur Way seem full of big happy families. Even though I can't see into the windows, I picture the parents I saw on the Christmas cards with their three or four children, gathered around dinner tables telling each other about their days. Everyone's healthy, self-assured, and confident about the future. More of the same: that's what they'll have, just more of the same, please. Health, happiness, peace, and goodwill, just like the cards say.

"Rach? You coming?"

Ned breaks my reverie. He's holding the car door open, having strapped Josh into his seat.

We drive in silence out of the Jensen development and through the winding country roads of North Hawthorne. The one remaining farm in these parts is on our left. Timothy Schools, whose wife died a couple of years ago, is the only farmer who hasn't sold off his land to Jane and Arthur. His old clapboard house is dark, save for one small light to the left of the porch. It must be hard to be alone out here, surrounded by the families in their McMansions.

"How's Tim Schools doing?" I ask Ned.

He shrugs, giving a quick glance to the vast hilly expanse of land.

"He's a fool," says Ned. "Do you have any idea how much money he could have in the bank?"

"Maybe it's not about money for him."

"Oh, he's just holding out. Figures he can do even better if he waits a while. All the market's done is go up, up, up."

"When did you get so—"

"What, aware of reality?" Ned's fingers tighten on the steering wheel. "Welcome to the world, Rach. Money may be something we never gave much thought to, but everybody has to grow up some time."

I watch Ned out of the corner of my eye as we drive around the traffic circle in the center of North Hawthorne and head home. Is the man who broke through and painted those gorgeous paintings still alive and kicking, trapped in some small place inside him? Is that man letting out a furious wail of helplessness?

NED NOTICES *KATE IN THE SNOW* THE SECOND HE WALKS through the front door, carrying Josh. I see his eyes widen as he takes it in, but he doesn't say a word. I walk ahead of him into the kitchen and set a pot of water to boil on the stove as he carries Josh upstairs to bed. I hear the floorboards creak and know he's gone into our room, where *Rachel in Bloom* looks out over the rumpled bed. I feel elated, frightened. I don't know how he's going to react, both to seeing his work after such a long time and to the obvious fact that I went into the barn and messed with his stuff.

A box of spaghetti, a can of tomatoes, some basil, and chopped garlic. It's been a while since I've had the slightest desire to cook a meal. I look across the kitchen at the painting of Kate with her girlfriends; they're sitting at a shady picnic table, making some kind of elaborate macramé. It should be titled *Kate, Before.* But still—I find myself sinking into it, until I am there on that early summer day, and the laughter of the girls is piercing and loud. The pitcher of iced tea is just outside the frame of the painting, and the smell of fish sizzling on the grill.

"What are you doing?" Ned asks.

"Making some pasta."

"Rachel."

I stop chopping garlic, set the knife down, and look over at him.

"They're the best work you've ever done," I say quietly.

He doesn't respond. Just stares at the painting of Kate and her friends.

"Can you see that?" I ask. I'm afraid I've blown it—that he's going to be so furious with me he'll head out the door and never return.

"She was so sweet," he says, his voice thick. "I remember what I was trying to capture there—the amazing sweetness of those girls. How old were they, seven? Eight?"

"Eight, I think."

Ned shakes his head.

"But the *work,* Ned."

He waves his hand dismissively.

I walk over to him and hold him by his upper arms, force him to look at me.

"The work is brilliant. You were on to something important—something big for you."

He sits down heavily at the kitchen table with his back to *Kate with Friends.*

"That's all gone now," he says.

"It's not." My voice starts to rise, and I can feel myself lose whatever control I have. "You're a terrible real estate broker, you were a good teacher, but you are a truly gifted artist and you can't just give that up! Listen to me. I know something about this!"

"Let's have some dinner," he says.

I go back to the stove and sauté the garlic, add the chopped tomatoes. I don't have to push it—not now. Ned just needs to keep looking at those paintings. He's an artist, and he will see, if he lets himself, the quality of what he abandoned in that barn.

"Smells good," he says.

He gets up behind me and puts his arms around me. I sink into him, and we stand there, like that, for a while as I wait for the water to boil.

"Thanks, Rach," he whispers. I don't know if he's thanking me for dinner or for bringing his paintings in from the cold. But I don't ask.

TEN O'CLOCK, AND WE ARE SITTING AT THE KITCHEN table, our plates of spaghetti pushed away, a bottle of red wine nearly finished. A single candle is burning, honey-colored wax splattered across the dark metal base of the candlestick. Josh is asleep upstairs, and it seems possible to imagine, for just a moment, that our lives have continued uninterrupted, that Kate is upstairs as well, sprawled on her bed doing her math homework. Wasn't this the way it was supposed to be? Night in, night out, until our children grew up and had children themselves?

"We need to talk about Kate," I say.

"I think we're going to disagree about this," says Ned.

"Okay, but at least hear me out."

Ned tilts his chair back, clasps his hands behind his neck.

"She's not thriving there," I say.

"Of course she's not thriving, Rachel. She's—"

"I thought you were going to hear me out."

"Sorry."

"The school feels like a punishing place to me. The doctors there are so cold, I just don't see how she's going to get better. You saw them; they're so quick to throw around awful diagnoses. I think they're treating her like some kind of freak. I think the only thing that's going to heal her—if anything can—is coming home. She needs to know we love her."

"Oh, come on. She knows."

"I don't think that's true, Ned. She fucked up so royally. She can't imagine how anyone could love her. She thinks she ruined our lives."

Ned looks at me, his eyes cool and steady as he drains the last of his glass of wine.

"Maybe that's what *you* think," he says quietly.

"What do you mean?"

"Maybe, underneath it all, you're as angry at her as I am."

"I've been angry," I say, "but I'm over it now. I just want our family to—"

"To what?" Ned asks. "To go back to being the way we were?"

"No. I know that's not going to happen."

I stand up and walk around the kitchen, suddenly unable to remain still.

"Look," I say. "I just don't want her to feel like we've given up on her. Like we're passing her off because things have gotten too difficult."

"But things *did* get too difficult," says Ned.

He pours the remainder of the bottle into our two glasses. His calm infuriates me.

"So we just gave her away," I say.

"Rachel, you're distorting this. We sent her to the best therapeutic school in the United States. That's hardly like driving to the edge of town and dumping her on the side of the road."

"Don't even say such a thing!"

"It seems to me that somewhere in your mind you've turned this into a way of punishing yourself," says Ned.

"You should be painting!" I blurt out.

"Oh, go ahead. Change the subject."

"That's not the point, Ned, you can't just—"

"I thought we were talking about Kate."

I take a breath. "You're right. We were."

"So what are you saying, exactly?"

"I want to bring her home." The words come out in a rush. "I want to be a family again—all of us."

Ned rakes his hands through his hair.

"If this is what you really want, I'm not going to try to stop you. But you need to realize what might happen. We can't trust her—she's going to have to be looked after every single second. And I doubt the academy will let her back in. It's going to be really hard on everybody."

"You're not even around, so don't talk about how hard it's going to be for you."

"Well, maybe I'll be here more."

"Maybe? What does *maybe* mean? You're either living with us or you're not." The wine has made my head fuzzy, but it's also made me bold.

"If I were to move back in—" Ned starts, then interrupts himself. "Do you trust me, Rachel?"

"What do you mean?"

"I need to know if you trust me. To take care of you. To take care of Kate and Josh."

"Of course I trust you."

I guiltily think of myself sifting through his paintings in the barn, searching for—what? I've been with him for twenty years. What is it I think I don't know?

"You haven't always."

"That's not true."

"When Kate—"

His face is paler than usual, a mottled rash rising along the sides of his neck. This is the first time he's brought it up. I've tried a hundred different ways to get Ned to talk about it, but he's always shut me down.

"That was different, Ned." I measure my words as carefully as I can, given my current state of tipsiness. "I had no choice. I had to at least consider—"

"No." His expression hardness again. "You knew me. You had to know that what she was saying was impossible."

"Of course I knew that, but try to understand. We had just come home from the hospital with Josh, and Kate told me this insane story. What was I supposed to think? She's my daughter—I couldn't just dismiss it. I needed time to sort it all out."

Ned shakes his head.

"What?" I hear a pleading note in my voice and try to banish it. "What should I have done differently?"

"If the situation had been reversed, I would have believed you. No—more than that. I never would have doubted you for a moment."

"You can't know that."

"Let's stop this," says Ned. He pushes his chair back and comes around behind me. *Please stay.* I want to say it. I want to—but I stop myself. All my years with Ned have taught me that he can't be pleaded with. He lifts my hair off my neck and holds the weight of it in his hands. He leans down and kisses me, his breath soft against my cheek.

11

A LIE—IT MUST HAVE SEEMED A SMALL THING TO KATE, something she blurted out, safe (or so she thought) in the cocoon of her psychiatrist's office. Perhaps she never even thought about confidentiality. Why would she? What fourteen-year-old thinks of consequences? For her, it was merely the testing out of an idea, a way of loosening the tourniquet of guilt and shame she had no way of handling. On some level, I understood why she did it. Even as our lives shattered around us, I understood that Kate was a child and she had no idea of what she had done.

But Ned knew no such thing.

"Katie. What are you saying?" He stood in the middle of Kate's room, all of us crowded in there: me, Liza, Joshie, Kate, and now Ned.

Kate didn't look at him. She had climbed back into her bed and curled into a little ball, her long thin spine curved away from us.

"I should leave," said Liza. Ned was frozen in place, and I wanted to wrap my arms around him—I wanted to protect my husband from our daughter. But I couldn't. It was impossible to move. I was caught between the two people I loved most in the world.

"Kate? Why are you doing this?" Ned's voice was shaking; the lower half of his face had caved in. I was terrified for him—for all of us.

"Liza, could you watch Josh for a few minutes?" I asked softly. "Please?"

She nodded.

"I'll take him back to his room."

"Thanks." We were all of us being very polite.

"Apparently Kate told Zelman this whole story." I turned back to Ned.

"It's not a story," said Kate. Her voice was muffled by her blanket, which she had pulled halfway over her head.

"Look at me, Kate."

She didn't budge at the sound of Ned's entreaty.

"Please. Let's stop this craziness."

Not a muscle moved. It was infuriating. Ned and I stared helplessly at each other. And then Ned started for the bed. I don't know what he was thinking. All I knew was that it would be a disaster if he touched her.

"Ned!" I said. "Don't!"

My voice was sharp and it stopped him. He turned to look at me, his face as uncomprehending as a toddler's. I was trying to protect him. I'd had a few more minutes than he had to understand that the rules had changed. He'd better not lay a hand on his daughter.

"Kate, your father and I are going downstairs. I'm going to make us some food. It's been a very long day." I spoke in a measured monotone, a Stepford mom. "I hope you'll join us for dinner."

"I'm not hungry."

"Fine," I said. "That's just fine."

I WAITED, THAT NIGHT, UNTIL EVERYONE IN THE HOUSE was asleep. Josh was finally settled in his crib, his little chest rising and falling evenly, the bandage on his head cushioned by his soft cotton crib sheet. Kate had passed out after hours of weeping, the door to her room once again closed—probably locked—sealing herself off from the rest of us. Liza and Tommy had gone back to Boston. And Ned had fallen asleep watching *Nightline.* He had spent the evening glassy-eyed, like a shock victim, staring beyond me, past me, as if looking at a ghost over my shoulder. *Why?* we kept asking ourselves. *Why would she do such a thing?* We understood that she must feel terribly responsible for what happened to Josh. But still—to then turn around and accuse her father? It made no sense. I couldn't help it, I was angry at Ned. An uncomfortable feeling rose up inside of me, the feeling that somehow Ned had brought this on himself. He had a temper. Kate pushed his buttons, and he reacted. He had yelled at Kate—really screamed at her—on a number of occasions. And then there was that terrible moment in the hospital when he shook her.

I climbed out of bed, careful not to disturb Ned, and tiptoed down the hall, avoiding the floorboards that creaked. I walked down the stairs and into the kitchen. I was feeling my way through the house, looking for answers in the shapes of things: the way the ladder-back chairs cast shadows, like bars, across the wide planks of the kitchen floor; the way the sheer white curtains never quite closed, a crescent-shaped sliver of the outside world peeking through. I kept an emergency pack of cigarettes in the pantry—it had probably been there six months—and I found it behind some canned cranberries. I slipped my down jacket over my nightgown and went out to the back stoop.

It was then, finally, that I started weeping. In the middle of the freezing night, with no one to hear me. What was going to become of us? I couldn't imagine how we were ever going to find our way out of this mess we were now in. My mind wandered in search of a tiny patch of peace, but all I felt was more fear than I had ever known. I was afraid I would lose them all.

"Rachel?" Ned opened the back door behind me. He was barefoot in his flannel pajamas. "What are you doing?"

I waved the cigarette at him.

"You're going to get sick to death out here."

My eyelashes had frozen solid, and my cheeks felt stiff. I was afraid to say anything to him—afraid that if I opened my mouth I would start to scream and never stop.

"I just need some time," I said.

Ned nodded slowly. "You think I did it," he said.

"Ned—"

"You do. Don't you."

"No! I don't think you did it. I think she's deeply troubled, but beyond that I don't know anything!"

Ned wrapped his arms around himself. His breath was vapor in the night.

"Can you say that you absolutely, positively know in your heart that I didn't do anything wrong?" he asked softly, slowly. And I felt a sudden flash of fury at him. Didn't he realize how impossible this was? She was my daughter. Because of that—and nothing but that—a splinter of doubt had wedged itself into my heart. I could feel it stabbing me with every breath I took. *Could it be?*

"No, I can't," I said sharply. "How can I say I *know*?"

Ned nodded again, that slow ominous nod.

"I'm going back inside now," he said. "I'm going to sleep on the couch tonight, okay?"

"Ned, please." I stubbed out my cigarette in the snow.

"What, Rachel? Do you think I can lie in bed next to you, knowing what you think of me? That you think I'm"—his voice caught—"some kind of monster?"

"I don't think that. I don't. Ned, you have to understand; this is all so fucking bizarre. I need time to process it."

"There should have been no question."

"Look, she's my daughter."

"Oh. So now she's *your* daughter."

"No! No, that's not what I meant!"

"That's exactly what you meant."

He walked away from me, closing the door behind him. Even though I was freezing, I stayed outside for a few more minutes, trying to find some comfort in the stars overhead, the smooth crust of snow leading to the barn in back. Never once in fifteen years had we ever slept apart under the same roof. If you had asked five hours earlier if it were possible—if things could be bad enough between Ned and me that we couldn't resolve them enough to go to sleep together—I would have laughed. *No way,* I would have said. *Ned and I, we can talk about anything.*

THE NEXT MORNING, WHEN I AWOKE, IT WAS STILL DARK outside my bedroom window. For a single blissful second I remembered nothing. I rolled over onto my stomach to try to fall back asleep and reached my arm over for Ned. It wasn't until I felt the cold, empty space on his side of the bed that it all came flooding back to me. Josh's poor bruised head. The long drive home from the hospital. Liza's pale tearstained face. And then Kate, her eyes as bright and unblinking as headlights, spewing forth a mouthful of ruinous lies.

I sat on the edge of the bed, feeling for my slippers, then padded down the hall to Josh's room. I had nursed him to sleep in the middle of the night and he had seemed fine, but still I wanted to check on him. At the hospital, they had come by each hour, shining a light into his eyes to make sure his pupils were dilating. It was all I could do not to wake him, as I stood by the side of his crib watching him sleep on his back, his little legs open like a crab's. The first streaks of daylight cast him in a bluish gray light. His head was turned to the side, where a small puddle of drool had gathered on the crib sheet.

I tiptoed out of the room and closed the door. I wanted to be sure to get downstairs and straighten the den before Kate woke up, so she'd have no idea her father and I had slept apart. I saw the kitchen light spilling across the floor when I got to the bottom of the staircase and assumed that Ned was up early. He had probably opened the front door and picked up the *Globe* from the stoop, folded in its blue plastic wrapper.

But it wasn't Ned sitting in the kitchen. It was Kate, hunched against the wall by the far side of the table, her hair hanging over her face, her head bowed.

"What are you doing up?" I asked. I was thinking fast, trying to figure out what to say to her about her father sleeping on the couch.

"Nothing."

I walked into the den and saw the sofa, cushions all fluffed up. The pillow and blanket were neatly stacked on the club chair. Had Ned even slept here? Where was he?

"Dad must have had an early appointment at school," I said, as I walked back into the kitchen. Normalcy—or at least a semblance of it—was all I wanted. I poured water into the coffeemaker. That was usually Ned's job, to make the morning's coffee the night before. I stood there with my back to Kate for a minute, trying to breathe.

"Mom?"

Her voice was tiny, but to my ears it sounded like a shout, and I whipped around. It was then I saw the dish towels she had wrapped around her forearms and wrists, and the splattered drops of blood on the kitchen table and the floor.

"Kate!" I screamed, and ran over to her. I was afraid to pull off the towels, afraid to see what kind of damage she had inflicted upon herself. What had she done?

"It's not so bad," she whispered. "I just cut myself a little."

"How long ago? How long have you been sitting here?"

"I don't know. Not long."

"We're going to the hospital."

"I don't need—"

"Stop. We're going." My mind was racing. Josh. I had to go upstairs and get him. I'd bundle him into the car in his pajamas. Or was there a neighbor I could call?

"Look."

Kate unwound the towels, and even in my terror I could see that she was right. She didn't need to go to the hospital. The cuts were superficial, etched up and down her forearms. There was a little blood beading out of a few of the cuts.

I sank into a chair, my knees suddenly wobbly.

"Oh, God, Kate. Why? What's happening to you?"

Josh started crying upstairs, his thin first-thing-in-the-morning wail. *Come get me!* he was saying in his own way. All he knew was that he was hungry. He wanted his mother's breast. Well, I could do that. That, at least, I could do.

"I have to go get Josh. Just stay here, okay? Don't move from that chair."

Kate nodded. I ran upstairs, stopping in my bedroom to get the portable phone. I was afraid I might pass out, my heart was pounding so fast. And why not? Why not a stroke or a heart attack? I was thirty-nine. Couldn't a thirty-nine-year-old woman have a heart attack, given the right circumstances?

"Ned, it's me."

I had dialed Ned's office at the academy.

"We have an even bigger problem with Kate," I said, into his answering machine. "Are you there? Please. If you're there pick up."

I was begging my own husband to answer my call. I just knew he was there. He had probably gone in the middle of the night. He had one of the nicer offices at the academy, with a big arched window overlooking the quad. I could picture him curled up on his old creaky recliner, surrounded by sagging shelves of books.

I leaned over Josh's crib, cradling the phone between my ear and shoulder.

Ned's groggy voice finally answered. "Yeah."

"Kate's cut herself," I say. "It's not serious, but—"

"What do you mean?" He sounded suddenly awake. "Cut where?"

"Her wrists. She—"

"No, she wouldn't."

"She didn't really hurt herself. She—"

"I'm on my way."

Josh was soft and squirmy against my chest.

"Let's go downstairs, Joshie," I said in a singsong. "Let's go find Katie."

It occurred to me, then, that I should keep my two children apart. That the image of his sister with her arms cut up, of white towels splattered with Jackson Pollock drips of blood might imprint itself on Josh's little brain. But I had no choice. I was being ripped apart, pulled in opposing directions by my children. I cradled his head as I carried him down the stairs, taking each step one at a time. Kate was exactly where I had left her, too weak or too freaked out by what she had done to have moved an inch. I sat down across the table from her, opened my robe, and started to feed Josh.

"Mommy?"

She hadn't called me Mommy in as long as I could remember.

"Yeah, baby?"

"I'm sorry."

Tears leaked from her eyes and she swatted at them. I didn't even ask what she was sorry for. Which thing.

"What's going to happen now?" she asked.

"I don't know."

I was crying too, hot tears spilling down.

The phone rang, and I figured it was Ned calling back. Who else would be calling at—what was it—seven-thirty in the morning?

"Where are you?" I said into the phone.

"Hello?" A man's unfamiliar voice responded on the other end.

"Oh, I'm sorry. Who's this?"

"Rachel, it's Dan Henderson. Is Ned around?"

"No, he isn't. He'll be back in a minute, though."

Dan was the assistant headmaster at the academy and one of Ned's closest friends. They played squash a couple of times a week and went out for beers once a month. But Dan almost never called the house—and certainly not at the crack of dawn.

"What's wrong, Dan?" I asked.

"I—nothing. Would you have Ned call me?"

"Okay," I said slowly. I stopped myself from asking any further questions. I knew. Somehow this was all connected. I could hear the strain in Dan's voice, though I didn't recognize it as a strain that would be echoed again and again in all our friends and neighbors.

I was just hanging up when Ned walked in through the front door, his coat hanging open, his face ruddy from the cold.

"Katie, Katie." He shook his head, taking in our miserable daughter. She wouldn't look at him. She just stared straight down at the floor. "What are you doing to yourself?"

He pushed a chair out of the way and moved toward her.

"Let me see your arms."

She cringed, making herself smaller.

"Just stay away from me," she whispered.

"Come on, will you stop it?"

Ned reached down and tried gently to pull Kate's arms from beneath the table, where she was hiding them.

"Don't touch me!" she shrieked, but Ned didn't move away from her. He crouched down and held her hand. He just looked her full in the face, calmly, quietly.

It was then she started screaming. I had never heard anything like it—it was the sound of someone who had completely lost control, and it was so loud I was afraid the people next door would call the police. Josh stiffened in my arms, startled, and started to cry himself.

"Kate!" I gasped.

Ned dropped her hand and stood up, backing away from her as if from a pointed gun.

"Ssshhh," he said. "Get hold of yourself."

"No-o-o-o!" she screamed, even louder.

I walked out of the room with Josh in my arms. My first

thought was to get him away from the madness. He was crying harder, clutching around my neck.

"It's okay, Joshie," I whispered. "It's okay," I repeated as I climbed the stairs to his room. Once inside, I closed the door behind us, muting the sound of Kate's screams. I lowered Josh onto his play mat and sat down on the floor next to him. I don't know how long I stayed there, watching Josh swat at the black-and-white stuffed animals hanging from the bar above his play mat. After a while Kate stopped screaming; she had worn herself out. And then I heard the clatter of pans and the beeping of the coffeemaker as Ned made breakfast. We still had to eat. I was sure that was what he was thinking. The normal sounds made my mind drift to practical questions. I had called Zelman three times but kept getting his service. Did we need to get Kate looked at by a medical doctor? Maybe she was having some kind of psychotic reaction to her anti-depressants. That was possible—wasn't it?

When the phone rang again I remembered that I hadn't told Ned about Dan Henderson's call. I heard Ned say hello on the phone downstairs.

"Hey, what's up, buddy?"

A long pause.

"What do you mean, come in?"

Another pause. He had stopped the kitchen clatter.

"It's winter break—why does McGrath want to see me? What's going on, Dan?" Ned's tone was careful. "Okay. I'll be there."

I didn't know what to do or where to go. Downstairs, to Ned—I knew he must be shaken up. And Kate—I should be tending to her somehow, dealing with her wounds, mental and physical. And there was Joshie, lying on the floor, happy enough, but still with that enormous bump on his head; I didn't want to be away from him for a single second. I wanted to divide and morph into several versions of myself, each tending to the different people who needed me.

I picked up Josh and went back down to the kitchen. Ned and Kate were sitting calmly at the table, eating scrambled eggs.

"That was Henderson," said Ned.

I resisted saying I knew.

"He wants me to come in for some secret meeting."

"What about?"

"I don't know. It's a secret."

Kate's eyes darted back and forth between us. I wondered if she suspected, then, that the ball she had put into play was bouncing uncontrollably, smashing into every possible corner of our lives. Henderson knew. The academy knew. Someone had called them. It was possible. All these people were connected. All it would have taken was Liza telling one person. Or Tommy. Or Zelman.

"Do you realize what you did, Kate?" Ned asked, chewing.

She didn't respond.

"You've ruined our lives," said Ned. He was eerily calm, just the way he had been when he crouched down next to her a short while before.

"Ned, don't."

"But she has, Rachel."

"She's a kid."

"Don't talk about me like I'm not here," Kate blurted out.

"You're *not* here," said Ned. "The daughter I know—she's not here."

Kate started crying again.

"What do you suppose is going to happen now, Kate? How are the bills going to get paid around here? Who's going to send you to school, or to shrinks, or whatever else you need?"

Ned's lips were white with fury, but his tone was cool, and it scared me more than anything until I realized what he was doing: he was reining himself in, trying to control his temper.

"You need to call Dr. Zelman and tell him the truth," Ned said.

Kate kept her head down and pushed the scrambled eggs around her plate with a fork.

"You need to fix this thing. If it isn't already too late," said Ned. "It's fine for you to hate me. You're a kid, and I'm your father—sometimes we hate our parents. But it's not fine for you to make accusations that aren't true. I don't think you realize what you've done."

"No." Kate raised her head and stared straight back at Ned.

"Kate—" I started, but Ned held up a hand.

"Let me handle this, Rachel."

"Fine," I said, storming out of the room. I went into my bedroom with Josh and turned on the television. I heard sounds from downstairs—some yelling and slamming—but I kept my eyes on the screen, not even knowing what I was watching. Josh had found a tube of hand cream by my bedside table and was doing his best to open the top.

"No, Joshie." I took it from him, and he started to cry.

"Okay, fine." I handed it back. What difference did it make, after all?

I waited until it had gotten quiet before I ventured downstairs again. Ned was sitting at the kitchen table, his half-eaten eggs in front of him.

"Where's Kate?" I asked.

"She left."

"What do you mean, she left?" I looked at him like he was insane. "How could you have let her walk out of here?"

"How could I have stopped her? What was I supposed to do, grab her?"

"Ned. She cut her wrists this morning. She can't be on her own. She can't—"

My heart started pounding. I ran back upstairs and threw on my jeans and boots, a sweater.

"You're going to have to watch Josh," I said breathlessly, back downstairs, as I looked for my house keys and wallet.

"I can't. I have to go see McGrath."

"Shit." I slammed my hand down on the table.

"I'm sorry. I was just so angry at her—"

"But she's still a kid, Ned. She's just a teenager."

I bundled Josh into his jacket. He pitched a fit when I tried to put his hat on.

"Come on, Joshie. Cooperate," I said, as I squeezed him into the Bjorn. I was halfway out the door before I turned and looked back.

"Ned?"

He raised his head.

"Are we going to be okay?" I asked.

He looked at me for a long moment.

"Yeah, sure," he said. But there was no one inside of him when he said it. My whole family—Ned, Kate, even Joshie—had fled somewhere where I couldn't find them.

"Listen, I have my cell phone. Call me the second you get out of McGrath's office, okay? And I'll call you when I find Kate."

Ned was searching through his pockets.

"Where are my fucking car keys?"

"Ned?"

"Yeah?"

"You'll call me, right?"

"Will do."

THE SIDEWALKS WERE COVERED WITH SLUSH, AND A little treacherous with the hard winter ice still beneath. I was conscious of each step, planting my boots firmly, making sure I had a good grip. The houses along Liberty Street were bedecked with wreaths and tiny Christmas lights that were turned off during the day, but still their glass glittered in the sun. I passed the Baskin house, with its usual over-the-top holiday decorations that got the whole town up in arms. Santa and his reindeer pranced across the snow-covered lawn.

"Kate!" I cupped my hands and called. "Katie!"

She had slammed out of the house with no destination in mind, I was pretty sure of that. Most of her school friends were back home for the holidays, and her town friends—at least the ones I could think of—were still away on winter vacations with their families. It was three days before New Year's and the town was dead.

Stew, our mailman, was driving slowly up the hill in his truck. He waved when he saw me and Josh, and I flagged him down.

"Stew, have you seen Kate?"

He shook his head.

"Nope, sorry. I'll keep an eye out for her. You want her home?"

"Yes," I said. I wanted her home.

I rounded the corner of Liberty and Main and walked through town, looking in the windows of all the logical places: the Dunkin Donuts, Bruegger's Bagels, even the Hawthorne video store where she and her friends sometimes hung out. Where the hell was she? Images flashed through my mind of blood seeping into snow, my Katie spread out in some field somewhere, hurting herself.

"What are we going to do, Joshie?" I jostled him up and down, trying halfheartedly to keep him amused. I was grateful that he was still a baby. He had no sense of what was going on.

I took a quick tour through the library; maybe she was in the back room where they have some comfortable chairs. She might even have been asleep in a corner somewhere. But no Kate. I walked down Main Street all the way to the academy and saw that the place was pretty well locked up, except for the lights in Henderson's office, where Ned was having his meeting. The campus, devoid of students, was eerily still.

An hour passed before it seemed to me I had looked in every nook and cranny in Hawthorne. I rang Ned's cell phone, but I got his outgoing message.

"We're going to the police, Joshie," I whispered. He was finally asleep, bundled warmly against my chest. "We're going to get the police to find Katie."

Skip Jeffries was at the desk at the station. That was a small piece of luck. He looked up as Josh and I walked in from the cold.

"Rachel Jensen! And there's the boy! Heard you all had a bit of a scare down there in New York."

I looked at him, puzzled. It had never stopped amazing me, the way word traveled through town—especially when it came to misfortune.

"How'd you hear about that?" I asked.

He shrugged and then took a look at me. I can't imagine what a sight I must have been. I had been crying, and my voice was hoarse from calling Kate's name up and down the side streets. I thought I knew all her usual haunts; I had even walked through the small cemetery on the edge of town where I knew she and her academy friends had been hanging out. My whole body felt stiff and cold, though Josh was warm, close up against me.

"Kate's missing," I said.

Skip put down his pen and pushed his paperwork aside.

"What do you mean? For how long?"

"Not long—only a couple of hours—but it's serious, Skip."

"Why's that?"

"She—"

I stopped. I didn't want to say it out loud, say it in a police station: *She cut herself.* But I didn't have any choice.

"She tried to hurt herself this morning," I said quietly. I looked around to see if anyone else in the station was listening. "And then she ran off. I'm worried."

"Hurt herself how, Rachel?"

"She cut herself." I started to cry again. "Her wrists."

"Okay—we'll get a couple of guys out looking for her," said Skip. "Right away. We'll find her."

FROM THE POLICE STATION IT WAS A SHORT WALK TO MY mother-in-law's office. Jane's Range Rover was parked in front of Jensen Realty, and Arthur's Jaguar was parked right behind it. Those cars were my in-laws' one flashy indulgence; they considered them a legitimate business expense. Customers in the market for million-dollar houses liked to be driven around in fancy cars. I unstrapped Josh as I walked through the front hall of Jensen Realty, past photographs of their exclusive listings: a Victorian in Marlborough, an inn for sale on Nantucket, the usual golf-course condos and new construction. The air smelled like lemon-scented Lysol.

"Look who's here!"

"Hello, Gladys."

I gave Jane and Arthur's longtime receptionist a hug.

"Will you look at the little honey bear!"

Gladys tickled Josh under his chin.

"Is he all right? I heard he had a tumble."

"He's fine."

"Hit your head, did you? Poor little munchkin."

I knew she meant nothing by it, but still I bristled.

"He's *fine,* Gladys."

She blinked and stopped. "Sorry, hon."

"No, no. I'm sorry. It's just been a hard week, that's all."

She looked hurt, and I felt bad.

"It's just—everybody's been so nice, but—"

"I know. You're worried about him. How could you not be? You're his mommy."

This was more empathy than I could bear, and I was afraid I'd break down right there in the anteroom of Jensen Realty.

"Is Jane around?"

"Sure, hon. She's in her office."

I walked down the carpeted hall to Jane's office. Through the glass door I saw the back of her gray lacquered bob as she sat in her leather swivel chair, facing the windows. Her feet were up on the console, and she was talking on the phone.

I knocked, and she waved me in without even turning around.

"I know, Louisa. But that's the way the market is right now. Crazy, isn't it?" She laughed, then swiveled around and saw me. "It's what I call Jensen's Law. The minute you're interested in a property, someone else comes along and starts getting real interested too."

Jane motioned me to the couch against the wall and waved her manicured fingers at Josh. "Listen, my daughter-in-law just walked in with my grandson. I'll talk to you later, after I get some feedback from the owners, okay?"

She hung up and rolled her eyes at me.

"Customers," she said. "We're looking at over two million bucks for the old Troubh farm on Goose Neck Road. Can you believe it?"

She crouched down next to Josh on the floor.

"There's my precious boy," she said. "Let me see that little boo-boo."

She started to lift Josh's knit cap, and he let out a wail.

"I think it's pretty sensitive," I said quickly. "But he's doing great."

"Of course he is."

"Kate hasn't stopped by this morning, has she?" I asked, trying to sound casual.

"No, why?"

Jane peered at me over her gold-rimmed bifocals. Her eyes were the same piercing blue as Ned's, but her gaze was colder, more unnerving. I found myself wondering what, if anything, she already knew. Jane had her ear to the ground in Hawthorne. Very little came as a surprise to her. Arthur and she had built their business by knowing who had been fired, who'd had a death in the family, who was about to file for bankruptcy.

"We're in trouble," I said, and sank back into the soft cushions of the sofa as if physically pushed. The world was dissolving around me—the family photographs on the walls of Jane's office jiggling and blurring, coming apart, scattering like pieces of a puzzle.

"What kind of trouble?"

I took a deep breath and tried to steel myself.

"Kate has accused Ned of molesting her."

The words tumbled over one another. I watched as the blood drained from Jane's face, and for the first time since I had known her my mother-in-law looked old and frail.

"Sweet mother of God," she said.

She walked back around to her desk and sat down in her chair.

"Molest—what—"

"Sexually," I said. "Sexual molestation."

Jane looked so sick I was afraid she might faint, or worse.

"Why would Kate say such a thing?"

I shook my head. "I don't know." I felt relieved for having blurted it out. It wasn't just my problem now. It was all of our problem—and somehow all of us would pull together to get through it.

"Who knows? Have you told anyone else?"

I could see the wheels inside Jane's head starting to whir and click. She was regaining her equilibrium.

"I haven't, no. But—"

"Good," Jane cut me off. She picked up a pen and started drumming it against the side of her desk.

"Jane—"

"We'll get Kate some help. Clearly she needs—"

"Jane," I repeated.

She stopped drumming. "What?"

"I think this has more momentum than you realize," I said slowly.

"What do you mean?"

"Dan Henderson called this morning. The academy—"

"Oh, no, don't tell me the academy—how could they possibly know?"

"Kate told her doctor."

"What doctor?"

I had forgotten that we had never told Jane and Arthur about Kate's weekly excursions into Boston to see Dr. Zelman. It wasn't their business, we reasoned. Grandparents didn't need to know every single thing.

"She's been seeing someone. A therapist. Someone Tommy and Liza recommended."

"Oh, fabulous." Jane glared at me. She raked a hand through her hair in a gesture that reminded me of Ned. Then she looked at me so intensely that I had to look away.

"Did he?" she asked.

"Did he what?"

"You know," she said. "Did he do it, Rachel?"

"My God, Jane. You're his mother. How could you possibly think such a thing?"

"I didn't say I thought it. I want to know what *you* think."

Gladys poked her head in the door.

"Mrs. Jensen, your eleven-thirty is here."

"Hold them off, Gladys. Offer them some tea," Jane said, without looking over at her.

As Gladys retreated, I tried to form a coherent thought. Was Ned's own mother doubting him? And if she was, shouldn't I be? Wasn't a mother's first loyalty to her children? How could I trust Ned if his own mother didn't?

"He never laid a hand on her, Jane," I said quietly to my mother-in-law. "I'm horrified that you'd even ask the question."

"I wasn't questioning it," said Jane, "but I had to be sure we understand each other."

"We understand each other," I repeated slowly. As I said the words, an even deeper understanding dawned on me: I was an outsider. Blood was blood, and marriage was marriage. The Jensens were going to rally the troops, and they needed to know who was for them and who was against them.

"I'm going to phone Buzz Hall," said Jane. Buzz was the family attorney.

"Why involve Buzz?" I asked. "Wouldn't it be better if—"

"Ned's going to need a lawyer," said Jane.

I thought about Kate. Where was she right now? Hitchhiking to Boston? Hiding out someplace she knew I'd never find her? The truth was, all I really cared about was that she was alive and in one piece, no matter what she had done.

"Mrs. Jensen?" Gladys appeared at the door again.

"Not *now,* Gladys," Jane snapped.

I pushed my chair back. "I need to go," I said. Josh had dozed off in the Bjorn, but I could feel him stirring. "I have to find Kate."

"What do you mean, find her? Where is she?"

"She stormed off this morning."

Jane's pen resumed tapping.

"This is a huge mess, Rachel," said Jane.

"I know," I said.

"Maybe she should go to one of those schools," said Jane. "Trish Dovell's granddaughter went to one in New Hampshire—straightened her right up."

"We're not sending her away," I said faintly. I pulled on my coat and wrapped it around Josh.

"Think about it." Jane came over to me and gave me a hug, then bent over and kissed Josh's cheek. "Don't you worry."

I WALKED WITH JOSH STRAPPED TO ME BACK UP THE HILL to our house. It was blindingly bright out, the winter sun reflecting off the snow-covered rooftops. I tried to piece together the chain of events, the phone calls that had led all the way to Ned's being summoned to the academy. Did Zelman call the authorities? Who had called the school? Of course no one would want an accused child molester teaching at a boarding school—or any school.

When I reached the top of the hill, I saw our house in the distance. The boy who shoveled our walk had been by in my absence, and the winding brick path from the sidewalk to our front steps was clear. As I picked up my pace, I thought of the very first time I saw the house, fifteen years earlier. We were in Jane and Arthur's car, and I was about four months pregnant with Kate.

"That one." Jane pointed. "It's a real fixer-upper, but the bones are there."

Ned and I were holding hands in the backseat, and he squeezed my fingers as we looked at the old clapboard house. We both knew. The instant we saw it, we knew. It was going to be okay to leave the city—more than okay. This quiet country life was going to be just fine. Ned would have all the space and time he needed to work, with none of the financial pressures that had been chipping away at him. And I would get private commissions and work out of the sunny top-floor studio. We were so intent on not feeling defeated by this move that we barely noticed any of the house's flaws: the cracked walls, the sagging floors (*nothing a good contractor can't fix,* Jane said, unable to turn off the broker-speak). All we saw, like images from a shared dream rising between us, were our children—would we have only this one? or two or three?—and the meals we would cook in the sunny kitchen, and the old rugs and deep comfortable couches where we would sprawl, reading all the great books we never had time to read in New York. *Matisse didn't live in a city,* Ned leaned over and murmured in my ear. He pointed to a stained-glass skylight. *Gauguin didn't either,* I whispered back. There was even a fireplace in the bedroom, and I imagined us curled up in bed, making love in the flickering light. I didn't have any real idea what it would be like to have a baby in the house; I wasn't thinking about the baby gates we'd need at the tops of the stairways, or childproofing the windows, or how fireplaces and toddlers don't mix. It wasn't reality I was buying. It was the fantasy of our future, a bright seamless new life in an old country house—romantic, cozy, and safe from harm. Ned would paint in the barn out back—a huge studio, five times the size of his Chinatown space.

Josh was fussing by the time I pushed open the front door. He'd had enough of the cold air; his nose was pink, his eyes tearing.

"Let me take all this stuff off, Joshie," I said as I unstrapped him. "Okay, here we go." I laid him down on the living room floor and undid his fleece snowsuit. "That's better, isn't it?"

He looked up at me and gave a little grin, his two tiny front teeth gleaming.

I heard a door slam upstairs. I hadn't seen Ned's car when I came in, but maybe he had left it at the academy and walked.

"Ned?" I called upstairs.

There was no answer.

"Honey?"

Nothing.

"Kate?"

No one responded.

"Come on, Joshie."

I hoisted Josh onto my hip and climbed the stairs. There was music coming out of Kate's room, from behind the closed door. She was home. Thank God. I threw the door open and she was lying on the floor. I stopped for a minute and watched her. Then I walked down the hall to Josh's room and put him down in his crib, where he couldn't hurt himself. Sometimes he stayed there happily for half an hour, watching the pastel animals of his mobile circle above his head.

"Mommy will be right back," I whispered, pulling off the knit cap. I peeked beneath the padded bandage. The bump looked nastier, if that was possible: a deep bluish purple. Now I understood why people compared bumps and tumors to regular household items. A tumor the size of a tangerine. A pea-sized lump. This bump was the size of a golf ball.

I bent down and kissed it, then kissed his tiny lips.

"Love you," I said.

Then I went down the hall to Kate's room. She was still on her back on the floor, her hair fanned out around her face like a halo. Her eyes were open and she was staring at the ceiling as the music blared.

I walked to the stereo and lowered the volume.

"Kate?"

Her eyes looked glassy, and for a split second my heart lurched. Had she taken something? She blinked, and I took a deep breath.

"We need to talk," I said.

Not a muscle moved. Once again, she was giving me the silent treatment. I stood there and watched her, wondering where my happy lighthearted girl had gone. Kate had never looked like a little kid. From the time she was a toddler her features were so distinct

I'd swear I could picture her at thirty, a stunning woman. A heartbreaker, as Ned used to say. Well, that much was true; she was breaking our hearts. I looked around her room at the accumulated stuff from her childhood, from the ratty old Steiff teddy bear Jane and Arthur had given her when she was born to her brief obsession with one of the *Dawson's Creek* actors, a pretty boy whose posters were now rolled away under her bed. Her field hockey trophies were lined up on a shelf.

I had to fight the urge to swing my arms wildly around the room, knocking everything down.

"This has now become public," I said. "You should know that Daddy's been called in to school."

I paused. No sign of recognition, much less remorse.

"They're probably going to fire him," I continued.

Nothing. Not a blink, not a peep.

"You've wrecked us." My voice started to get louder. *Stay calm,* I exhorted myself. *Just stay calm, don't give her what she wants.* "You"—I bent down over her now and got right up close to her face—"You've wrecked your family!" I yelled. "How can you not care about that?"

Her forehead wrinkled, but beyond that she didn't respond.

"Please, Katie." I changed course. "Please—just say something."

She didn't answer me. I stood up, blood rushing to my head, and picked up the phone on her desk.

"I'm calling Dr. Zelman," I said shakily.

The doctor's voice mail picked up—of course it did. He hadn't responded to my three previous calls that morning.

"Dr. Zelman, this is Rachel Jensen again," I began. "I'm standing here looking at Kate. She's lying on the floor and is completely unresponsive to me. Please call me as soon as you get this message. I don't know what to do."

I placed the receiver back in its cradle.

"I called the doctor," I said. I felt like I had to keep talking to her. "Kate? We can't keep doing this."

A big tear rolled out of the corner of her eye, down the side of her face and into her hair. I was simultaneously relieved and saddened beyond belief.

"Oh, Katie." I lay down on the floor next to her and buried my face in her shoulder. "What happened to hurt you so much?"

"I don't know, Mommy," she said. Her whole body was trembling, and I held her tightly. I could feel her heart pounding in her thin, narrow rib cage. She was so cold; I wanted to engulf her. I pulled her as close to me as I dared, trying to warm her inside and out. We stayed there until her heart slowed and her breathing grew steady and even. My arm had fallen asleep beneath her, but I didn't want to move. I heard the front door slam. Ned was home. He walked up the stairs and paused for a moment in the door frame of Kate's room, looking down at the two of us. *I'll be out soon,* I mouthed to him, not even daring to whisper. I had my daughter safe in my arms. Deep down I knew that it would be a long time—longer than I could bear—before she would let me hold her again.

OUR HOUSE GREW QUIETER OVER THE NEXT FEW MONTHS, so still and silent it seemed no one lived there. Boxes from Ned's office were piled up in the front foyer—more than a decade's worth of books and papers thrown haphazardly into crates. We drifted through the house like ghosts, mourning our former selves. Everywhere, there were reminders: tickets to a Yo-Yo Ma concert in Boston tacked to the kitchen bulletin board; Club Med brochures I had sent away for, thinking about a spring vacation; cooking magazines with dog-eared recipes for lasagna and beef stews.

Kate went back to school, but she was having a hard time. The kids all knew Ned wasn't there. They'd heard rumors. He had been fired; he had resigned; he was taking a leave of absence. They kept asking Kate, *Where's your father? What happened to him?* I don't know what she told them; they stopped hassling her—in fact, they stopped talking to her at all—when a small article about the allegations against Ned finally appeared on page 3 of the *Courier.* Now there wasn't a farmer or a mailman in the vicinity who didn't know our business.

Zelman had finally called back and we'd had a number of long conversations, all of which ended up in the same place: we needed to send Kate away. A therapeutic school was his only solution. He didn't feel she could be kept safe at home, and beyond that he implied that the current level of tension in our house might be making matters worse. Of the possible alternatives—wilderness camp, psychiatric hospital—Zelman felt that a special school would be the gentlest, most effective way of helping her.

Certainly our home environment wasn't healthy or productive. I knew Ned was avoiding Kate as much as he could. He was afraid of her. What else might she do to him? And though he never said it, I believe he was afraid of his rage toward her. He spent most of his time sitting in the wing chair by the fireplace in our bedroom, with the door closed and music playing on the small stereo we kept in there. He often had a book in his lap, but I never saw him turn the pages. Occasionally he roused himself to do a chore around the house, waiting until Kate wasn't home before he oiled the creaky front door or took out the garbage.

IT WAS EARLY SPRING BY THE TIME I APPROACHED NED to discuss sending Kate away. I sat on the floor next to the wing chair and stroked his leg, his hand. As time had gone on, his sadness had become palpable. His shoulders were hunched, his back tensed against the weight of it.

"Zelman thinks we should send Kate away," I said quietly.

"Away where?"

"To one of those schools. Where they have therapy."

I tried the words on for size. They felt like poison in my mouth, but it was poison I had no choice but to swallow. "I'm afraid she's going to kill herself if she stays here. We can't control her. Zelman says he can facilitate—"

"Why does that fucker have anything to do with this?" Ned asked.

"Because he's already involved. And anyway, maybe we can get him on our side. It isn't easy to get a kid into these places—"

"What do you know about these places?"

"I've been reading a lot. On the Internet."

"Right."

"I also talked to Liza, and she says the best place is—"

"Liza would know."

"Look, Ned. We need to do this, and we need help."

"What kind of help?"

"We need some strings pulled." I paused. "There are wait lists."

"Unbelievable."

"Yeah, well. And then there's the money. It's expensive. Your parents—"

"We are not going to my parents for money," said Ned.

"We may have no choice."

"We can sell something. We'll sell the Fischl."

Eric Fischl had gone to art school with Ned. His large paintings now fetched upward of half a million, while Ned's sat in our barn out back.

Ned swallowed, then reached down and grabbed my hand. It was the first time he had willingly touched me in weeks. He cleared his throat.

"Rachel."

Something in his tone set my heart racing.

"I have two things to tell you." He took a deep breath. "The first is that I've rented a place over in Pine Dunes," he said, stroking the inside of my palm with one finger. "A condo."

"What do you mean? For whom?"

He paused. "For me."

"I don't understand."

"I'm going to move out. For a while."

He held my hand tightly, as if he were afraid I might bolt.

"I don't want you to do that."

"I know. But I have to."

The chair creaked as he shifted in his seat.

"The other thing is that I'm going to work for my parents."

I shook my head hard, raked my fingers through my hair. I was trying to shake loose what I was hearing, as if the words were merely debris flying between us.

"What?"

"For Jensen Realty. I've been studying to take the real estate exam."

"Ned." I removed my hand from his and struggled to my feet. "You can't do this."

"This is what I have to do, Rach." His voice was calm, measured. Obviously, he'd been thinking about this for a while. Long enough to make plans.

"It's impossible," I said. "It's impossible that you're doing this."

"We're going to need the money. And this is a way of making a whole lot of cash."

"I can work more," I said. "I can get a regular job."

"That's not the point."

"Why not?"

I was leaning over Ned, standing facing him while he sat still in his chair. I felt desperate, as if I would physically block him if he tried to leave our house.

"We can't go on like this."

"Like what? We're not fighting. We're sorting things out."

"Rach, there are huge things we're not talking about. And we can't talk about them, because right now there's nothing to say."

"What about Josh? You're just going to disappear from his life?"

"Of course not! I'll see him all the time. And I'll see you too. Who knows—maybe it'll be easier."

"Easier." My voice was flat.

"For now." Ned stood up, and I backed away from him. "Until the air is clear."

"When will that be, Ned?"

He started walking toward the door, and I realized he meant to leave right then.

"Don't go now," I said. "Please—at least let's have dinner."

He shook his head. "I've got to go, Rachel."

He handed me a piece of notepaper, on which was scribbled an address and phone number. I followed him down the stairs, through the front hall, and out the door. I left the door open, since Josh was napping inside.

"Ned—"

"Please, Rach. This is hard for me too," he said hoarsely.

He hugged me to his chest, and I could feel his heart beating rapidly. Then he walked away, climbed into his beat-up car, and drove away from our house.

THE NEXT MORNING, KATE HAD JUST LEFT FOR SCHOOL when the phone rang and the caller ID flashed ZELMAN.

"I have excellent news," he said. "I've spoken with my colleague Frank Hollis, who runs Stone Mountain. He's just had a cancellation."

What could a cancellation mean in these circumstances? I didn't even want to think about it.

"Maybe we're overreacting," I said. "Kate doesn't need—"

"Mrs. Jensen," interrupted Zelman. "I don't think you understand. This is a real opportunity. Stone Mountain is the best facility on the East Coast."

I paused, stopping myself from asking him if he believed Kate's accusations. Did he really think she had been the victim of sexual abuse—of incest?

"How could this have happened?" I asked. "How could she have gotten so sick so quickly?"

"Perhaps it wasn't so quick. These things tend to be incremental," said Zelman.

I felt dizzy, nauseated.

"My husband moved out last night," I blurted out.

Silence.

"I'm sorry to hear that," he said.

"Do you think—maybe it would be better if—"

"No." He cut me off. "I can't state this any more strongly than I already have. Kate needs to go."

"So what do we do now?"

"They're expecting her tonight," Zelman said.

"How am I supposed to get her there?" I asked. I was suddenly furious at the doctor's implacable tone.

"I suggest that you and your husband pick her up after school and take her," said Zelman. "It's about a two-hour drive."

"She's not going to go willingly."

"I'll prescribe some Valium. You can give her a five-milligram pill once she's in the car."

"This sounds so awful," I said quietly. "Like we're kidnapping her."

"I know it feels that way now," said Zelman, his voice softening a bit. "But you're doing the best thing possible for her."

AT FOUR-THIRTY, NED AND I WAITED BEHIND THE BLEACHERS by the softball field for Kate to finish practice. I caught glimpses of her through the wooden seats. She was wearing her blue-and-white Hawthorne jersey, her hair pulled back in a headband. She was totally focused, the long muscles in her legs straining as she caught a sharply hit ground ball and tagged a girl out at second base. She looked so healthy. How was it possible that we should be sending her away?

Ned cleared his throat. "She's not going to take well to this," he said.

"We'll just get her in the car," I said grimly. "Like Zelman suggested."

I had packed her canvas duffel bag with the few things Stone Mountain allowed: some warm sweaters, jeans, underwear, socks, and sneakers. Tiny name tags were sewn into her socks and underwear from her summer-camp days. I went into her bathroom and took her toothbrush and toothpaste. My hands were shaking and sweaty, my muscles tense. I thought we were doing the right thing—the only thing we could do in the circumstances—but what if we turned out to be wrong? I placed her old teddy bear at the bottom of the bag. They'd let her keep her teddy bear, at least. Wouldn't they?

"How's your new place?" I asked Ned.

"Rachel, don't."

"No, really. I want to know."

"It's dark and depressing, and it smells bad."

"Good."

"Oh, that's really nice."

Kate bounded off the field, zipping up her hoodie. Her posture changed, as it always did, the moment she saw us waiting for her.

"What's up?" she asked.

"Let's get into the car, honey," I said.

I took her elbow and started to steer her to the parking lot. She shrugged me off.

"Where are we going?"

I didn't want to lie to her, but I didn't want to say anything until she was safely in the backseat with the doors locked.

"We think you need help, Kate."

She examined her thumbnail, her hair falling into her face.

"I'm getting help," she said quietly.

"Dr. Zelman agrees with us that you need something more," I said.

"What does that mean?"

We climbed inside the car and I locked the doors. I hoped she hadn't noticed.

"There's a place not far from here—" Ned began.

"It's just for a little while," I interrupted, and Ned shot me a glance. The truth was, we had no idea how long she'd be away.

She looked up at us, her face paling.

"No way."

"It's not a bad place, Kate. It's a school, but they have some extra—"

"I already have a school."

"You can't stay there right now," I said.

"But it's almost the end of March! School ends in two months!"

She jutted out her chin, a gesture she'd had since she was a little kid.

"I know. But we need to do this now."

"Why? I have nothing to be ashamed of."

"It has nothing to do with shame, Katie."

She glared at Ned. "*You're* the one with the problem."

"Here we go," he muttered. He pulled the car away from the curb and drove away from campus.

"Fuck you."

"That's not going to get us anywhere," I said.

She pulled at the door handle. "I'm not going."

"It isn't up for discussion, Kate."

"You can't make me."

"Listen," I cajoled, "just give it a try."

"Let me out of the car!"

I rummaged through my bag for one of the Valium pills I had picked up from the pharmacy that afternoon and a bottle of water.

"Here." I handed them to her. "Take this."

"What is it?"

"A little Valium. It'll make you feel calmer."

"I don't want to be calm!" she screamed. "Let me the fuck out of here!"

She started rattling the door handles.

"It's not safe to do that when the car is moving, Kate," Ned said evenly.

"I don't care. I'm not going and you can't make me!" she yelled.

"Everyone thinks this is what's best for you."

She glared at Ned. "This is your idea, isn't it?"

"Actually, no."

Then, to my surprise, Kate popped the pill in her mouth and drank the whole bottle of water. Maybe she realized she really didn't have a choice.

"I won't be staying long," she said.

"Okay, honey. That's fine," I said. I didn't tell her about the duffel bag in the trunk of the car. Instead, I climbed over the arm rest and squeezed myself into the backseat next to her.

"Rachel, what the hell are you doing?" asked Ned.

I knew it was dangerous, but I needed to be near Kate. The school had strict rules about parent-child contact, and I had no idea when I would see her again. She was sobbing quietly, and even though she kept pushing me away, I reached over and stroked her hair, her hot wet cheek. By the time we had gotten on the highway, the Valium had kicked in and her head was resting on my shoulder. She was sound asleep. I closed my eyes and felt her warmth, breathed her in. In sleep, her face softened and she looked like a peaceful little girl. Thousands of times she had slept in the back of this car as we went on family outings, overnight trips. When she was a child we played the license plate game, picking out cars from as many states as we could find. *Look, Mom! There's Alabama! There's Oregon!* We sang silly songs, pulled into roadside stands, ate ice cream and drank lemonade, lowered all the windows and screamed into the wind rushing by us. We told bad jokes—*Ever hear the one about . . . ?*—and we wouldn't even have gotten to the punch line before Kate would be laughing. That was the point: just to make her laugh.

We hurtled along Route 93, the interstate shiny and black in the dusk of an early New England spring. There were hardly any other cars on the road, but there were trucks, huge eighteen-wheelers driving too fast. Ned turned off the highway, and we drove the hilly, steeper terrain of southern New Hampshire, the state where we were going to leave our daughter in the hands of strangers.

12

WHEN I WAKE UP WITH NED'S ARM FLUNG ACROSS MY hip, I think I must be dreaming. I close my eyes and try to shake the dream. I don't want to start my day with the dull ache of disappointment I have felt every single morning since he left almost a year ago. But then I hear snoring—a light guttural sound that used to drive me crazy—and I slowly open my eyes again. His face is inches away from mine. No one else gets to see him like this, I think to myself fiercely. No one but me.

"You're here," I whisper, moving closer to him so that our noses are almost touching.

He slowly blinks open. "So it seems."

He kisses me, his lips soft, our morning breath mingling. I watch him as we kiss, his features blurring together, and I realize that this—this is what I've missed the most. For fifteen years I saw the whole world through a transparency of Ned's face, as if he were always right there, close to me. Wherever I was—working, or driving Kate around to play dates, or cooking dinner—there was Ned, clinging to me like an invisible cloak. It made me feel safe in the world—and then, with no warning, it was ripped away.

"Are you—"

I start, but then I stop myself from asking: *Are you staying?*

"What?" Ned leans up on one elbow.

"Nothing. Can I get you some coffee?"

He flops back down again. "That would be great."

I walk naked to the closet and pull my robe from its hook. I try not to worry about my body, its sags and lumps and scars. As if he can read my mind, Ned calls softly across the room.

"You're beautiful."

I wave him away, embarrassed. "Stop," I say.

"No, really."

He looks at me then, with his painter's eyes, and I find myself glancing up at *Rachel in Bloom.* What more could any woman want than to have her husband register her at her most lovely?

I feel heat rise up my chest to my face. I pull my robe on and tie the sash tight around my waist.

"Let me get you that coffee," I say.

He holds my gaze, and there it is again: as if it has never slackened, the rope of feeling between us is as taut as it ever was.

"We're going to get through this, Rach." It's the first time he's ever said it. Since everything began to fall apart, I've had to be the cheerleader, the one saying it's going to be okay.

"I hope so," I say, and instantly regret it. That's not what he needs to hear. "I *know* so," I go on—even though in truth I know no such thing. How can I know anything anymore? My faith in the world—precarious to begin with—has been shaken to the core. You can live a good life, be the best mother and wife you know how to be, and still it can explode all around you. God isn't up there in the sky doling out equal amounts of pain and confusion and despair, and it's possible that we've gotten more than we can handle. Josh is a big question mark, as the doctor said. And Kate is an even bigger one. What will happen to Ned and me if either one of our kids doesn't make it?

"I'll be right back."

I pad down to the kitchen and stop in my tracks. All around

the kitchen cupboards are more paintings from Ned's series. They cover almost the entire surface of the walls and are leaned against chairs. He must have gone out to the barn in the middle of the night. Tears spring to my eyes when I realize what it means—that he sees, he gets it. At least he knows these are paintings worth looking at. And he brought them in here, to our house. A gift.

It's a little before seven; the first pink streaks of dawn are outside the kitchen window. Josh is still asleep. Usually he doesn't wake in the morning until the sun hits his window at about seven-thirty. I open the fridge and pull out the milk for my coffee. Ned takes his black. I pick up one of the paintings and study it, looking for a map of our future, as I have countless times since we sent Kate off to Stone Mountain last spring. We're in Jane and Arthur's backyard, Kate and I lying in a hammock strung up between two pine trees. Kate looks to be around twelve, so it was the year before I got pregnant with Josh. I was thirty-seven. My hair was long and loose—a wild mess of curls, the way Ned likes it—and I was wearing jeans and a faded sweatshirt, not a stitch of makeup. But looking at the painting, the eye travels to Kate. She's laughing, lying almost on top of me in the hammock. Her head is leaning into mine, her straight silky hair mixing with my own. It is a measure of our lives together that I have no memory of that moment. There were so many like it: easy, intimate. Nothing special. I search Kate's face for a hint of what was to come, but all I see is the open innocent face of a girl at home in her own self.

I lean the painting against a chair and pour milk into my coffee cup, then stick the cup into the microwave to warm up the milk. *We're going to get through this.* I remember, after my father died, thinking that it was as likely as not that there was life after death—that somehow he was watching over me from wherever he was. It was as easy to believe as it was not to believe, because really, who knew? And so, as much as possible, I carried that idea with me into the rest of my life, and over time it became something ingrained in me: a kind of blind hope that things ultimately worked out. I clung to that hope as a hedge against the dark cloud that always seemed to hover nearby, threatening to engulf me. When did that cloud begin to take over? I feel the need to pinpoint it to a single moment: Kate's arrival back from camp? Josh's accident? Kate's accusations against Ned? No, I think it was later than that. Even through the troubles that besieged us, I had hope. I only lost it, I realize, when Ned moved out. When I saw that something I believed was unbreakable could be broken.

I climb back upstairs and give Ned his mug. Josh is stirring; I can hear the rustle of his quilt, the little moan he gives when he first wakes up. I crack his door open and poke my head in.

"Good morning, Joshie," I sing softly.

He smiles at me from his crib. He's old enough for a bed, but I just haven't been able to bring myself to make the switch yet.

"How did you sleep?" I ask.

He grins and reaches up his hands, clasps me around the neck. "Want out," he says. "Want out of crib."

My throat tightens and my eyes tear when I hear him speak in almost a full sentence. I don't care what he says, I'm just so grateful that he's saying anything at all.

"Guess who's here," I say, as I lift him up. "Guess who's in the other room."

"Grandma?" he asks.

"No."

"Poppy?"

"No."

I carry him down the hall to the bedroom and plunk him down on the floor. He looks up at the bed, where Ned is sitting up, sipping coffee.

"Daddy!" he yells. "Daddy!"

"Hey, munchkin," says Ned. He pats the bed next to him. "Climb on up."

Josh scrambles onto the bed and snuggles up to Ned.

"Big hug," he says.

I stand there in the middle of my bedroom, watching. My husband and my baby boy, lying together in a rumpled bed in the early morning light—it's a sight I had given up hope of ever seeing again.

"Mommy, get in!" Josh commands. And so I do. I get under the covers on the other side of Josh.

"Joshie sandwich," says Ned. That's what we used to say all the time when Kate was a baby. I can see that Ned is trying to contain himself. The tip of his nose is pink, and his lips are trembling.

"Joshie sandwich," I repeat, holding him close as he squeals in delight.

IT HAS BEEN ALMOST EXACTLY A YEAR SINCE WE FIRST drove Kate to Stone Mountain. When Ned and I dropped her off there, I never imagined she'd be there that long, or that we'd be going back to pick her up against the school's judgment. But here we are. It's noon, and we're on the road to New Hampshire once again. This is our third trip to Stone Mountain together, but it's the first time my heart doesn't feel heavy. The sun is brilliant and the temperature has warmed a bit, patches of grass visible through the melting snow.

"I forgot my sunglasses," says Ned.

"Wear mine."

I hand him my metal-framed glasses and he slips them on. They look silly on him, improbably small against the bridge of his nose.

"Should we tell them we're coming?" he asks.

"No way. They'll call in the troops."

"It's not like it's prison," says Ned. "They can't keep her there against our will."

"They can try."

"I think you're giving them too much power, Rach."

"They have a lot of power—they have Kate."

"Going playground?" pipes up Josh from the backseat.

"No, Joshie," I say. "We're going on a drive. Going to see Katie."

He looks at me blankly. His sister's name means almost nothing to him. The last time he saw her was the day we took her to Stone Mountain a year—almost half his life—ago.

"Can you say 'Katie'?"

"Katie," he repeats dutifully.

"I wish we weren't bringing him," says Ned.

"We have no choice."

Preschool is closed for parent-teacher conferences, and I didn't want to ask Jane to baby-sit. This is private, what we're doing. It's nobody's business but our own. I'm so tired of people giving us advice, no matter how well-meaning. *Bring her home. Leave her there. You're her mother, you know best.*

"Mommy?" Josh calls from the backseat.

I swivel around and look at him.

"Truck." He points to a tractor-trailer passing us.

"Yes, honey."

He grins at me, dimples flashing.

I grab Ned's hand, resting on the gearshift, and dart a quick glance at him. He's squinting in my sunglasses, one hand gripping the steering wheel, and he's smiling.

"What are you smiling about?" I ask.

"You. Us." He pauses. "Joshie back there, checking out the world."

"He's a pretty cool kid," I say.

Ned and I hold hands for most of the two-hour drive, disentangling only when he needs to shift gears. Every once in a while, Josh points something out. *Cow! Bus!* Ned squeezes my hand, and I know we're both remembering Kate. She was once this excited by the tiniest things she saw: a bird, a spider, a firefly. Before I'm remotely prepared, we are on the winding two-lane road leading to the monarch-butterfly sign for Stone Mountain.

"MAY I HELP YOU?" THE RECEPTIONIST ASKS, AS NED AND I walk through the front doors, with Josh running ahead of us. She's a different woman from the one who was sitting in the corner typing just a few weeks ago.

"We're here to pick up our daughter," says Ned.

She glances down at a schedule on her desk. "Your daughter is . . . ?"

"Kate Jensen."

She looks confused. "Do you have an appointment?"

"No."

"Excuse me one moment."

She picks up the phone and punches in an extension.

"Dr. Hollis, the Jensens are here."

She pauses, listening. Her eyes flicker up at us, then away.

"Yes," she says. "That's correct."

Another pause.

"Very well."

She hangs up and folds her arms. "Dr. Hollis will be with you in a moment."

We walk over to the armchairs by a fireplace that looks like it hasn't been used in years. Josh has plopped himself down on the floor and is crawling under a heavy glass coffee table. Ned picks up an old issue of *Newsweek* and starts thumbing through it. I feel sick, just being in this place. I've felt, ever since the first time we came here, that parents dump their kids here when they've run out of options, when they just don't know what else to do with them. I've never felt right about Kate being here—never. How does a mother let her daughter go? I haven't been able to do it. Even though every single day for a year I've stayed away from her, a part of me has been broken off and is living here at Stone Mountain, just waiting for her to be well enough to take home. I wonder if Hollis has ever had a problem with his children—if he even has children. Maybe he's a bachelor. Maybe at the end of every day at Stone Mountain he retreats to his cabin in the woods and thanks his lucky stars that he's alone.

"Mr. and Mrs. Jensen," Hollis says, striding across the worn carpet. Ned stands up abruptly, the magazine falling from his lap to the floor.

"We're back," I say, lamely trying to inject some humor into a humorless situation. Hollis doesn't crack a smile. He tilts his head slightly to the side and observes us as if we're subjects in a medical study. Rats in a maze. *See parents run. Run, parents, run!*

"I see you've brought your younger child," he says.

"No baby-sitter," Ned apologizes.

"That's fine, just fine," says Hollis, in a tone that implies it's anything but fine. "Please. Let's go into my office."

We trail after him and sit on the hard-backed chairs next to his desk. He sinks into his leather office chair and leans back, hands behind head.

"What can I do for you today?" he asks.

"We're here to pick up Kate," I say.

"I see." He looks over to Ned. "Mr. Jensen, are you in agreement?"

Ned nods.

Hollis studies us for a long minute.

"I'd like to hear your reasoning," he says mildly. "Why the change of heart?"

"I think she'll do better at home," I say.

"And what makes you think that?"

"I don't know. It's just my instinct."

"Mrs. Jensen, Kate is really beginning to make progress," says Hollis.

"It hasn't seemed that way to us," interjects Ned. "Please. We're not here for a discussion about this. We want to pick up our daughter and take her home."

Hollis takes a long pause, looking first at Ned, then at me.

"Would you both excuse me? I need to make a phone call."

Ned and I exchange a glance.

"But we just want—" Ned starts to say.

"I'm going to try to arrange something," Hollis interrupts. "I think you'll find it worthwhile."

"But we don't want any—"

Hollis puts up a hand like a traffic cop.

"Please, Mr. and Mrs. Jensen."

Ned and I get up to leave the room.

"Just give me a minute," he calls after us.

"What do you think he's up to?" I whisper to Ned, as we wait just outside Hollis's door.

"I don't know. But whatever it is, I don't have a whole lot of patience for it," says Ned.

"Of course he's going to try to talk us out of it," I say. "She's worth a small fortune to them."

"I don't even know if that's what it is. I think maybe it has more to do with their egos. Like they don't want to admit they've failed."

Hollis opens his door.

"Okay, I've made arrangements with Dr. Esposito," he says. "Can you wait around until two?"

"We'd really just like to get going," says Ned.

Hollis leans into the door frame, towering over us.

"If you'll both bear with me, there's something I'd like to show you this afternoon. I think it would be helpful in making your decision. If you'll meet me back here at, say, a quarter of?"

"I don't see what difference—"

I put a hand on Ned's arm, stopping him. "We've waited this long," I say quietly. "Let's just see it through."

"Very well," says Hollis. He checks his watch. "See you back here in an hour, then."

THE TOWN OF WARREN, NEW HAMPSHIRE, CONSISTS OF A gas station, a post office, and a diner. The population of the whole town must be under a thousand, unless you count Stone

Mountain—which I'm sure the good citizens of Warren are none too happy about. We pull into the driveway of the diner.

"Happy Burger," says Ned.

"Sorry?"

"That's what this place is called."

He points to a small unlit neon sign above the door.

"Maybe we'll eat our burgers and be happy."

"Right."

We slide into a booth. Ned flips through the selection in a jukebox.

"Hey, check it out. They've got Pink Floyd on here."

I look up from the place mat, on which the all-day menu is printed.

"Groovy. Do you want a quarter?"

"Are you humoring me?"

"Would I do such a thing?"

"Here, Joshie, look at this." Ned points to the jukebox.

Josh stands on the vinyl seat of the booth and starts pressing buttons.

A kid who was pouring coffee behind the counter walks over to us with an order pad in hand.

"What can I get for you?"

"Cheeseburger," says Ned.

"Me too," I say. "And a grilled cheese sandwich for my son."

The kid nods and saunters away.

"He didn't ask how we like our burgers," says Ned.

"Go outside?" Josh asks hopefully.

"In a little bit, Joshie," I say. I look across the table at Ned and try to imagine how we're going to handle it all, what will happen once Kate is back at home.

"Where's she going to go to school?" I ask.

"Not the academy, that's for sure."

"Maybe we should keep her out of school for a semester. She can see Zelman, or someone else—"

"The public school's fine, Rach."

"I know. But do you think she can deal with it?"

The waiter brings our food. Josh promptly picks up half his grilled cheese sandwich and dumps it on the floor.

"Joshie!" I scold him. "No dumping!"

"Dumping," he repeats.

"We have no idea what she can deal with," says Ned. "We're just going to have to wait and see."

He takes a bite of his burger.

"I'm sorry to ask this—but are you sure, Rach?"

"Absolutely," I say.

Ned's attention is caught by something on the other side of the room. I follow his gaze to a table on the far side of the restaurant. A couple about our age is sitting on one side of the table, and a girl of about thirteen is on the other side. The girl is crying, and the mother looks stricken. The father puts his arm protectively around the mother's shoulders.

"Where do you suppose they're headed?" asks Ned.

I am transfixed, watching them.

"Those poor people," I murmur. I feel like I know too much about their lives, without our exchanging a single word: the fury, the silence, the late nights staring at the ceiling trying to figure out what went wrong.

"I feel like we should go over there and talk to them," I say.

"What for? What can we possibly tell them?"

"Don't you think it makes a difference just to know other people are in the same boat?"

"No. It just means the boat is more crowded," says Ned. "It doesn't change a thing."

The girl raises her voice loud enough so that it carries across the clatter of the restaurant.

"You can't make me!" she cries.

Her parents try to hush her, while the few people sitting at the counter turn to see what the fuss is about.

"I can't stand this." Ned pushes away his half-eaten burger.

"Me neither," I say. "Let's go."

JOSH STARTS FUSSING IN THE CAR ON THE WAY BACK TO Stone Mountain. I sit with him in the backseat and try to distract him with a series of his favorite songs, stopping so he can fill in the words.

"Puff, the magic dragon, lives by the—"

"Sea!" sings Josh.

"You're teaching him a song about marijuana," says Ned, from the front seat.

"He doesn't know."

"But he will someday."

We pull back into the driveway and Ned parks the car. Hollis is standing by the front doors of the main building, wearing his overcoat.

"Here we go," says Ned under his breath. "More adventures in crazyland."

We head across the small campus of Tudor buildings. Josh is wriggling in my arms, not wanting to be carried. A cluster of girls passes us, led by a woman in her thirties. They walk along in their jeans and sneakers, and in my mind I compare them to the girls at the academy. I look for a sign, anything that sets them apart from other high school kids. But to me, they are indistinguishable from the academy girls with their perfect SAT scores, field hockey trophies, and Ivy League dreams. A few of them glance curiously in our direction, and a laugh rises from the group. We are so obviously parents, being given the grand tour by Hollis.

"We're heading over there." He points to a low gray stone building, built to blend in with the older buildings around it. He guides us through the sliding glass doors. A chalkboard is set up in the lobby, on which a schedule is written: GROUP A, ROOM 102. GROUP B, ROOM 300. We follow Hollis down a long empty hall and into a small dimly lit room with an oval table at its center. Along one side of the table, four chairs are lined up, facing three television monitors on the wall.

"We generally use this room for professional observation," says Hollis as he picks up a remote and points it at one of the monitors. "Please, have a seat."

The picture opens up across the screen, and it takes a moment for me to register Kate. The camera is pointing at her from above, and she's slumped down in a metal folding chair, her arms crossed. Her bruises are healing nicely—that's all I can think. The swelling has gone down, and her black eye has faded to a pulpy yellow. I'm filled with relief just to see her.

"She's screwed it up for all of us," a young girl's voice is saying.

"What do you mean, Zoë? How did she screw things up for you?" I recognize Esposito's measured tone.

"Now all of us are back on Level One. Do you know how fucking hard I worked to get to Level Two?"

Kate stares straight ahead—that same glassy stare I've become familiar with.

"Will you answer me, you fucking asshole?"

"Hey, hey, hey. No name calling in here," says Esposito.

"I can't help it. She just makes me so mad."

Kate brushes her hair off her face. The gesture strikes me as defiant.

Josh starts whimpering. I can't blame him. A toddler shouldn't be cooped up like this. I put him down on the floor and give him my cell phone to play with—always a last resort.

"What about you, Jessica?" Esposito asks.

"What about me?"

"Is that why you hit Kate? Because she made you mad?"

Ned reaches over and holds my hand. He knows—it's all I can do not to burst into the room and grab that faceless girl around the throat.

"I hit her because she hit me first."

"Is that true, Kate?" Esposito now materializes behind Kate's chair. "Did you hit Jessica first?"

Kate doesn't say a word.

"Did you?"

She starts rocking back and forth.

"Don't start with that bullshit in here, Kate. I'm on to you," says Esposito. He crouches down until he's inches away from her. "Answer me."

He stares at her for what must be a full minute. Finally, he stands up.

"Fine," he says quietly. "Have it your way. All privileges revoked. For all four of you. You thought Level One was bad? We're talking Isolation."

He walks out of the picture.

"No!" a girl shouts.

"You can't do that!" yells another voice.

"I can. I just did."

"Why are you punishing all of us?"

"Because that's the way it works around here."

"But that's not fair!"

"Who said life was fair?" Esposito says. "When one of you behaves badly, the others pay. Actions have consequences—not just for yourselves, but for others."

"You shouldn't do that," Kate says, lifting her head up for the first time. She speaks quietly, but her voice cuts through the girlish shrieks of the others.

"Oh!" Esposito says. "Now she speaks!"

"You shouldn't punish them on my account."

Kate pulls her knees up and hugs them to her chest. It's strange, being able to look at her this way—undisguisedly, ravenously. I've been so careful around her for so long. *What are you looking at? Stop staring at me!* She's physically changed since her arrival at this place. At a glance, she looks like the same Kate, but when I study her closely I see that she's both hardened and hollowed out. Though still beautiful, she's like an outline of her former self.

"Everything's your *fucking fault,*" one of the girls spits out.

Kate recoils, as if the word is a physical blow.

"Watch it, Zoë," says Esposito.

Kate says something under her breath. I lean forward, straining to hear her.

"What did you say, Kate?" Esposito asks.

"You heard me."

"No. Actually I didn't."

She buries her head in her knees, and her voice is muffled but clear.

"I want to die."

"She's just trying to get attention," says one of the girls. But I'm no longer listening. I'm just looking at my daughter. My precious, beautiful daughter, curled into herself, trembling. I feel as if I were suddenly trapped inside a glass globe, watching the video monitor that separates me from Kate.

"What does that mean to you, Kate," prods Esposito, "Zoë saying it's your fault? What does that make you feel?"

"I don't know."

"Come on. You can do better than that."

I see something soften in Kate's eyes.

"What's your fault?" Esposito continues to push. "What's your fault so much that you want to die?"

"It was an accident!" Kate cries out.

Around her, the room grows still and silent.

"What are you talking about, Kate?" Esposito asks. "What was an accident?"

"I slipped and fell!"

She covers her face with her hands.

"On the stairs. I wasn't thinking, I wasn't watching my step, and—I never, ever would have hurt the baby, I never, *ever*—"

"What is she talking about?" mutters one of the girls.

"Ssshh." Esposito silences her.

"Then why did you think it was your fault?" he prods.

"Because—I" She gulps, sobbing openly. "Because—"

She stops. She can't go on.

"Sometimes accidents happen," says Esposito. His voice is gentle. "Sometimes accidents happen, Kate, and it doesn't matter what we wished or didn't wish, what our darkest fantasies might have been."

My poor, poor girl. All I want to do is comb her hair away from her face, kiss her forehead, wrap my arms around her.

"Rachel?" Ned squeezes my hand. "Rach?"

"Mrs. Jensen?" Hollis steps forward. "Are you all right?"

I nod slowly and try to still my mind. Breathe in Josh's sweet animal scent. Then I turn to Hollis. I search his face for something solid, something to trust.

"She's been saying that a lot," he says quietly. "About the accident."

"I know she blames herself," I say. "I tried, afterward—but then she accused Ned, and everything just—"

"Spiraled," Ned finishes for me. "We could never get a grip."

Hollis nods.

"It's a good sign, though," he says.

"What?"

"That she's talking about it."

"Is she talking about all of it?" asks Ned.

"You mean her accusations?"

"Yes."

"Not yet," says Hollis, "but give it time. That's why I hope you'll reconsider."

"If we keep Kate here, can you help her?" I ask.

"We hope so," he says quietly.

"It hasn't been going well up until now," says Ned.

"There's always a question with an adolescent," says Hollis. "Will she grow out of this? How solid is her foundation? How's her constitution? Is there genetic loading?"

"So you can't guarantee that—"

"I can't guarantee anything, Mrs. Jensen. But I truly believe she has a better chance here than she would anywhere else."

"I want to see her," I blurt out.

Hollis thinks for a moment.

"I'm not sure it would be productive," he says slowly.

"Please. I think it will help us make a decision."

"All right," Hollis says, checking his watch. "I'll show you to her room, and Dr. Esposito will bring her to you when group is over."

Hollis leads us to one of the old Tudor buildings at the far side of the quad, which has been outfitted with bars on the windows. Ned has his arm around me, shepherding me, keeping me close to him as if he's afraid I might fall. And I'm carrying Josh, who has just about dozed off in my arms. Hollis presses a code into a security system at the side of the front door, and a buzzer sounds.

"This is where the Level One girls live," he says. We pass a guard, who nods at him, and walk up a flight of stairs to a long hallway that looks like a college dorm except for the small glass windows in each door. Inside, Kate's room is spare as a prison cell: a single bed, a chair, and a small desk. The last remaining patch of afternoon sunlight streams through the window bars and casts striped shadows on the floor.

"She'll be here in about half an hour," Hollis says. "And Mr. and Mrs. Jensen"—he pauses, and for a moment his professional veneer drops and I see the weight of his responsibility—"I do hope you'll keep her here with us."

"Do you mind if we take a walk?" I ask abruptly. I can't bear the idea of sitting in Kate's room. I can feel her despair all around me: the nights she's spent weeping on the thin mattress of the bed with no one to comfort her, the walls she's punched and clawed. She must have felt like a prisoner. She *was* a prisoner. The desk in the corner is empty. Of course she isn't allowed pens or pencils. What did she do, how did she pass the hours alone in this room?

"Of course," says Hollis. He ushers us back out the door. "Meet us by the bench out front at three o'clock."

A BRICK PATH LEADS AWAY FROM THE DORMITORY AND around the quad. We walk its perimeter slowly, taking turns carrying Josh. The dark buildings with their peaked roofs, the bare trees swaying, the tiny green shoots of the spring's first crocuses poking their heads from the flower beds lining the front lawn—if not for the buzzers and the bars on the windows, we could be visiting any institution: a sanitarium, a hospital, a home for the elderly. I suddenly imagine us, Ned and me, as an ancient couple, shuffling along on grounds similar to these. It's a comforting image, in its own way: I'm envisioning the distant future and seeing us together. We're propping each other up, holding canes instead of babies, walking even more slowly than we are now. And where will our children be? Will Kate come to visit us—a robust middle-aged woman with pink cheeks, the belt of her trench coat tied smartly around her waist? Will Joshie drive up the driveway with his wife and two children, hop out of his car, and engulf us in a hug? Will our children survive us?

"Tell me what you're thinking," says Ned.

I jostle Josh in my arms and say nothing. I don't trust myself to speak.

"It's the right thing, Rach," Ned says, after a few minutes.

I know exactly what he's talking about. There can be no question. When we leave this place at the end of the day, once more we'll be leaving Kate.

"Yes," I reply. "It doesn't make it any easier, though."

We fall into silence. The two of us watch Josh as he struggles to stay awake, his mouth stretching into a big yawn. I wonder if Ned is filled with the same kind of worries as I am. He's always been better at pushing things away. I can't seem to push anything away.

"Are we terrible parents?" I ask out loud.

"I don't think so," Ned says. "I think we've done the best we can."

"I hate that. I just hate that," I say. "My mother always used to say the same thing. What does that even mean?"

Ned puts his arm around me again.

"Stop it," he says softly.

We keep circling the quad. Josh has fallen asleep in my arms, his head heavy against my shoulder. I feel his squirmy little body go limp, his breath moving in and out. All the girls at Stone Mountain must be in classes or therapy. Not a sound mars the perfect stillness of the afternoon, only the slow thud of our footsteps on the brick. I think about Kate—specifically, the Kate I saw on the video monitor. She seems both better and worse, raw in a way almost impossible to comprehend. She looked less like a fully formed girl than a mass of muscle and skin and bone. It is as possible to imagine her as a healthy grown woman as it is to picture a helpless creature, forever trapped by her own biochemistry, her own genetic—what was the term Hollis used?—*loading.* But will she be stronger than her troubled mind or will she be beyond reach?

"I have questions," I say to Ned, as we come to a stop by the wooden bench outside Kate's dorm. The sun is warm, the bench out in the open.

"But you're not going to have answers," says Ned. "At least not now."

A door opens across the quad. Kate and Dr. Esposito emerge into the daylight, then stand and talk intently on the front steps of the group therapy building. He pats her on the back, then watches as she walks toward the bench where we sit. Kate's head is bowed, her gait tentative, almost a limp, as if the very act of moving through the air is painful for her.

She doesn't look up until she is standing directly in front of us, and when she does the first thing she sees is her little brother asleep in my arms. She raises a hand to her mouth and just stares at him. She kneels down on the ground and touches his cheek.

"He's so big," she finally says.

Up close, I can see that her face is still bruised and her eyes swollen from crying. She reaches out a finger and traces the back of his partially opened hand. The gesture strikes me as maternal; I've done it myself a thousand times.

"Why are you guys here?" she asks, without taking her eyes off Josh.

"Because we love you," I say. "We want you to know that."

"What about you, Daddy?" she asks. "Why are *you* here?"

"Because I love you," says Ned.

Kate's long slender fingers stroke Josh's dark curls.

"How can that be?" she asks.

"What do you mean?"

"You must hate my guts," she says softly.

"Is that what you think?"

Ned doesn't move a muscle, and neither does she.

"Yeah."

"I can't hate you," says Ned. "Not at all." He pauses. "You're my daughter."

"You love me *because* I'm your daughter?"

Ned watches her carefully. "Well, yes, in part," he says. "That's how it works."

She pushes herself to her feet, then looks at us. She still has the face of a little girl, but her eyes are more knowing than any sixteen-year-old's ought to be.

"I did a terrible thing," she says.

Ned winces a little. "We're not taking you home, Kate. So don't start saying things you think we want to hear, because—"

"I mean it." A breeze ripples across the quad, and she lets out a violent shiver, but she doesn't move away from us. Her voice is so thin it almost disappears. "I did a terrible thing, and I hurt you."

Ned's face begins to crumble, slowly contorting itself into a mask of grief. He doubles over at the waist with a sob.

"Oh, *God,* Kate," he cries.

Josh stirs in my arms as I stand up and hold Kate as close as I can. Her body stiffens, then melts. We sway together, and then I feel Ned's arms wrap around both of us, and we all hold on to one another for dear life.

ACKNOWLEDGMENTS

My gratitude to Jonathan Wilson, Jennifer Egan, Hilary Black, and Sue Shapiro, who made valuable comments on early drafts; Dr. Laura Popper and Dr. David Kaufman for generously sharing their medical expertise, and a whole lot more; Jennifer Rudolph Walsh for being the best friend and agent a writer could hope for; and the brilliant Jordan Pavlin, whose attention to this book has been a gift and a revelation.

ALSO AVAILABLE FROM VINTAGE/ANCHOR

DISOBEDIENCE

by Jane Hamilton

When seventeen-year-old Henry Shaw discovers that all is not as it seems with his ordinary midwestern American family—his mother is having a passionate affair—he is unable to tell anyone. Neither his amiable father, a history teacher, or his high spirited younger sister has any idea how drastically their world is about to change.

Fiction/0-385-72046-7

BEE SEASON

by Myla Goldberg

Eliza Naumann, a seemingly unremarkable nine-year-old, expects never to fit into her gifted family: her autodidact father, Saul, absorbed in his study of Jewish mysticism; her brother, Aaron, the vessel of his father's spiritual ambitions; and her brilliant but distant lawyer-mom, Miriam. But when Eliza sweeps her school and district spelling bees, Saul takes it as a sign that she is destined for greatness.

Fiction/Literature/0-385-49880-2

LOVE AMONG THE RUINS

by Robert Clark

In the summer of 1968, William Lowry and Emily Bryne fall deeply in love despite their family's differences. Soon, the young lovers decide to escape to the wilderness to start anew. Left behind to grapple with the shifting mores of the nation and the sundering of their families, the liberal Lowrys and the conservative, Catholic Byrnes must search for both their children and their own lost innocence.

Fiction/Literature/1-4000-3030-7

A BRIEF HISTORY OF THE FLOOD

by Jean Harfenist

A strong-minded, backwoods-Minnesota girl, well-versed in the basics of survival, Lillian Anderson barrels through adolescence with no illusions about her future, honing her clerical skills while working the nightshift at the airport kitchen. Just as she's on her feet and moving out, her family's house is literally sinking into the marsh.

Fiction/0-375-71335-2

BURNING MARGUERITE

by Elizabeth Inness-Brown

After his ninety-four-year-old "Tante" Marguerite Deo dies, James Jack Wright sets out to fulfill her last wishes, as the narrative reveals an illicit passion and an unforgivable crime, and the unsuspecting relationship between a small boy and a tough, reclusive woman.

Fiction/0-375-72622-5

SUMMER GONE

by David Macfarlane

When Bay Newby is twelve, he loves the life of ritual, beauty, and stark privilege of summer camp. With the death of his baby sister, he waits twenty-three years for his next "perfect summer" with his son.

Fiction/Literature/0-385-72075-0

SCHOOLING

by Heather McGowan

After her mother's death, thirteen-year-old Catrine Evans is uprooted from her home in America to an English boarding school. There she finds the sympathetic chemistry teacher Mr. Gilbert, who offers Catrine the friendship she so desperately needs—a friendship that takes on sinister and obsessive overtones.

Fiction/Literature/0-375-71432-4

MOTHERKIND

by Jayne Anne Phillips

Formerly free spirited, Kate suddenly enters roles of great responsibility: a new marriage, complete with her own beloved infant and two lively young stepsons, and caregiver to her ailing mother, the strong woman who has been her guiding star.

Fiction/Literature/0-375-70192-3

POBBY AND DINGAN

by Ben Rice

Pobby and Dingan are Kellyanne Williamson's best friends, and only she can see them. Kellyanne's brother, Ashmol, can't see them and doesn't believe they exist. Only when Pobby and Dingan disappear and Kellyanne becomes heartsick over their loss does Ashmol realize that he must believe and convince others to believe in them, too.

Fiction/Literature/1-4000-3188-5

THE TINY ONE

by Eliza Minot

Via Mahoney Revere is eight years old when her mother is killed in a car accident. Confused by anguish, bewildered by her mother's absence, and mystified by the notion of death itself, Via retells the day of her mother's death in minute detail, trying to discern the crack in the world through which her mother must have slipped.

Fiction/Literature/0-375-70633-X

SISTER CRAZY

by Emma Richler

The sprawling Weiss family—as recalled by Jemima—live an almost idyllic existence. In a darkly humorous voice, she tells of playing elaborate war games with toy Action Man figures, composing a survival book, observing her beautiful Mum to fathom her magic, and weaving the story of the Grail quest into her brother Jude's life.

Fiction/Literature/0-385-72089-0

HIGHWIRE MOON

by Susan Straight

Serafina is an illegal migrant worker living in California when the police catch her and send her back to Mexico—without her three-year-old daughter Elvia. Twelve years later, Serafina begins a journey back across the border to find her daughter. At the same time, Elvia, now fifteen and pregnant, resolves to track her mother down.

Fiction/0-385-72261-3

I'M NOT SCARED

by Niccolo Ammaniti

A sweltering heat wave hits a tiny village in Southern Italy, sending the adults to seek shelter, while their children bicycle freely throughout the countryside, playing games and getting into trouble. On a dare, nine-year-old Michele Amitrano enters an old, abandoned farmhouse, where he stumbles upon a terrible secret that turns out to be closer to home than he ever could have imagined.

Fiction/Literature/1-4000-7563-7